"WHO ASKED YOU TO INTERFERE?" REENA GLOWERED AT CAID.

"I could easily have handled that obnoxious rancher myself."

"Right. I suppose you were going to toss him over your shoulder," he scoffed.

"That's *exactly* what I was going to do." She added fiercely, "I could, you know. My brothers showed me how to do it—and a lot of other things too, Mr. Helpful Hero."

"Honey, you're just a tiny drink of water. You need strength and muscle to toss a man." Caid's lips twitched as if he was trying to keep from grinning.

Reena saw red. "Don't you honey me!" She tapped him hard in the middle of his broad chest. "Don't you dare."

"Now just a moment!" He wrapped his large hand around hers, completely enveloping it. A tingling feeling flowed through his fingers into her hand, and she frowned in confusion. "Lady, you are something else," he murmured.

Feeling strangely breathless, she backed away.

ARIZONA RENEGADE

KIT DEE

AVON BOOKS ◆ NEW YORK

This is a work of fiction. Names, characters, places, and incidents either are the product of the author's imagination or are used fictitiously. Any resemblance to actual events, locales, organizations, or persons, living or dead, is entirely coincidental and beyond the intent of either the author or the publisher.

AVON BOOKS, INC.
1350 Avenue of the Americas
New York, New York 10019

Copyright © 1998 by Melitta Dee
Inside cover author photo by Image Bureau
Published by arrangement with the author
Visit our website at **http://www.AvonBooks.com**
Library of Congress Catalog Card Number: 97-94769
ISBN: 0-380-79206-0

First Avon Books Printing: June 1998

AVON TRADEMARK REG. U.S. PAT. OFF. AND IN OTHER COUNTRIES, MARCA REGISTRADA, HECHO EN U.S.A.

Printed in the U.S.A.

WCD   10 9 8 7 6 5 4 3 2 1

*To Camille Kolb Ostrow, my own Auntie Mame,
an adventure-loving lady who challenged life
and dared to do things before ladies did them*

Chapter 1

⌒◯◯⌒

Saturday, September 19, 1885

"**W**e have to find the Simpsons and stop them." Caid Dundee spoke loudly over the metallic clickety-clack of the train wheels.

"*If* the information Goodie Hensen gave you is correct. And that's a damn big if." Tanner Stewart stood beside him on the rear platform of the private railcar. "Why would they be holding up banks and trains here in northern Arizona? It doesn't make sense."

"A lot of gold is coming out of the mines around the Grand Canyon. And look around you." Caid gestured at the high, windswept plateau they were crossing.

They could see for a hundred miles in every direction. Rugged mesas in every shade of red, from garnet and ruby to scarlet and vermilion, dotted the

1

plain like giant sand castles. On the horizon snow-capped mountain peaks raked the deep blue sky. And the land was as wild as the hawk soaring overhead.

"The Simpsons don't have to run back to Mexico to hide, when a wilderness like this has thousands of places." Smoke and cinders swirled around them and Caid brushed a still-smoking cinder off his black jacket.

"But why Lost Gold, instead of a bigger town like Flagstaff?"

"Because Goodie heard her father say the Simpsons have a spy in Lost Gold. And we're going to find him." He raked his fingers through his black hair. There was no need to mention that he knew the Simpsons, Caid decided. No one needed to know that. Or that he wouldn't rest until they were in jail. Or dead.

"You're getting soft, Caid, using your father's railcar. Shouldn't we slip into Lost Gold more anonymously?"

"Would a government agent call so much attention to himself? Of course not. I'll be labeled another rich dilettante from the East with nothing to do but ask questions. And as usual, you'll pretend to be my secretary."

"What do you plan to do when we get there?"

Caid gazed at the rails unfurling behind them in a silver ribbon tying faraway towns together. Once he sprang the trap, he'd make sure the Simpsons knew who had captured them.

And it would be over. Justice would be done. Finally.

"We'll stay at the new Fred Lowry Hotel and say we're checking out the Lost Gold area for railroad investors. It gives us a reason to be nosing around." He turned to the younger brown-haired man. "I'll tell everyone that I'll be reporting what I find and that you're writing the reports. I think that about covers it. Can you think of anything I missed?"

"Nope."

"Just remember, the Simpsons shoot to kill and are as dangerous as rattlesnakes."

He pointed at a distant cluster of buildings shimmering in the afternoon heat waves, looking lost and lonely on the vast plain. "I'd say that's Lost Gold coming up."

"Let me go ahead and make sure no one sees you leave," Belle Livingston said, stealthily opening the bedroom door and peeping out into the hall.

"What if they do? No one will recognize me." Rowena Simpson tucked the last of her long blond hair up into the crown of her battered sombrero, then tried to edge past her plump friend. "They'll just think I'm a man."

Belle put her arm out, blocking Rowena's way. "Oh, right, we'll just let Miss Abigail think a man's been up here on the women's floor. That's not going to raise any questions at all! You've never lived in a dormitory before, have you, Reena?"

Surprised by the unfamiliar name, Rowena started to correct her, but stopped herself in time.

Reena Sims was the name she'd given when she'd applied for work as a waitress at the new Fred Lowry Hotel in Lost Gold, and she'd better get used to it. She couldn't afford to slip up—not when she was working for The Cause and spying for her brothers, Jefferson Davis and Robert Lee.

"Do you know what happens in a women's dorm when someone yells 'Man on the floor'? Talk about causing a commotion to beat the band! Believe me, you'd never again be able to sneak out of here dressed like a man. And that's if we weren't all fired on the spot. Remember, Mr. Lowry is very strict about his Lowry Girls having spotless reputations."

Rowena studied her roommate thoughtfully. "All right, let me know when the coast is clear."

Belle opened the door a crack and peered out, then, still keeping watch, motioned behind the door to Rowena. "Quick! There's no one in the hall."

A few moments later, Rowena eased down the back stairs. Outside, she zigzagged through the grove of oaks that shaded most of the hotel garden. The last roses of summer perfumed the air. When Rowena reached the wooden gate in the adobe wall, she paused and tipped her sombrero forward so it shadowed her face, then pulled her motheaten wool serape forward on her shoulders so that it hung down and disguised any curves that weren't already hidden by her baggy shirt and pants.

Lifting the latch, she slipped out and walked down to Main Street, where she turned toward the railroad depot. The piercing shriek of the engine whistle announced the arrival of the train from the

East, and she began to hurry. She came around the depot just as the engine chugged slowly past her, its bell clanging. Clouds of steam and smoke belched from the engine, and the whistle blew twice more.

Slowly, with screeching brakes, the train ground to a halt. The engine always stopped beside the water tower to take on water, so each of the railcars always stopped in the same place, too. Behind the engine tender came the baggage car, then the passenger cars.

Rowena slouched against the depot wall. From there she could see what was happening in the baggage car, while also keeping an eye on the passengers. Hooking her thumbs in her front jeans pockets, she braced a booted foot against the wall. It felt good to be back in her well-worn jeans and old shirt, instead of those constricting, high-necked, stick-in-the-mud black dresses she had to wear while working at the hotel.

When she'd first arrived in town, she'd tried gathering information properly garbed in a dress, but she'd noticed that men stopped talking whenever she went by and she never heard anything useful.

Taking a gamble, she'd dressed in the shirt and pants she wore at the ranch, and found that when she sauntered down Main Street dressed as a boy, no one gave her a second glance. Rowena could linger in the vicinity of a conversation and no one ever worried about what the "boy" was hearing. She'd picked up a lot of information that way.

She was at the train station for the same reason she was working as a waitress: to help the Cause. So far she'd gathered information, acted as a courier, and helped send new recruits to the Second Confederate Army her brothers were raising. Rowena ensured that the recruits had horses and guns and a map to get down to the Colony in Mexico. Then it was up to her brothers to train them for the coming takeover of Arizona.

Rowena wrinkled her nose at the biting odor of hot engine oil. A lanky cowboy, his saddle hoisted over his shoulder, jumped down from the second passenger car and ambled toward the depot. Two burly miners in work shirts and dirty blue coveralls, carrying pickaxes and coils of rope, stepped off the third car and stomped into the station. The cowboy's eyes met hers. He bypassed the depot entrance and came toward her.

"Know where I could buy a horse, boy?" he asked, shifting the saddle slightly. He tapped two fingers of his left hand against his belt, following the code she'd set up.

"The stable out behind the new hotel might have some," she replied. She tugged on her left ear to let him know he'd contacted the right person and that she'd meet him behind the stable late that night.

He walked on and her attention returned to the train as she watched for more recruits. The last railcar was a private one, by the looks of the red velvet curtains in the windows and the name painted on its side in large gold letters—Senator Dundee. Recognizing the name, Rowena stiffened. Papa often railed against the senators who'd been elected since the end of the Confederacy, and the senator he hated most was Senator Dundee.

Who was on the car? If it had been Senator Dundee, everyone in town would have known he was coming and been at the station to greet him. So it had to be someone else. A man in a black jacket and trousers jumped down from the railcar's rear platform. He was followed by a brown-haired man who disappeared around the corner of the railcar.

The first man's black Stetson hid his features, except for a square don't-mess-with-me jaw. Rowena straightened away from the wall as he snagged every bit of her attention.

He moved with the lone-wolf vigilance of a gunslinger. Pacing forward beside the passenger cars, he watched two workmen drag a large wooden ramp toward the baggage car. The wood screeched as they positioned it beside the car and lifted the end into the doorway. With the help of a man in the car, they wedged it into the opening with a clatter and thud, and one of the workmen started up the ramp.

"Stay out of there," the stranger commanded, in a dark voice rumbling with gravel.

The workman turned sharply and gave him a long look, then silently backed down the ramp and waited. The stranger ignored him as he walked past him into the car, and soon reappeared in the doorway leading a bay horse. He glanced around as though looking for someone, his gaze sliding past

Rowena without stopping. Then he led the horse down the ramp.

She still couldn't make out the stranger's features, but his jacket was drawn taut over barn-wide shoulders. Something about him reminded Rowena of a painting she'd once seen of a magnificent black stallion. The stallion's neck was arched and he pawed the earth and breathed fire from his nostrils. She had a feeling this man could also breathe fire.

Just as he reached the ramp's bottom, a commotion erupted in the baggage car. Hooves crashed against wood, and an enraged neigh sounded. Someone cursed loudly inside the car.

"Here, boy. Hold this horse for me." He held out the rope.

Rowena glanced around. Was he talking to her?

"Yes, you. Quick."

She dashed forward. He flung the coils of rope at her and turned back up the ramp.

"Easy, boy." Rowena rubbed the horse's neck beneath his mane as she led him away from the ramp. She walked in a circle, keeping the animal moving while she listened to crash after crash as a horse tried to kick out the side of the railcar. A string of curses accompanied each crash, but slowly the curses and crashes subsided.

The man reappeared leading a spirited white horse who pranced down the ramp as though he hated having his hooves touch the ground. All he needed were wings and he would fly away—like Pegasus. Near the bottom, a sparrow landed almost beneath the horse's hooves, sending it into a snorting, bucking frenzy. The man loosed the lead rope to keep from being jerked off his feet, then, slowly, talking to the animal all the while, reeled it back in, close to his side.

He was good with horses. Very good.

The stranger walked over to her, with the white horse prancing and snorting at his side. "Thanks for taking care of the bay, son." His voice rumbled across her nerve endings like distant thunder, and her heart skipped a beat. He reached for the bay's rope, but the white stallion suddenly reared, jerking him back.

"Easy, boy, easy." He drew his hand along the stallion's arched neck in long, soothing strokes that made her wonder what his hand would feel like on her.

Rowena felt a flash of respect that he hadn't gotten angry at the horse, just soothed him. Most men she knew, including her brothers and father, would have sworn at the animal and tried to control it with brute force.

"It looks like I'm going to have my hands full with my horse, son. And my partner is busy seeing that our railcar is separated from the train and shunted onto a siding. Could you lead the bay to the hotel stable?" He stood loosely, not fighting the white horse as it sidled around and whipped its head up and down, continuously jerking on the lead rope.

"Sure, mister," she replied in her gruffest voice. "It's this way." She started walking beside him, the horses flanking them on the outside. His stride was so much longer than hers, she had to take two quick steps for his one.

"That's a beautiful horse you've got there," she said. Yet it wasn't the prancing horse, but the man who claimed her attention. He radiated tension and something else that she couldn't quite identify—yet. But she knew that eventually she would.

"Thanks. Normally he isn't such a terror." He reached up and scratched the horse behind the ears. "But he was cooped up in the baggage car for too long."

"You can run him for miles here."

"I intend to." Suddenly he looked at her and his nostrils flared, as he inhaled deeply. "Strange, I could swear I caught a whiff of lilacs."

"Must be a plant out here that smells like them." Rowena edged away from him. Damn, she'd forgotten to wash off her lilac scent. She couldn't slip up like that when she wore her disguise.

She flicked him a sharp look. He was still watching her. His alertness seemed to be part of him, as natural as breathing, not something that he put on and took off like a coat. And it made him dangerous as hell.

"Are you going to be staying at the hotel?" She turned left on Main Street, toward the hotel.

"Yes. I want to see how it's doing, now that it's open." He slanted an assessing glance at her. "I'm here to check out the Lost Gold area for investors back East."

"You're a businessman?" Not in her wildest

dreams would she ever have pegged him as pouring over ledgers.

"Something like that. I represent investors."

"Oh." He looked like he should wear a gun at his hip, not represent rich people. "The hotel dining room has been open for weeks, but they haven't had anybody stay in the rooms yet. They haven't even finished hiring the hotel staff."

"Sounds like you've been there."

"Uh-uh. Too rich for my blood." Her throat was getting sore from talking so gruffly. "It takes money to go there. But I've heard the food is good."

"Beds better be, too," he muttered wearily. "Is that it?" He gestured at the four-story adobe that stood on the corner and spread welcoming wings of rooms along Main and the side street. "That's one grand hacienda."

She turned to him, surprised. "That's what it's supposed to look like—a luxurious hacienda. There's a lovely garden behind the walls. That is, there will be in a few years, after the plants grow. This way," she said, indicating the side street.

"And what do you do, when you're not showing strangers around town?"

"Oh, this and that." She didn't look at him as she turned into the alley in the middle of the block. He was asking too many questions, noticing too much, and her alarm bells were jangling. "The stable is back here so the smell doesn't bother the guests."

"I can take the horses now, son." He fished in his front pants pocket. "Here." He flipped a coin at her and caught the rope when she dropped it to catch the coin.

"Thanks, mister." She'd seen boys bite coins when they caught them, so she did, too. It was real.

"Thanks." When he turned away, the stallion shook his head, knocking the man's Stetson off and revealing his rugged features.

Rowena studied him from beneath her lashes. His hair was a shade between brown and black, like black coffee. His bronzed face was all hard angles and planes, arresting and rugged as the mountains on the horizon. High cheekbones underlined piercing silver-blue eyes. Penetrating, seeing-too-much eyes.

He was too rugged, too harsh and stern looking ever to be called handsome. Power, strength, and taut control—that was what he radiated. Handsome was a civilized word for a civilized man. And instinctively she knew he wasn't civilized. Not in the least.

"Son, are you all right?"

Rowena gulped. Lordy, she'd been standing there, staring up at him, stunned as a poleaxed calf.

"Sure." She ducked down to pick up his hat and break eye contact, although she had a feeling he'd already seen too much. "Here's your hat, mister," she added, in as gruff a tone as she could muster. She started to hand it to him, but realized his hands were full.

"Put it on my head." He bent his head so she could.

She hesitated, not wanting to get that close to

him. But a boy wouldn't even pause, so she stood on tiptoe and jammed it on his head, then took a quick step back—so she could breathe again. "There you go."

"Thanks." He turned and led the horses away, but as he entered the stable, he glanced back at her.

Only after he disappeared inside did Rowena release the breath she'd been holding.

Turning, she hurried along the adobe wall surrounding the hotel to the gate. Once inside the gardens, she leaned back against the gate and took a long, relieved breath, inhaling the scent of roses. She'd be safe there, hidden among the trees and rosebushes and winding paths.

Surprised by the thought, she stiffened. Then she recognized what her instincts were telling her. Danger clung to his broad shoulders. Danger came in the touch of his hand and the gaze of his too-knowing eyes. Danger flickered around him like flames flickered around a log in a fireplace.

And she didn't want to get burned.

Chapter 2

〜⟩◯◯⟨〜

"I met a man today who was really something!" Rowena said to Belle, as she joined
her in the butler's pantry off the dining room in the
hotel.

Belle stared at her. "You actually noticed a man?
Who is he? He must be as handsome as a Greek
statue."

"He's not handsome." How could she describe
him? "He's rugged and strong and . . . good with
horses."

"You finally notice a man, and he isn't even
handsome? But he's good with horses—" Belle
rolled her eyes. "That's really important when
you're thinking of dating a man."

"I'm not going to date him! I just mentioned him
because—oh, never mind. I'm sorry I said anything." She couldn't explain him anyway, because

14

she didn't understand why she could picture him so clearly in her mind.

"Don't be. He must have made quite an impression, if you remember him at all. I don't think I've ever heard you mention *any* man—at least, one you weren't having trouble with. I'd like to meet him."

"Attention, ladies." Miss Abigail clapped her hands, silencing the buzz of talk filling the butler's pantry. "Mr. Kincaid Dundee, son of Senator Dundee, will be staying with us in the new hotel."

Rowena elbowed Belle. "That's him," she whispered.

"*Him?*" Belle mouthed, her eyebrows arching.

Rowena nodded, impressed. He was the senator's son, yet he hadn't mentioned it, hadn't even given her a clue, which meant that he didn't use his father to get special treatment for himself. Rowena respected that kind of independence.

"Since the hotel is barely completed and most of their staff haven't been hired yet, I will need a couple of volunteers to clean rooms in the hotel as well as waitress while Mr. Dundee is with us," Miss Abigail continued.

"We'll do it, Miss Abby." Belle stepped forward.

"We?" The tiny, white-haired woman pursed her lips as if she were sucking on a lemon. "Who's we?"

"Reena and me."

Rowena blinked owlishly at her roommate. "Me?"

"Reena doesn't make her own bed. Why would she make someone else's?" Miss Abigail snapped.

Rowena felt a telltale flush on her cheeks, surprised that the older woman knew that she didn't believe in making her bed every morning. After all, she'd just be getting back into it that night.

"I'll supervise," Belle said. "We'll do a good job, we need the extra money, and you know we can be trusted."

Miss Abigail studied Belle for several moments before nodding abruptly. "All right. You'll start tomorrow morning after serving breakfast." Then she glanced around at them all. "Now, ladies, you need to get your tables set for the first dinner seating tonight. Remember, it's Saturday and we will be busy. And Reena, straighten your apron. Why isn't it ironed?"

"I ironed it yesterday, ma'am." This ironing business was an awful lot of bother for nothing. Pa and the twins were just glad to get clean clothes—wrinkles didn't matter.

"Not a very good job, if you ask me."

"I'll take care of it, Miss Abigail," said Belle, stepping in front of Rowena.

"See that you do. All right, ladies, check your dresses. Are they buttoned completely? No flashes of flesh, please. Are your aprons spotless and tied straight? Each of you, check the person beside you."

"He's back," Belle whispered, as she checked the top button on Rowena's high-necked black dress. "Turn around so I can tie your apron."

"Who's back?" she said over her shoulder.

"Your rancher." Belle straightened the apron ties and tied them into a bow.

Rowena twisted around and looked at the taller girl over her shoulder. "Tell me you're kidding."

"Hold still. Nope. I saw him on the street. He was going into the Wild Women Saloon, though, so maybe he won't come here. If he does, I'll change tables with you."

"That doesn't solve the problem. But thank you for offering. Now turn around so I can tie your apron."

"Look on the bright side. Maybe you finally got through to him last Saturday."

"I doubt it. I didn't the week before, or the week before that. The man just doesn't hear the word no. I guess I'm going to have to be blunt with him. All right, you're done."

"What do you mean by 'blunt'?" Belle leaned back against the oak cabinets, resting her elbows on the cool marble countertop. "What are you planning?"

Reena pulled spoons and forks out of the silverware drawer. "I'll think of something."

"To tell you the truth, Reena, I don't know why you don't go out with him. He's a good-looking devil."

"Devil is right. I get shivers up and down my spine when he's around. And they're not good shivers." She couldn't put her finger on it, but there was something evil about the persistent rancher. "Besides, I'm too busy."

"Too busy doing what? Going around town disguised as a boy? How much fun can that be?"

"You'd be surprised." She opened the lower cabinet door and pulled out a stack of heavy dinner plates.

"I'm sure I would," Belle said dryly. She waggled her finger. "Honestly, Reena, you need to go out and have some fun. Enjoy yourself." She flashed an impish grin. "You should smile more. And you always wear black."

"So do you." Rowena couldn't help smiling back. Mr. Lowry required that all the girls who worked in his railroad restaurants wear properly modest black dresses, topped by spotless white aprons.

In the few short years since Fred Lowry opened the first Lowry Houses, they had become famous for fine food. At food stops, passengers and train crews rushed off the train and poured into the Lowry House. By the time the train pulled out an hour later, they had eaten meals worthy of the finest restaurants in New York.

"Come on, let's get to work." Rowena said.

"Let's start by checking out the saloons to see if we hear anything that might give us a clue to who's spying for the Simpsons here in Lost Gold." Caid surveyed the parlor of his suite. It was mahogany paneled like his father's library—the library where he'd stood before his father's huge desk and endured so many lectures. "Come on, let's go outside." He opened the French doors and stepped out onto his private balcony overlooking Main Street. "Once we find their spy, he'll lead us to them."

Tanner leaned over the wrought-iron railing, idly watching the people going by on Main Street. "You know, Caid, every time I think about Goodie's story, I'm struck by how unbelievable it is. Are you sure she wasn't setting you up or trying to get you out of Savannah?"

"What for? She doesn't know what I do. Hell, she thinks I'm a dilettante, like everyone else she knows. The only reason she came to me is because I'm the only Yankee she knows."

A wagon heavily laden with beer kegs rattled by and the aroma of beer drifted up to them.

"I find it incredible that the Simpsons still could be trying to set up a Second Confederacy. Robert E. Lee surrendered twenty years ago. Don't they know the War Between the States is over?"

"Not to the diehards. Just because Lee surrendered doesn't mean they did. Plenty of Confederate families fled the United States to avoid living under Yankee rule, and many, including the Simpsons, settled in Mexico. I'd already heard rumors that the gold stolen in the Southwest was going to a Johnny Reb plot to take over Arizona."

Tanner shook his head. "Are they crazy? How can they think they'll succeed?"

"You're forgetting that Arizona was a Confederate state. It lost its statehood and now is back to being a territory. A lot of people here aren't happy about that. The Rebs think there are enough malcontents to revolt and take over the territory. And they may be right."

"Then we have our work cut out for us."

"That we do." Caid drummed his fingers on the iron railing. "The Simpsons are the ringleaders. We capture them and we stop the take-over."

"But why was a conversation about Arizona taking place in Savannah?"

"Colonel Hensen, Goodie's father, has kept in close touch with the Simpsons. They're distant cousins."

"Oh ho, now I'm beginning to get a better idea of this whole Reb plot." He slanted an assessing glance at Caid. "Is it my imagination or are you getting a soft spot in your heart for Goodie?"

Caid snorted. "The soft spot would have to be in my head to get involved with a southern belle. I lived in South Carolina: I know how much trouble southern ladies can be." He wouldn't touch one with a twenty-foot pole, not with their fluttering eyelashes and lying mouths.

"Beside the Simpson lead, my Aunt May has a ranch not far from here. Her husband died about six months ago, and my mother is worried about her."

"Why don't you have her come into town, then? Your visit with your aunt will be another reason to linger."

"Exactly what I thought. Especially when I remembered that her husband was a Southerner."

"You think he was involved in the Simpsons' plot before he died?"

"I doubt it, but she's bound to know other Southerners around here. And who knows where that trail will lead? May will be joining us in the next few days."

"There's just one other thing, Caid."

"What's bothering you?"

"You."

"Me? Hell, I haven't chased a skirt since I left Savannah ten days ago, and I haven't shot anyone in weeks. In fact, I've been disgustingly respectable."

"You seem wound way too tight on this assignment. You didn't take any time off after the last one, and I'm worried you're pushing yourself too hard."

Caid raised a dark eyebrow at him. "Aren't you supposed to be my secretary?" he asked coolly. "Not a squawking mother-hen."

"Mother-hen, my foot! I'm the only one besides the President who knows what you really do. Damnation, man, not even your father knows."

"And we will leave it like that," Caid snapped. He turned away and walked into his suite.

Reena pushed open the door from the butler's pantry and sailed into the dining room. Dinner was in full swing and the deep rumble of men's voices engulfed her. All the windows and French doors were open, allowing the crisp mountain air to breeze through the room and cool it. Gaslight flickered from the walls and ceiling chandeliers. Since it was Saturday night, almost every table was occupied.

Although some of the ranchers and miners had

merely washed their hands and slicked back their hair, most of the men had dressed more formally in black jackets or frock coats. Scattered among them were a few women in dresses of violet, sky blue, emerald, and ruby, with matching ostrich feather hats. They dipped and bobbed like flowers waving in a field of black.

Putting on her professional smile, Rowena glided across the room toward her tables. She took the first man's order at a table of eight, then worked her way around the table.

At her next table, an all-too-familiar voice growled, "Hello, doll." She glanced up and found the rancher who wouldn't take no for an answer. Sprawled on his chair, with one arm hooked over the back, he grinned at her.

His dark green mail-order suit crackled with newness. His close-cropped hair curled over his head in a deceptively babyish cap, but his eyes had lost their innocence long ago. Ducking her head to break eye contact, she started taking orders quickly, anxious to get away.

"What would you like, sir?" She asked him the same question she'd asked everyone else. Up close he stank of whiskey, as though he'd rolled in it. Unable to hold her nose as she wanted to, Rowena tried not to inhale.

"You know what I'd like, missy." His low voice coiled around her like a snake. "It's Saturday night."

"Which entree do you prefer?" she asked, ignoring everything else.

"Chicken. Breasts and thighs would do nicely." He gave her a slow up-and-down look that left no doubt whose breasts and thighs he was talking about.

Embarrassed and outraged, Rowena gripped the folds of her black dress tightly to keep from slapping him. Somehow she finished taking orders and escaped to the kitchen.

She gave the chefs her orders quickly, before she forgot them in her blazing anger. Then she looked for Belle. Her friend was loading a tray with plates of chicken and sage dressing.

When Belle looked up and saw Rowena, she put down her tray. "Whew! I ain't never seen such red cheeks. You look like you got a mighty big burr under your saddle blanket. Want to spit it out?"

"I wish I could," she gritted. "The rancher's at table three."

"Enough said." Belle added a plate of sliced lamb and mint jelly to her tray. "I'll pick up the orders and serve that table; you take my table in the corner."

"Thanks, Belle. I owe you."

"Don't mention it. I'm the one that owes you, for teaching me to read and write."

"That has nothing to do with this!" She didn't want Belle doing things because she felt she owed her.

Taking several deep breaths to settle herself, Rowena squared her shoulders and went back out to her last table. It was partially hidden by a potted palm, so she couldn't see who was seated at it until she rounded the palm—then stopped short.

Kincaid Dundee sat there with the brown-haired man who'd gotten off the train with him. Damn! They were talking in low tones and broke off at her approach, but she managed to catch the words "Johnny Rebs."

"What would you gentlemen like?" Could he and the other man be Southern sympathizers? No, probably not, if they were talking about the Johnny Rebs. That was a damn Yankee term.

Dundee's silver-blue eyes met hers for a long, probing moment, until she broke the contact by picking up the printed menus they'd laid aside.

"Do I know you?" He studied her openly.

Nervously she touched the top button on her dress. His gaze followed the movement of her hand. Flustered, she folded her hands over the menus, flattening them against her chest like a shield.

She swallowed to moisten her suddenly dry throat. "I don't think so. You haven't been here before, have you?"

"No, but you seem—I don't know, but I feel as if we've met somewhere." The rumble in his deep voice sent a shiver cascading down her spine.

"Are you ready to order, or would you like me to come back later?" she asked coolly, to distract him.

"I'll have roast pork," the other man said. "What about you, Caid?"

"Roast beef, and wine." He ordered a bottle of the most expensive wine in the well-stocked cellar.

"Yes, sir." She walked away slowly, hoping to hear more of what they'd been talking about, but they didn't speak.

His friend had called him Caid. It fit him, she decided, rugged and hard-edged, like him.

The headwaiter took the wine to Caid's table personally, rather than trusting her. Rowena followed him, relieved. The ritual of opening the wine made her nervous.

The headwaiter slowly drew the cork out of the bottle, but instead of holding it out to Caid to sniff, handed it to her. "Monsieur," she gasped, "I—"

"It is time you learned. I must go to another table."

Stiffly, she took the cork and held it out to Caid.

"Closer," he growled, closing his large hand around hers and drawing it beneath his nose. She had to move a step closer to him. His thumb slid across the sensitive skin on the inside of her wrist, and his warm breath whispered across her fingertips.

"You may pour," was all he said as he released her. Then he looked up at her and she realized his caress had been no accident. Her hand shook so badly that the bottle clinked against the crystal wineglasses. Then she put the wine down on its coaster and left.

As she served her other tables, Rowena felt that prickly feeling on the back of her neck that told her someone was watching her. Finally she looked at the table beside the palm. From where she stood she could see Caid—and his eyes met hers. Her heart skipped a beat when he didn't turn away or pretend that he hadn't been watching her.

Later, coming around the palm with their dinners, she found the two men again talking in low tones. Again they broke off, but not before she heard Caid quote Tacitus, "When they make a peace, they wind up with a wilderness."

As she put their plates before them, she murmured the correct quote under her breath, "When they make a wilderness, they call it a peace." She started to walk away.

"Just one minute, miss," Caid said quietly.

"Yes, sir?" Damn! When would she learn to watch her tongue?

The curiosity in his eyes was even more alarming than anger would be. She didn't want anyone to be curious about her and asking questions.

"You know Tacitus?"

"Tacitus?" She shook her head innocently. "I don't think so. What does he look like?"

Tanner snorted and patted the corner of his mouth with his linen napkin to hide his smile.

"You know what I meant. You just corrected me."

"That's just something my father used to say. I thought he made it up," she hedged quickly.

"Is everything all right, gentlemen?" Miss Abigail's high, chirping voice came from just behind Rowena and she glanced over her shoulder at the tiny, birdlike woman.

"Yes, it's fine," Caid replied.

"Are you sure?" Miss Abigail gave him a searching look. "Perhaps you'd like another waitress to bring the rest of your dinner, Mr. Dundee?"

"This one is doing just fine," Caid repeated, and lifted a dark eyebrow at Rowena. "As a matter of fact, we were just discussing a mutual acquaintance."

When Miss Abigail turned to leave, she gave Rowena a stern, you'd-better-be-careful look.

"Thanks," Rowena said after the gray-haired woman walked away. There was no need to say more. He knew what would have happened if he'd complained.

In the kitchen, she ran into Belle.

"Your admirer shore do smell," her friend said. "Must be drunker than a pig in a pile of overripe peaches." She sighed and patted her snood-covered hair. "Come on, we better get this apple pie and coffee out to everyone. I'll finish up your rancher's table."

Rowena picked up the heavy silver coffeepot and began working her way around her tables.

"There you go, sir." She poured Mr. Lowry's famous rich, strong brew into Caid's cup.

"Thank you," he murmured.

Steam drifted up from the cup, carrying the aroma of fresh-roasted coffee. Rowena touched the white linen tea towel in her left hand against the spout so it didn't drip, then filled the other man's cup.

She went to the next table and filled all the cups there. Turning to serve another table, she found her way blocked. Her gaze traveled from the freshly polished black boots, up the new dark green pants and jacket, to a new white shirt, already sporting gravy stains, to the jowly, whiskey-reddened face of the rancher.

"Didn't you forget a table, missy?" He swayed back and forth as if he were on a ship.

"No, I didn't." Lifting her chin, she gazed at him coolly. Damned if she'd call him 'sir,' no matter what Mr. Lowry taught his employees.

He leered at her and chucked her under the chin. "You're so damn cute when you're mad. I love those red cheeks."

She slapped his hand away. "Don't you dare touch me," she snapped. "Don't you dare."

His leer turned positively satanic. "And who's going to stop me, missy?"

"I will." Rowena glanced around. She was trapped on both sides by tables and people, but, thank heavens, no one was paying attention to them. And behind her was a wide aisle where she'd have room to maneuver. This time she would take care of the pest once and for all.

She backed up a step.

He stepped forward, almost falling over his own boots.

"If you don't stop bothering me, I'll..." She backed another step. He was so drunk, this was going to be as easy as taking candy from a baby.

"You'll *what?*" He rocked back and forth unsteadily.

"You'll find out." Only one more step. Just one more and—

She backed against a brick wall.

Startled, she glanced over her shoulder.

And looked up, past broad shoulders, to Caid Dundee's rugged features. He was looking past her, his eyes hard as steel.

"Get behind me," he said, without taking his eyes from the rancher. Turning sideways, he pushed her behind his protective bulk.

"Wait," she protested to his back. "I can handle this."

"What's your problem, mister?" he asked in a razor-edged voice.

The rancher's brow furrowed in confusion. "Hey, what are you doing with my gal?"

"I'm not your girl," Rowena snapped. She tugged at Caid's black jacket. "I said I can take care of—"

"Hear that?" he told the man, ignoring her. "She says she's not your girl." Caid crossed his arms over his broad chest, relaxed, yet solid as a mountain.

The rancher glowered at him. "Get outta my way," he snarled, trying to shove him aside.

Caid didn't move. Silence spread like ripples on a pond as more diners noticed them.

"Perhaps you'd like to go outside?" Caid said softly.

Instead, the rancher reared back and punched Caid in the shoulder, barely rocking him. Catching the rancher's wrist in his hands, Caid swung him around and held the rancher's arm behind his back.

"Now, let's go outside," he gritted.

"Hey, what the hell are you doing?" the rancher bellowed, drawing the attention of everyone else in the dining room. Caid hustled him across the dining room, through the French doors, and out onto the flagstone terrace.

Her cheeks flying flags of fury and embarrassment, Rowena put the coffeepot down on an empty table, then followed them outside. Caid and the rancher were standing beside the low stone balustrade that circled the terrace and Caid was trying to talk sense into the rancher.

But the rancher was too busy throwing wild punches to listen. Caid blocked two of them, but the third landed on his jaw, snapping his head back.

"That does it!" Caid balled his hand and punched the rancher on the chin, knocking him over the balustrade into the rosebushes. The rancher grunted and cursed loudly as he tried to disentangle himself from the thorns.

Furious at Caid for interfering, Rowena watched as he shrugged his shoulders, straightened his jacket, then tugged at his shirt cuffs. *Now he's going to dust off his hands*, she bet herself. As if he'd read her mind, he brushed his palms together, then strolled back toward the French doors.

Rowena stepped out of the shadows, directly into his path. Golden light spilled through the windows, highlighting his prominent cheekbones. He stopped and gave her a triumphantly superior smile.

"He won't bother you again."

"Who called you?" She clamped her hands to her hips and glowered at him. "Why did you interfere? Did I ask you to take care of him for me. Well? Did I?"

"What?" He frowned and straightened, as if taken aback. "But I thought—"

"You thought! Ha! You obviously *didn't* think. I could have taken care of the situation! I didn't need you mixing in and making a big scene of it, and letting everyone in the room, including Miss Abby, know something was going on. I could have handled that rancher more quietly than you."

"Right. I suppose you were going to toss him over your shoulder."

"That's *exactly* what I was going to do, after I backed down the aisle and had enough room." She leaned forward at the waist and added fiercely, "I *could*, you know. My brothers showed me how to do it—and a lot of other things, too, Mr. Helpful Hero."

"Honey, you're just a tiny drink of water." He smiled down at her. "You need strength and muscle to toss a man." His upper lip twitched as if he was trying to keep from grinning.

Rowena saw red. "Don't you honey me!" She tapped him hard in the middle of his broad chest. "Don't you dare."

"Now, just a moment!" He wrapped his large hand around hers, completely enveloping it.

A tingling feeling flowed down his fingers into her hand, and she frowned in confusion.

"You're very pretty when you're angry," he said softly.

Rowena rolled her eyes. "Can't you come up with an original line? I already heard that one from your drunken friend."

She felt the vibration of his laugh through the hand still pressed to his chest. "Lady, you are something else." He trailed his long fingers down her arm.

"And don't you forget it!" Feeling strangely breathless, she backed away from him.

"I won't." His voice was as warm as an afternoon in July. "You can bet on that."

Chapter 3

Rowena spent the night with Caid Dundee. At least that was what it felt like to her, for he haunted her dreams: pushing her behind him and protecting her in a gunfight in one dream, beckoning to her from another, and kissing her in a third. When she awakened from that one, she could still feel his lips on hers.

Tired, she turned over and vowed not to dream about him again. But she did. When she awakened before sunrise on Sunday she was still tired, from tossing and turning all night.

But she had work to do for the Cause, so she resolved to put Caid's image out of her mind. She dressed quickly, then stealthily opened her dresser drawer so she wouldn't waken Belle. Reaching way in back, she took out a map of the route to the Colony and two hundred dollars from her secret stash of greenbacks. She stuffed them into the hidden pocket she'd sewn into her petticoat, then went out to the long, low stable to meet her brother. It was almost sunrise but still dark inside the building, with its shadows and dark corners. She paused, listening for any sound that shouldn't have been there.

All she heard were soft hoof thuds as the horses moved around restlessly. Several snuffled at their empty hay racks, waiting for their morning feed. The sweet, grassy scent of alfalfa hay filled the building.

She began to walk down the long line of box stalls. A strange wheezing sound stopped her in her tracks, and it took her several seconds to recognize the snores of an old horse. She'd just taken another step when something brushed her leg and she jumped.

"Hi, Cat," she said, bending down to pet the huge tortoiseshell. "I don't have any milk for you today." She'd brought him milk twice before, and now he twined between her legs.

A stall door at the far end creaked open and a man emerged, but she couldn't identify him in the dim light. Was the groom here so early? Then he began to walk toward her, and she recognized her brother's distinctive rolling stride and the even more distinctive golden ostrich plume he wore in his Confederate-gray Stetson, so the girls would think him dashing.

"Ah, it's you Jeff." She hurried to meet him,

clasped his hands, and rose on her toes to give her tall brother a peck on his cheek.

"Morning, sis." He stroked his brown beard thoughtfully. "How did you know it was me and not Robert Lee?"

"You walk differently, and he's a bit taller than you. Haven't you ever noticed that when you two look in the mirror?"

"No, can't say that I have." He pulled one hand free and brushed it over her blond tresses. "I miss you."

"I miss you, too." She dropped his hand and stepped back to get a better look at him.

"How are you doing otherwise?"

"It all feels so strange. I'm still not used to wearing dresses—they're such a bother, with all the stupid rules about how many petticoats and a bustle and a damn corset, even. Sometimes I feel like I'm laced to within an inch of my life, and I'm afraid that someday I'll explode, like a volcano."

"You'll get used to it," he said unsympathetically. "After all, ladies wear corsets all the time."

"Thanks for your support, brother," she murmured in a wry voice. "And it's never quiet here, like it was when you and I went out to tend the cattle and we'd just sit there and listen to the breeze playing in the grass."

"You're not here to listen to the breeze, Rowena. You're here because we need you here. What you're doing is crucial to the Cause and the Second Confederacy."

"I know—but I want to be home. I miss Papa

and everyone." She wanted to be out on the range, riding her horse hell-bent-for-leather. She wanted to wear shirts and pants like her brothers, instead of dresses. She wanted to sit at the dinner table and listen to Papa talk about who should be President of the United States instead of Grover Cleveland.

"We need the information you're getting about gold shipments, and the work you're doing as a courier and recruiter is vital. No one could take your place here." His voice lowered to a conspiratorial whisper. "Besides using the gold to arm new recruits, like the ones you're sending us, we're using it to buy food and clothing for the widows and orphans of heroes who laid down their lives for the Cause. Always remember you're helping them, too."

"That's what I keep telling myself—that I'm doing it for the Cause. But it's really strange, Jeff. No one here seems to have ever heard about the Cause. It's as if they think the War for States' Rights ended when Lee surrendered twenty years ago."

"To them it did. They don't know that there are Southerners like us who never surrendered—that we may have retreated temporarily, but now we're ready to fight our way back. And when we do, we'll be stronger than anything the Yankees faced in the war."

She paced away a couple of steps, then turned to face him. "It sounded so much easier when we talked about it in Mexico. In our colony I knew that I was a soldier in the struggle to bring back the

Confederacy. But here in Arizona, no one seems to care."

"The Yankees have short memories. We don't."

"But it's not only Yankees. I meet Southerners who stayed, and they don't talk about the Cause. They've gone on with their lives and seem to be doing well."

"They're just putting up a good front, or else they were traitors right from the beginning."

"I don't think so." She clasped her hands together. "I've been here two months and the first time I heard anyone mention anything about the Cause was last night."

"Who? Southerners, I'll bet."

"Not from their accent." She thought back over the bits and pieces she'd heard. "Actually, they were talking about Johnny Rebs. That doesn't sound like Southerners to me." She didn't mention that one of them was the son of a man Papa hated.

"Maybe they're Northerners who've seen the light and want to join us."

"These men aren't from around here. They came in on the train yesterday. One of them has a beautiful white stallion."

"Whooee!" He slapped his Stetson against his leg, raising a puff of dust. "I saw that stud when I came in. That's the best horse I've seen since we left South Carolina. I'll bet he's got bloodlines that go back farther than Queen Victoria's."

"He's hot-blooded, all right," Rowena said, thinking of the way Caid Dundee had handled him yesterday. "I saw him buck his way off the train. His owner is good with horses."

"Maybe you should introduce me to him. If he's trying to join us, that'll make it easy for him."

"What if he isn't, though? What if he's gotten wind of our plan to take over Arizona and is here to stop us? After all, nobody talks about Johnny Rebs anymore. Why don't you let me see what I can find out about him first?"

"All right, sis. Try to get to know him—you know what I mean." He waggled his eyebrows rakishly. "Now, what else have you got for me in the way of news?"

Rowena brightened. "The President is coming to Arizona and he'll be going through Lost Gold. Everyone's all excited and talking about what they'll wear, and—"

"He's not your President, sis."

"I know. But it's still exciting." Why did he have to be such a wet blanket all the time? "And a new recruit came in on the train yesterday. I talked to him last night and he'll be joining us in the next few minutes."

"What about the bank? Any gold there?"

She rolled her eyes. "You've got a one-track mind, Jeff."

"Damn tootin'! I'm fighting for the Cause! You are, too: don't you forget that."

"Don't you think I know that? The Ranchers' Mercantile Bank has a strongbox full of gold bars from one mine and they're expecting another in about ten days. After the other one arrives, they'll ship both out on the train."

Jeff slapped her on the back. "That's the kind of information we need, sis."

"Thanks, big brother." At the edge of her vision she glimpsed movement at the back entrance to the stable and turned. "Hi, Terry, come join us." She waved at the lanky cowboy. "Jeff, I'd like to introduce Terry Alexander. He's our newest recruit in the Second Confederate Army."

"Welcome, Terry," Jeff said, shaking hands. "Glad to have you with us. Did my sis give you all the information?"

Terry glanced at Rowena. "Boy, did she! You're an amazing lady, Miss Rowena."

"Thank you, Terry, but I'm just doing my job, like everyone else in the Confederate Army. And I have something for you." Turning away from them, she lifted her skirt and pulled out the map and greenbacks from her petticoat pocket. "Keep this map with you in case you have to get out of the country, Terry. It'll get you through Mexico to the Colony. Jeff will see that you're outfitted with a horse and supplies and tell you what to do." She handed the money to her brother.

"Rowena is our banker in between jobs," he explained, folding the greenbacks and stuffing them in his rear pocket.

Footsteps crunched on the gravel outside the front entrance to the stable.

"Someone's coming. I'll see you next Sunday." Jeff wrapped his arms around her in a bear hug and gave her a quick buss on the cheek. "Come on, Terry," he said, darting out into the alley.

The footsteps came nearer, much nearer. Rowena glanced around frantically, looking for an excuse to be out there so early. There was no time to hide, or—

The white stallion extended his head over the half-height stall door and looked at her. He nickered softly.

"You're a help, love," she murmured as she hurried over to stroke his velvet-soft muzzle.

Suddenly a man stood silhouetted in the doorway and paused for a second, just as she had, as if listening.

As he approached her, an air of alertness and purpose clinging to his broad shoulders, Rowena moved closer to the stallion. She scratched the stud under the chin, in the spot that so many horses liked, and watched. Gradually the man's stern features became visible in the gloom.

Caid Dundee! Rowena stifled a groan.

She didn't want to see him this morning, not after her dreams last night. She still didn't know what to make of them.

"Hi, boy," he said, as he neared. "Ready for a— well, well, what do we have here?" She had to give him credit, he didn't slow a bit as he walked up to his horse—and her. "Isn't it a little early to be out here?" He rested his fingers lightly on the stud's muzzle.

He was standing so close she caught a whiff of lemon soap. She took a step back, too aware of the powerful muscles beneath his ruffled white shirt. "I'm on my way to serve breakfast."

"By way of the stables?" He raised a dark eyebrow at her.

"I miss our horses," she said simply, for it was true. "I rode every day at our ra—" she caught herself, "—farm. And your stud was so beautiful I wanted to see him again." She scratched the stallion's arched neck. "Right, love?"

"His name is Diablo." His low voice vibrated through her. He smelled of soap and leather and maleness, and for the first time in her life she found it an oddly enticing combination.

"Devil? But he's white." She combed her fingers through the stud's mane, straightening the long, silky-harsh strands. What would his owner's mane feel like if she combed her fingers through it? Would his shaggy dark hair feel silky, or straw-harsh? Good Lord, where did that thought come from?

"Appearances can be deceiving. Haven't you ever met someone who looked like an angel and lied like the devil?"

"Too many times!" Caid himself reminded her of the devil.

He didn't take his gaze from her as he reached into his jacket pocket and pulled out an apple, then held it out on the flat of his palm.

The stallion sniffed it, then whisked it out of Caid's hand. He crunched down on it, letting half drop out of his mouth as he crunched the other half noisily.

"He has no manners," Caid said, still watching her. He rested his hand on the horse's neck, possessively.

"What do you expect?" His hand was large, powerful, she noticed. Would it feel heavy on her, or light as—

Damn! What was he doing to her? Scrambling her brains? She turned all her attention to rubbing the horse's neck.

The stallion lowered his head to get the other half of his apple, and as Caid's hand slid down the horse's neck, his fingers tangled with hers. Suddenly there was nothing between the two of them.

She didn't want to look at him, yet something tugged at her, compelled her. Slowly, hesitantly, she looked up.

In that light, his eyes were neither silver nor blue, but a combination, like mists rising from a sunlit sea.

He drew his callus-roughened fingertips across the palm of her hand. Her heart thumped wildly against her ribs. "I . . . I . . ." She swallowed to moisten her suddenly dry mouth.

"Hey. Did you feed that damn devil horse?" the stableman yelled from the other end of the stable.

Startled, Rowena jerked away from Caid's touch. He didn't move and she stared at him, wide-eyed and confused. Then she shook her head, trying to make sense of the feelings swirling through her.

Thankfully the stallion raised his head, coming between them as he snuffled at Caid's jacket, looking for more apples. Caid ran his hands over the animal—almost, she thought, as if he needed to do something.

"Like I said, he has no manners," Caid said, but she detected a certain tension in his gravelly voice.

"He's a sweetheart," she murmured, rubbing the horse behind the ears. "Aren't you, love?" And he deserved extra apples for coming between them.

The stud turned to her and lowered his head slightly, as if to give her better access. She continued to rub him. His eyes half-closed and he exhaled a long gust of air, like a sigh.

"I'll be damned!" Caid leaned against the stall door. "Do you know this horse never lets anyone but me touch him?"

"He let me." She kept her gaze on the stallion, but she felt a shimmer of awareness that told her Caid was watching her.

"Do you have some sort of magic for taming savage beasts?"

"Ha! If I did, I'd have used it last night on that cowboy."

"Maybe it only works on horses."

"Well, it certainly didn't work on an ass." She clamped her hand across her mouth and gave him a stricken look. "Oh, Lord, I can't believe I said that. I meant a donkey."

He flashed her a lopsided grin that turned her knees to jelly. "I think the first term was perfect, Miss—?"

"S-Sims." Damn! She'd almost said Simpson. "Reena Sims. About last night?" She glanced at him—and was immediately sorry. He was closer than before and his broad shoulders blocked out the rest of the stable, so they were alone. "Thank you for helping."

"Glad I could. Where are you from, Miss Sims?"

"Kansas," she said, telling him what she'd told everyone at the hotel when she'd gone to work there.

"Really? I would never have guessed it with that southern accent of yours."

"Me? A southern accent? I never thought I had *any* accent."

"You do."

She thought fast. "My family was from the South, but they left after the war. Maybe that's where I got it."

"Maybe."

With the horse between them again, she was brave enough to study him. Crow's feet were beginning to form at the corners of his eyes, so she knew he spent most of his time outdoors. A thin white scar sliced across his left eyebrow and disappeared into his dark hair. The urge to trace its path with her fingertips surprised her.

Belatedly she remembered where she was—and why. "Heavens, I'm going to be late, if I don't hurry." She patted her upswept hair nervously. "I better get to work."

She whirled in a rustle of starched petticoats and hurried away. She wouldn't look back, she vowed. She wouldn't.

She'd almost reached the last stall when her steps slowed . . . slowed . . . and she glanced back.

He was still leaning against the stall door, still watching her. She drew a quick breath and hastened on, unnerved by the way her heart skipped a beat.

She didn't look back again. She didn't dare.

Caid watched her walk away. When she'd been standing close, he'd caught a tantalizing whiff of lilacs, just like last night. But today he'd detected something mixed with the lilacs, something spicy. Like her, he thought, spicy and sweet at the same time.

He'd had to shove his hands in his pockets to keep from reaching for her, testing the satin feel of her flesh, and combing his fingers through that golden river of hair, of tasting the promise of her so-sensual full lips.

It was strange that he was so aware of her, knowing she'd been out there to meet her lover. He'd seen the man ride away as he approached, and she'd been flushed when he walked up to her. From her lover's kisses? But what the hell did he care? The wave of anger that swept him surprised him—and answered his question.

"Hell!" He couldn't be attracted to her; she just intrigued him. Yet something about her bothered him, too. Something didn't quite ring true. He couldn't put his finger on it, but he knew eventually he'd figure it out. He'd learned long ago to trust his instincts. They had saved him more than once from a knife in the back.

The stud shoved him with his muzzle. He

reached for the bridle hanging on a peg outside
Diablo's stall. "Come on, Diablo, we're going for a
run." He slipped the bit in the horse's mouth, then
pulled the headstall over his ears and buckled it at
his cheek.

A good run on Diablo always helped him see
things in a clearer light. And he needed to see
Reena Sims in a much clearer light.

Otherwise he was liable to do something rash
and wonderful.

Chapter 4

Rowena slouched on the park bench in front of the Ranchers' Mercantile Bank and watched Caid striding toward her with his gun-slinger's walk.

He wore a height-of-fashion black Norfolk jacket with matching trousers, and his shirt's white ruffles foamed up around his bronze neck. From his clothes, she would have taken him for a dabbler from back East, a man who didn't need to earn a living and had nothing to do.

But her instincts said he was something hard and dangerous, and she believed her instincts.

She hadn't seen him since inside the stable the day before, and now her heart did a crazy hop, skip, and jump.

As he neared, she tilted her sombrero forward so she looked like she was dozing. Rowena watched his boots pass and waited until he was halfway down the block before she rose and sauntered in the same direction.

He pushed through the swinging doors into the Wild Women Saloon. When she got to the saloon, Rowena paused at the entrance, her nose assaulted by the stench of stale smoke and cheap whiskey and other smells she didn't want to think about. She'd never been inside, but she wanted to see who Caid was meeting and what they were talking about.

Someone was playing an out-of-tune piano. She swallowed, squared her shoulders, and slipped through the doors, barely making them swing with her slight shape. Inside she waited for her eyes to adjust to the dimness that also helped her blend in.

The saloon wasn't crowded, with only a few men standing at the mahogany bar that extended across the back of the room. A man stood behind it, wiping the bar with a white towel.

Caid had joined his companion, the brown-haired man, at a table. Many of the tables were empty, including one in the corner, next to Caid and his friend. She moseyed over and pulled out a chair. When it screeched across the floor, she cringed and glanced around, sure that everyone in the bar was watching her. They weren't.

Hastily she sat down and rested her hands on the round table. As soon as she did, a young woman in a short, tight, red satin dress sashayed over, swinging her hips so wildly it was a wonder she could walk. "What'll you have, stranger?"

"Whiskey," she said in her gruffest voice.

Caid flicked a glance at her and nodded, obviously recognizing the "boy" who'd led his horse for him. He told the woman, "I'll have a Bushmill's Irish Whiskey. What about you, Tanner?"

"A shot of your very finest Kentucky bourbon."

"Coming right up."

Rowena looked at the pictures of very well-endowed ladies wearing feathers and nothing else that adorned the walls, but listened with all her might to what Caid and Tanner were saying.

"Thinking about Miss Tacitus?" Tanner asked, casually making rings on the table with an empty shot glass.

Rowena's ears pricked up. Good Lord, was that what they called her?

Caid's brow furrowed into a frown. "Hell, no! Why *would* I be? And her name's Reena Sims."

"Fast work, even for you." Tanner grinned at him.

"Uh-uh. I happened to meet her down at the stables yesterday." Caid glanced around. "Where the hell are our drinks?"

"Happened?"

"She was meeting her lover," Caid growled. "Let's get down to business. What did you find out?"

Rowena stiffened, surprised that he'd realized she'd met someone, yet relieved. He didn't know it, but he'd just supplied her with a reason to be down at the stable from now on.

"There's one strongbox of gold in the bank right

now, and they're expecting another one in the next week. They'll keep them both in the bank vault until they go out on the train to the East. And I—" Tanner broke off as the saloon girl plunked their drinks down on the table.

Rowena almost snickered when she leaned far over, giving Tanner a good view of her ample cleavage. "Anything else I can get ya, sir?" she drawled, batting her eyelashes so fast, it was a wonder she didn't take off like a bird.

"Not right now, little lady."

The girl plopped Rowena's drink down and left. She lifted the amber liquid to her mouth and took a tiny sip. Even so, she choked as it burned all the way down.

It tasted awful and made her eyes water. Why did men like the stuff? She put the glass down and looked up to find Caid watching her.

"What about you?" Following Caid's gaze, Tanner glanced over his shoulder at her, then turned back to his friend. "You have any luck, Caid?"

"Hmm?" He swung back to Tanner. "I talked to the sheriff about the Simpsons and the Second Confederacy, and—" he lowered his voice and Reena couldn't hear what he said.

Shock froze the breath in her lungs. He'd been talking about her brothers and the Confederacy! Why? She didn't dare look up from the table because she wanted to scream at him, *Why?*

Several cowhands marched in, their heavy boots echoing on the floor. Talking loudly and slapping each other on the back, they bellied up to the bar.

"Bartender, double whiskeys," a cowboy shouted in an all-too-familiar voice. Her ardent admirer.

Rowena repressed a shudder of disgust. Hunching over her drink, she eyed him from beneath her sombrero. Would he recognize Caid? Probably not, she reassured herself; he was drunk Saturday night, too.

Resting his arms on the bar, the cowboy leaned over the polished surface. When the bartender slapped two shot glasses down, he drained one, then the other. "That's better," he said, wiping his mouth on his sleeve.

Rowena watched Caid from the corner of her eye. He hadn't moved, but she was sure he knew who the cowboy was.

Bracing his hands flat on the bar, the cowboy tried to focus on the huge mirror behind the bar, but he kept swaying. "Why's the mirror moving?" Suddenly he peered intently into the mirror. "Hey, there's the bastard who interfered on Saturday night."

"This is your chance to take care of him, Seth," one of his friends shouted, clapping him on the back.

"Yeah, you're right." Turning around, the cowboy braced his elbows on the bar and glared at Caid, who ignored him and went on talking to Tanner. "Look at the big man, pretending he doesn't hear me," he said, suddenly sober and as menacing as a rattlesnake. "Today there's no women around to protect you, big man."

"Ignore him," she heard Caid mutter to Tanner.

"He's not smart enough to go away. Here, show him your match trick," Tanner said, lighting a match and holding it out to Caid. "Maybe you'll get rid of him that way."

Caid took the burning match in his left hand and held it up so everyone could see it. He flipped back the ruffled cuff on his right arm, so it didn't get in the flame. Then he snuffed the flame between his thumb and forefinger.

"What's the trick?" Seth asked. "I can do that." He struck a match against the oak bar then held it up and went to snuff the flame between his thumb and finger, as Caid had. "Hey! That hurts." He shook his hand, then sucked on his finger.

"Of course it does," Caid said quietly, not even turning around to look at Seth. "The trick is not to mind the pain."

Rowena's respect for him went up a couple of notches, as did her wariness. What kind of man could control his instinctive avoidance of pain?

"Think you're so high and mighty, don't you?" Seth swaggered over to Caid's table and glared at him. Caid ignored him. The cowboy kicked the table over and grabbed Caid by the lapels of his jacket, jerking him to his feet. "What say, big man? How about we step out back and settle this?"

Caid brought his hands up in a swift movement that broke the cowboy's hold. "I already settled it, cowboy." His voice was deceptively soft, yet it had a steely edge.

"Naw, it isn't. Come on out back and settle this like a man. If you can, that is."

Caid gave him a slow, contemptuous scrutiny. "I don't engage in fisticuffs with common ruffians," he said, straightening his ruffled shirt cuffs.

"You don't, huh?" Even as he spoke, Seth's right fist came up in a wide-armed swing that would have staggered Caid—if it had connected with his jaw.

But Caid feinted away, than dodged back in and landed a powerful punch to Seth's jaw that sent him staggering backward until he slipped on spilled beer and sat down abruptly.

He sat there, legs outstretched, shaking his head. "Ain't any of you no-good saddle tramps goin' to stand by me?" he finally yelled. "Or am I goin' to be looking for a new crew tomorrow?"

"Looks like Seth needs help," someone shouted.

Suddenly all hell broke loose, as men launched themselves at others and landed heavy, thudding fists.

Rowena ducked as a beer bottle sailed past her ear and hit a bull-necked man in the back of the head. He roared like a wounded buffalo. Turning, he glared at her.

"You sniveling little coward." Head down, he charged straight at her. Reena was too astounded to move. "Too afraid to meet me face to face, eh?" Grabbing the edge of her table, he flipped it up. The big round of wood came straight at her.

She tried to get out of the way, but the edge caught her in the upper lip and nose, knocking her out of her chair and onto the floor behind the table. Her sombrero fell off and her hair tumbled down over her face. Scrunching down behind the table, eyes watering from the stinging blow, she frantically felt around for her hat, clamped it on her head, and tucked her hair back up into it.

When she finally peeked around the table, all she saw were men throwing punches at each other and rolling around on the sawdust-covered floor. The bull-necked man had leaped on Caid's back and clamped his arm around his throat in a stranglehold. Caid tried to dislodge the bull-necked man while he fought off the battering blows of another man.

Two against one wasn't fair. Rowena picked up her chair and swung it as high as she could, intending to hit the bull-necked man's back. But her aim was too low and she got him in the butt instead.

"What the hell?" He let go of Caid and turned to see who'd hit him. "Damn! You again?" He came toward her, his hands open in giant claws. "This time I'm going to break your scrawny little neck, boy."

"I don't think so," Caid said coolly, grabbing him by the shoulder and swinging him around to meet a knuckle sandwich. The bull-necked man looked surprised as he crumpled to the floor. Then Caid turned and polished off the other man who'd been using him as a punching bag.

In the momentary lull, he grinned over at Reena. "Thanks." Then surprise seemed to flash in his eyes. "Come on, Tanner," he yelled, "let's get out of here. You, too," he added, grabbing Rowena's arm and dragging her along as he headed for the back door.

Outside, the three of them ran down the alley past wooden buildings for a block before they slowed.

"Well, that was fun," Caid said, not even breathing hard. He clenched and unclenched his hand several times. "You all right, Tanner?"

"Sure, but it looks like your hand is going to be sore and swollen."

"It's nothing. What about you," he said, turning to Rowena. "Are you hurting anyplace?"

"No, sirree," she said in her deepest, gruffest voice. "I'm just fine. But I better get on home. Mama will worry about me."

"Wait, son," Caid said, grabbing her shoulder through the serape and stopping her in her tracks. "You've helped me twice now and I want to return the favor. I don't think you should go home until we take care of your bloody nose."

"Bloody nose!" Rowena clamped her hands across her face. When she pulled them away, she found a streak of blood on one finger. "Oh no!"

"I don't think it's broken, though. Here, let me see." He pinched her nose between two fingers and wiggled it slightly.

"Is it?"

Caid shook his head. "Uh-uh. You would have screamed." His upper lip twitched suspiciously.

Her eyes grew big. "I would have screamed?" she managed in a strangled tone.

"Come on, boy," he said, grabbing her elbow and towing her along as he strode purposefully toward the hotel. "We've got to get you cleaned up."

"Right," Tanner added, as he kept pace with them. "You don't want to scare your mama, now, do you? Caid will take good care of you—won't you, Caid?"

"Let go of me." She tried to dig in her boots, but the ground was too hard. "I can do it myself. I don't need any help."

"We're already at the hotel." Caid paused at the open gate in the wall surrounding the hotel garden. Beyond him, she saw Miss Abigail standing on the porch, frowning at the three of them as if they were making too much noise.

"Come on," Caid said, his hand still wrapped around her elbow. "We'll just go up to my room and take care of it."

Not wanting to make a ruckus in front of Miss Abigail and reveal her disguise, she walked quietly beside Caid as they started up the wide steps to the porch. Too quickly they were past Miss Abigail and walking up the back stairs to the second floor.

"Let go!" Rowena tried to jerk her arm free when they reached the second floor. It didn't work.

"It'll only take a second, and then you can go home." He hurried her along the second-floor hall. Caid stopped at his door and drew a key out of his pocket, but still kept his other hand wrapped around her arm. "By the way," he turned to her, "what's your name, boy?"

Name? No one had ever asked her before. "Ah, John."

"We'll get you cleaned up in no time, Ahjohn." He pushed the door open.

"Look, mister, I can take care of myself." Rowena clamped her hand around the door frame.

"Come on, we can't stand out here in the hall and discuss this. What if one of those nosy Lowry girls came by? You know how gossipy they are."

"You—I—" Rowena struggled to get something more out through the blaze of anger. She was a Lowry girl and she'd *never* engaged in gossip!

He hustled her through the doorway. "Yeah, you're right. They'd probably faint at the sight of you, with all that blood."

He slammed the door and leaned back against it, his hand on the knob, and eyed her the way the big bad wolf eyed Goldilocks. She swallowed, trying to wet her desert-dry throat.

He slowly advanced on her with a grim expression, and she backed up until she came up against the sideboard. Damn! If she got out of this mess, she was never going to dress up like a boy again. Never!

"I'll pour us a couple of drinks," he said, reaching past her and uncorking a bottle.

"No! I mean I don't drink."

He glanced at her, his brow wrinkled in confusion. "Wasn't that a drink you had at the saloon?"

"Yes, but that's different." She half-turned away

and leaned over the sideboard. How had she gotten herself into this mess?

"Are you all right?"

She nodded, aware that there was a warm tone in his voice and something that sounded suspiciously like a smile.

"I think we've had enough of this charade," Caid said quietly. "Don't you?"

Rowena blinked. Charade? What did he—She turned to him, wide-eyed. "Charade?"

"Yes." He swept her sombrero off and her long hair fell over her shoulders. He closed his hand around several strands and tugged gently. "This charade, Miss Sims."

"How long have you known?"

"I first suspected Saturday night. But today when you hit that cowboy with the chair, part of your hair was hanging down your back like a banner."

She groaned. "Oh, no. How many people saw it?"

"No one. But that's why I hustled you out of there so quickly."

"Why would you do that?" Tilting her head, she eyed him warily. "You don't know me."

"But you've helped me twice now. It was the least I could do. Besides, I was curious to see if I was right." He grinned. "You are quite an original, Miss Sims. Now, let's get you cleaned up." He drew her over to the sink in the corner, then wet a washcloth and turned to her.

"I really can do this myself." She tried to take the washcloth.

"Uh-uh. I can see the smudges and blood better than you can." Wadding up the washcloth, he daubed gently at her nose and cheeks.

"I feel like a child, the way you're wiping my face."

"It's what you get for going around dressed as a boy. You never know what kind of trouble you'll get into." He refolded the washcloth so a clean side was out and daubed at the corner of her nose again.

"So I've discovered," she said wryly. He was so close she could see the tiny scar that ran through his eyebrow. She traced its course across his temple up into his hair with her finger. "How did you get this?"

He stilled and she could see the bits of silver in his blue eyes. "It happened a long time ago. I lost a battle with some bullies." He gazed down at her lips as though mesmerized, and his fingers left shivery trails as he slowly threaded them through her curls.

He was going to kiss her.

And she wanted him to, she realized with astonishment. For the first time in her life, she wanted a man to kiss her. Nervously she swiped her tongue over her lips to wet them.

Caid's lips brushed hers. They slid to the corner of her mouth, then came back and settled with a warmth that enticed her into a new world of sensation. He slid his large hands to her shoulders and drew her closer.

She leaned into him, tantalized and wanting

more. His mouth moved over hers with delicious intent, making her breathless.

The clock on the mantel bonged loudly, startling them. Rowena listened as the clock bonged three more times, and twisted away.

"It's four o'clock! I'll be late for work." She glanced around frantically. "Where's my sombrero? I've got to skedaddle."

"Here." He watched as she hastily tucked all her hair up into the crown. "And don't worry if you're late. I'll tell your supervisor that I asked you to do a little extra cleaning in my room."

"But it isn't fair to the other girls if they have to cover for me. Is it all tucked in?" She turned so he could see all sides.

"Yes. But you may have some swelling tomorrow from getting hit by the table." He followed her to the door. "So don't be surprised if you have a couple of black eyes."

"Shiners?" She remembered how her brothers had looked with black eyes. "I'll look like a raccoon!"

She saw laughter dancing in his eyes. "But a delightful raccoon."

"Would you want your dinner served by a raccoon?" She started to open the door.

He stopped her. "Let me look in the hall first. I don't want anyone to see you leaving."

"That's very nice of you, Mr. Dundee, protecting my reputation like that."

"You've got it all wrong, Miss Sims. I'm protecting *my* reputation. I don't want anyone to see a boy sneaking out of my suite."

It took her a second to understand his meaning. Then she chuckled and gave him a very womanly smile. "Don't worry, Mr. Dundee. No woman would ever suspect that of you."

His answering smile howled of wolves and pursuit and seared her all the way down to her toes.

Chapter 5

Caid closed the door behind Reena Sims and leaned back against it. He'd barely tasted her before his kiss was cut short, but he knew he wanted to do it again. He was intrigued. She was an innocent when it came to kissing, he could tell that—and he'd be damned glad to tutor her.

He'd dreamed about her the last few nights—of undressing her, of taking off one piece of clothing at a time, starting with a perky little hat that sat atop her upswept hair. After the hat, he would remove the pins from her hair and catch it as it fanned over her shoulders and fill his hands with the golden strands.

Then he'd start at the top button of her primly buttoned dress and open one button at a time, savoring her unveiling. What would he find beneath her dress? She didn't wear a corset; he knew that already. Did she wear cotton or silk next to her skin? Silk, he'd bet; she was a sensual, passionate creature who'd like the feel of silk.

"Aw, hell," he muttered. What was he doing, dreaming such dreams?

He walked over to his writing desk, tapping it absently as something bothered him, ghosting along at the edge of his consciousness. He began to pace.

Something about Reena was wrong. His instincts were yammering that something was wrong. But what?

He grimaced and shook his head at the free-for-all in the Wild Women Saloon. He'd never forget the sight of Reena swinging a chair at a miner who outweighed two of her. What would the miner have done if he'd known the boy who'd hit him was really a woman?

She had been at the train station dressed as a boy, also—and she wandered around town dressed as a boy. Why?

Was she afraid of being accosted if she went walking alone? Remembering her response to the persistent cowboy, he knew she wouldn't be. So there had to be another reason. Such as . . . ?

What would be the advantage of dressing as a boy? Men would not accord her the courtesies they'd accord a woman. In fact, they probably wouldn't even see a boy.

He stopped pacing. That was it!

She could wander around town and people wouldn't pay any attention to her. They'd ignore a

boy, wouldn't even notice him most of the time.
Which meant . . . that she could listen in on conversations and gather information.

Very clever, he thought. As a waitress she picked
up information from overheard conversations, and
when she wasn't waitressing, she was wandering
around town, gathering more information.

But why? What could she use it for—unless *she*
was the Simpsons' spy? He banged his fist on the
writing desk. He hadn't even considered that their
spy might be a woman.

Come to think of it, he'd passed her sitting on a
bench on his way to the Wild Women Saloon. She'd
come into the saloon after him—and sat down close
enough to hear what he and Tanner said. Hell's
bells, she'd followed him!

But why? There was no way she could know that
he was a government agent. So why would she follow *him*?

He walked over to his humidor and took out a
cigar. There was only one way to get answers to
his questions. He was going to get to know Reena
Sims a lot better.

And, he thought with a smile, he was going to
thoroughly enjoy every minute he was with her.

"I'd like to send a telegram," Caid said as he
walked into the telegraph office in the train depot.

"Yes, sir. Would you write it down? And the address, too." The man handed him a pad, then
turned away as his key began to chatter.

Caid composed his message and handed it to the

balding older man. The telegrapher read it, then the address. He looked up at Caid. "This is the address?"

"That's right. I'll wait while you send it."

"Yes, sir, Mr. Dundee. I've never sent a telegram to the White House before."

Caid leaned on the counter and idly watched the passengers getting off the westbound train which had just arrived. The conductor walked toward the depot with the passengers.

And Reena hurried across the platform seemingly looking for someone among the passengers. Caid frowned thoughtfully. What was she doing at the train station?

Apparently not seeing him, Reena ran into the conductor.

Caid heard her exclaim, "Pardon me. I didn't see you." She bent to pick up her purse, which had fallen from her wrist.

"Pardon me, miss. Here, let me help you." The conductor also bent down to pick up the comb and wallet that had spilled out of her purse. "Here you go." He scooped up her purse and handed it to her.

"Thank you." Reena smiled at him as she took it.

"You're welcome, miss." He tipped his hat and walked on into the depot.

Had she passed anything to him or he to her? Caid wondered. Or had it been an innocent encounter? Reena backed away from the passengers crowding into the depot, while continuing to scan them. Was she looking for someone, or had she already made her contact?

Or was he getting suspicious of innocent encounters?

A young man barely old enough to shave caught his eye, because he had a piece of paper in his hand and kept looking up at the station, as if reassuring himself that he was in Lost Gold. Instead of coming into the station, he angled off toward the side.

Curious, Caid stepped outside to watch him.

"Excuse me, ma'am," the young man said, tipping his hat to Reena. "Could you tell me who has horses for sale in town?"

"Try the stable in back of the hotel."

"Thank you, kindly, ma'am." The cowboy touched his hat again and sauntered on.

"What are you doing here, Miss Sims?" Caid asked, walking up to her. The sun had just set and her hair was fire-gold in the luminous light, and he wanted to thread his fingers through it and finish their interrupted kiss.

She gave him a wide-eyed look of shock. Was it surprise, or dismay? he wondered. "Hello, Mr. Dundee, what are you doing here?"

"I came down to send a telegram."

She looked past him at the telegrapher's office. "I'd forgotten the telegrapher is here."

"What about you?" he probed. "Meeting someone?"

"No! I just love to watch the trains and think about where they've been and where they're going.

Someday I'd like to get on a train and just keep going and going."

"Where to?" So, she couldn't tell him why she was at the depot.

"I don't care. Anywhere. Just to go."

"It can get pretty boring on a train, you know, especially after a few days. There's not a whole lot to do besides read and play cards." If she were with him, he'd never get bored—no matter how many days they traveled.

"I wouldn't be bored. Not when I could look out the window and see new towns and cities and meet new people. And at night when it was dark out, I'd read."

"You've got it all figured out, haven't you?" He couldn't tell if she was lying or not.

"I've been thinking about it for a long time."

Caid glanced at the steam engine. "The train is about to pull out and it's getting dark. Would you like to walk back to the hotel with me?" He crooked his arm for her.

"Yes. I would." She placed her hand on his arm.

"Mr. Dundee." The telegrapher ran after them waving a yellow telegram. "Mr. Dundee, sir, I've got a reply already."

"Thank you." Caid took it and gave him a coin. "There may be more for me. I'm at the hotel."

"Yes, sir. I'll remember, sir."

She waited while Caid opened the telegram and read it. Then he slipped the yellow paper into his jacket pocket and wrapped his hand around her elbow.

"Tell me, do you ever get a day off?" He short-ened his stride to accommodate her shorter legs.

"Today. That's why I'm not wearing one of those awful black dresses." She was wearing an apple-green dress with white lace at the collar and cuffs.

"You look very nice in that one, much nicer than in your boy clothes. Would you like to go to din-ner?" It wasn't that he was attracted to her, he re-assured himself, but because he wanted to investigate her since she might be the Simpsons' spy.

"Why yes, I'd like that very much. And why don't you call me Reena?"

"All right, Reena. My name is Caid."

A few minutes later Rowena walked into the ho-tel dining room on Caid's arm. As they were shown to a table, she knew the kitchen was already buzz-ing with news of her escort.

Caid took the chair next to her instead of sitting across the table. After they'd ordered, he turned to her. "Now that we're in good light, I can see you avoided the raccoon look."

Reena rolled her eyes. "Thank heavens. Can you imagine my trying to explain them?"

"You do have a little smudge of bruise here." He brushed his thumb over her cheek, just below her eye. "But no one will notice it."

"You did." Her voice had a breathless catch.

"I was looking for it." He rested his hand on the white linen tablecloth, afraid that he'd reach up to touch her again.

She fiddled with the silverware nervously and when she finally spoke, her voice was so low he barely heard her through the dining room din. "How's your hand?" She drew her finger across his bruised knuckles lightly.

"Not very swollen at all." Her finger left a tingling trail in its wake.

"I'm glad." She looked down, studying her plate, and her brown lashes were so long and thick he couldn't see her eyes at all.

The headwaiter brought the wine Caid had ordered and uncorked it for his approval, then poured it.

Reena sipped the wine. "What did you say you do, Caid?"

"I have my own business. Right now, I'm in Lost Gold checking out possible investment opportunities for some investors back East. Why?" Was she looking for information? Most people out West knew better than to ask a man a lot of questions.

"I just wondered, that's all."

She dipped her head to sip the wine and the light from the chandeliers caught and coiled in her hair, turning it to the gleaming yellow gold of Kansas cornfields.

"It isn't very interesting work," he added. "How long have you been in Lost Gold? Did you come here to work in the hotel?"

"About two months. I was looking for a job and the dining room was just opening."

Their dinners came and Reena cut a piece of her

roast chicken. She knew which of the four forks lined up beside their plates to use, Caid noticed, so she was educated in more than just the classics.

"There's something I wanted to ask you, Caid."

"I think you're going to have to hold the question, Reena." He focused on Tanner and the tall, raw-boned, older woman coming across the dining room toward them. "It looks like we're going to be joined by two more people." He had a lot of questions to ask her, too, but now they'd have to wait. "I hope you don't mind."

"No, of course not." She looked over her shoulder.

"Look who I found, Caid." Tanner said with a smile.

He stood up. "Aunt May, it's good to see you after so many years." Her black dress proclaimed that she was still in mourning.

"Caid, you've grown tall as a tree. Last time I saw you, you weren't big enough to paddle." Her iron-gray hair was pulled back in a no-nonsense bun.

"And you're as lovely as I remember."

"Pshaw, boy! Don't you start trying to wind me around your little finger," she said, even as she wrapped her arms around his waist and gave him a big hug. "Or I will paddle you."

For a moment Caid stiffened, then he hugged her back. "Now, that strikes terror into my heart."

"Nothing ever struck terror in your heart. That was the problem. Lord knows where you dreamed up the stunts you pulled." She brushed a lock of hair off his forehead as if he were eight instead of thirty.

"Would you and Tanner like to join us for dinner?"

"Sounds good to me, my boy."

Caid pulled out a chair for her as Tanner slid into the chair next to Rowena. "Aunt May, this is Reena Sims," Caid said, "and you already know Tanner Stewart, my secretary."

"Hello, young lady." Caid's aunt looked across the table at Reena. "I'm Margaret Winters, but everyone calls me May. You too, Caid. I don't need Aunt added to my name. And why do you need a secretary?"

"I'm checking out business opportunities for some Eastern investors and have to write reports about what I've found. Tanner takes down my observations."

"You should have learned to write, boy. Just because the teacher whacked you across the knuckles when you were learning your letters was no reason to give it up."

Caid smiled. "If I had let that stop me, I would never have learned anything. Tanner writes better than I do, that's all." Reena had hidden her smile behind her linen napkin, he noticed.

May chuckled softly. "I used to laugh so hard when your mother's letters would come. Of course, by the time she wrote, everything would have settled down again. Until the next time. You were a little terror."

"That was a long time ago, May."

"Not so long ago that I've forgotten. Caid, your antics brightened some of my darkest days." She smiled across the table at Rowena. "My favorite happened when Caid was about six. One Sunday afternoon his father lay down on the library davenport to take a nap. This was before Tom was a senator, you understand. In fact they were still living in South Carolina. While he was sleeping, Caid tied the shoelaces from both Tom's shoes together. Then Caid went out in the hall and yelled 'Fire!' " She giggled like a young girl. "Tom leaped off the sofa, and of course he fell flat on his face."

She glanced over at Caid. "I understand he chased you all over the house."

"After he untied his shoes." He'd forgotten about that.

"Sounds like you were a little devil." Rowena giggled, intrigued by this glimpse of Caid as a boy. Probably it was just training for when he became a big devil.

He shot her a look that made her heartstrings hum wildly. Devil or not, she thought, she wanted to kiss him again and see if the sensations were just as enticing the second time.

"And what do you do, dear?" May asked Reena.

"I'm a waitress in this dining room," she replied.

"Ahh, good work. Pays well and makes you independent so you don't have to depend on a man to take care of you."

Reena laughed. "That's right."

Caid leaned back in his chair and his leg brushed

Reena's under the table. She flicked him a glance through her downcast lashes and decided it wasn't an accident. She moved her leg, then brought it back against his, liking the hidden contact. He didn't look at her, but he didn't move his leg either.

"How can you say that, Aunt May? Weren't you happily married for over thirty years?"

"May, not Aunt. I was, but my Sydney was special. Now, how was your trip out here? Tanner said you came from Savannah, not home."

After that the conversation swirled around the table. Gradually the dining room emptied until only a few tables were still occupied. Finally Caid put down his coffee cup. "Let's get you up to your suite, May, and get you settled."

"Suite! Land sakes, I don't need a suite, Caid. A room is fine."

"But you may want to entertain friends while you're in town and it'll be like your parlor at home."

"Let's hope not," May said dryly. "My parlor is a mess."

Reena noticed that Caid let Tanner escort May, while he hung back with her.

"Your aunt is delightful, Caid." As they walked out to the lobby, his large hand settled in the middle of her back, and she liked it. It felt right.

"She's always been a character."

"To hear her tell it, you're the character," she said, with a hint of laughter in her voice. "I want to thank you for a wonderful evening."

He clasped her hand in both of his and looked deep into her eyes. "I'd rather we'd been alone." Then he lifted her hand to his lips and kissed it.

Her hand was still tingling as he walked away.

Chapter 6

Lordy, Rowena mused, she was glad they were standing in the middle of the lobby. She'd almost gone through the floor with shock—though it had been a pleasant shock. She could still feel the exact spot on the back of her hand that his lips had touched.

Maybe he really was a businessman, she thought hopefully, as he started up the stairs with his aunt. May had asked a lot of questions and he'd given her the same answers he'd given Reena. Maybe she'd just become suspicious of everyone because of her work for the Cause.

But what had he said to the sheriff about her family and the Second Confederacy yesterday? She'd been trying to bring the subject up in a roundabout way when they'd been interrupted by the arrival of his aunt and Tanner.

She glanced once more at Caid as he reached the top of the stairs with his aunt. Had he noticed the young recruit who'd asked where to buy a horse? Had he realized she'd passed money to Jim Spekes, the conductor, when she'd accidentally-on-purpose run into him at the train station?

Was she being overly cautious? No. Businesspeople were pasty-skinned from being indoors all day, poring over accounts. They weren't tanned and didn't have the mile-wide shoulders and the vigilant gunslinger's walk that he had.

Besides, why had he been in Savannah? No one in the South had money for investing! And what was in that telegram he'd received?

Maybe it was time to do a little nosing around in his suite.

The next day Caid walked into his parlor and shut the door. He walked directly to the desk and glanced down at the telegram he'd left lying strewn on top of the papers. He'd penciled in very light lines from the telegram to the papers below it. Now the pencil lines didn't line up and the hair he'd laid across the desk drawer was gone, so he knew it had been opened.

He heard his bedroom door to the hall click shut.

He ran out into the hall, but it was empty. Checking the back stairwell, he heard running steps down at the first floor. And he knew that by the time he got down there, whoever it was would have blended in with the people in the lobby or dining room.

Back in his parlor, he surveyed the room to see if anything else had been disturbed. A very faint scent lingered in the air. Was it lilacs?

He didn't want to believe it, but it was beginning to look more and more as if Reena was the Simpsons' spy. Why else would she have searched his room?

A knock at the door summoned him. He slipped the telegram into his jacket pocket, then opened the door and gazed at Reena, who stood there with an armload of folded white sheets.

"Oh, Caid, I didn't know you were here," she said, taking a hasty step back. "I came to clean your room, but I'll just come back later."

"No, come in." He gestured her in, surprised to see her. If she'd just fled his room, she wouldn't return to clean it.

"Are you sure? Because I can do it later."

"No, come in. I was just leaving."

Maybe he'd been wrong, he thought, fingering the telegram as he walked down the hall. Maybe someone else had searched his room. He hesitated and looked back. Or maybe Reena was smart enough to come back with the sheets, knowing that would allay his suspicion.

Shutting the door behind Caid, Rowena leaned back against it and took deep breaths. Her mouth was still parched and her heart pounding with the fear that had flooded her when he'd almost caught her in his room.

Caid was a government agent!

Still in shock from her discovery, she walked over to a chair and collapsed in it. She'd been trembling so badly as she talked to him, she feared her legs wouldn't support her. But she'd faced him and hadn't given him a hint that she knew what he really did.

She glanced at the desk, but the telegram was gone.

Not that she needed to see it again—the words were seared into her mind. *You are authorized to use all means necessary to stop the Simpsons. Signed G. A. Cleveland.* President Cleveland's initials were G.A.

She felt as if she'd been hit by a wagon loaded with bricks. Her instincts had been right all along.

He'd been lying from the beginning. He'd come to Lost Gold to stop her brothers and the Second Confederacy.

Caid was her brothers' enemy. He was *her* enemy!

"Slow down, Reena. You walk like a man." Belle puffed as they walked along Main Street.

"No, I don't." Rowena talked over her shoulder to her friend, who'd fallen five steps behind. She paused in front of the bakery, where the aromas of nutmeg and cinnamon floated out the open front door.

"Yes, you do. Long strides and fast."

"Who cares how I walk?" She clamped her hands to her waist and frowned. Sometimes Belle was so picky.

"A lady doesn't hurry. She promenades, like this.

See?" She slowed and took small steps.

"It looks like you've got your knees tied together," Rowena said, unimpressed. She slowed to look in the window of the saddle shop. "Look at that great saddle."

"Who cares about saddles? Walk with small steps."

Rowena rolled her eyes and took ridiculously tiny, mincing steps. "Like this?"

"That's right, if you do it without the exaggeration. Yes, that's it. See how we're gliding gracefully along? And you twirl your parasol like this." She demonstrated with the new parasol that matched her dove gray dress.

"Oh, puhleeze! This is ridiculous."

"And when you see a handsome man you want to watch, you look in the store windows and watch his reflection."

"Why?"

"Because you'd seem forward if you watched him openly."

Rowena made a face. "All these rules. It's so silly."

"But it's how a lady acts. And if you want a man to treat you like a lady, you have to act like one."

"Do you know what Miss Abigail would say if we walked like this when we were serving meals?"

"That's different. Then we're doing our job. Now, we're ladies promenading and seeing the sights."

"What sights?"

Belle gave her a disgusted glance. "You mean

you haven't noticed the two cowboys lounging on the chairs in front of the Wild Women Saloon? They've been watching us for the last block."

Rowena looked at them. "So?"

"No! What did I just tell you about not openly watching men?"

"I'm not watching them. I'm looking because you said they were watching. What's wrong with that?"

"Oh, Reena, didn't anyone ever teach you how to flirt?"

Rowena slanted her a wry look. "Who? My father? Or my brothers?"

Belle snapped her fingers. "I've got an idea. I'm going to teach you how to flirt and act like a lady to repay you for teaching me to read."

"You don't have to pay me back. I enjoy helping people."

"I want to do it, though, Reena. I've never had such a close friend, and if I can teach you something, I want to."

"All right." Maybe there were things about this flirting business she should know.

"Good. Why don't we start by going down to the dressmakers? We could both use some new dresses."

Rowena stopped dead. "I don't need any more dresses! I've got three already." It wasn't as if she'd be wearing them when she went home to the ranch; then they'd go into Mama's old trunk and she would return to wearing pants and shirts.

Belle rolled her eyes. "I don't believe you. No woman ever has enough dresses. Besides, you want a new dress for the church-raising next Sunday, don't you? After the building is up, there'll be a picnic with games and dancing in the evening."

"But I don't need any dresses." She didn't want to go to some boring picnic. And dancing was just an excuse for men with sweaty hands and bad breath to try to hold her close.

She'd decided not to go out dressed as a boy for the time being. Since Caid knew it was a disguise, he might wonder why she did it. And she didn't want him wondering about anything.

Besides, going around in disguise was almost as bad as lying, and even if it was for the Cause, she didn't like having to lie. Especially to people like Belle, whom she liked.

Belle chewed her lower lip and took a couple of steps. "Then come with me, please, and give me your opinion on how I look."

"Oh, all right." She crossed her arms over her chest. "But I'm not staying long."

Belle stopped and looked at her. "You're unbelievable," she said, raising her head and hands as if she was imploring help from heaven. "Not only do you walk like a man, but you even think like one. That's exactly what a man would say."

"What's wrong with that? Why do you want to waste time looking at dresses?"

"It's something ladies do. Now, let's go." They walked down Main Street, their shoes echoing loudly on the wooden sidewalk.

As they neared the dressmaker's, Rowena noticed the man lounging on a bench in front of the shop and her steps slowed.

"Damn!" It was so nerve-wracking, treating him no differently than before she'd learned he was a government agent. But she had to. She had to! She was the only one who could warn her brothers. "What's he doing here?" she muttered under her breath.

Belle paused and glanced at her uncertainly. "Something wrong?"

"No. What could be wrong? Do I look like something is wrong? Come on." Rowena glided forward, using the small steps Belle had showed her, down two steps, across the rutted side street, and up two steps to the dressmaker's. She nodded as she passed Caid but didn't stop, although she could feel his gaze following her.

The bell tinkled as they entered. "I'll be with you in a minute," Madame Fifi called out from the back room. A curtain across the doorway hid whoever was back there.

"Take your time. We'll just look at fabric," Belle replied.

Rowena looked around with interest. Shelves and large tables were covered with bolts of cloth in all colors, from palest yellow to intense purple and blackest black. Used to getting only serviceable ginghams and plain cottons in limited colors at the Colony store, Rowena wandered around, browsing through the large selection.

"Reena—either of these colors would look great on you." Belle stood across the table from her, holding bolts of challis in forest green and fawn.

"They are nice, but I want to look around."

She didn't look up when the bell over the door jangled. She didn't have to. She could feel the warmth of Caid's gaze on her back. Unconsciously she smoothed a hand down over the nipped-in waist of her russet dress.

"Hello, Mr. Dundee," Belle said from the other side of the table.

"Hello, Belle." Caid nodded at her. "Shopping for dresses?"

"We're getting new dresses for the church-raising picnic this Sunday. Are you coming?"

"I wouldn't miss it," he said, looking at Reena.

"Darn it," Belle said, snapping her fingers, "I forgot I have to go to the bank. I better get there before they close. I'll just be gone a minute." The bell jangled again as the door closed behind her.

Rowena fingered a blue-green silk on the table. The muslin she bought at the Colony store felt like coarse hay compared to it. An emerald green velvet drew her to the next table. She filled her hand with its plush folds, luxuriating in its opulent color and texture.

A warm breath stirred the fine hair at the back of her neck and sent a cascade of shivers skittering down her spine. Surprised, she turned her head just enough to see Caid. He was watching her.

"Hello, Caid." She stroked the emerald velvet, watching the sheen of the pile change in the light.

"It was nice of Belle to leave." He brought a drape of the velvet up to her cheek and held it there, caressing her without touching her. "You'd look lovely in this color." His low voice throbbed through her.

In spite of her resolve, she rubbed her cheek against the velvet, relishing its feel. She felt his fingers tighten in the folds of cloth.

Shocked at herself, she pulled away sharply. "It's way too expensive." She had no idea how much the velvet cost and she didn't care. She wanted it more than she'd ever wanted anything.

He let the velvet slide down her arm. "Not for you. It picks up the green in your eyes."

"I don't have green in my eyes," she replied indignantly. Did he think he was going to flummox her?

He framed her face with his hands, and catalogued her features slowly and thoroughly. "Yes, you do, Reena." His voice vibrated through her, putting all her nerve endings on full alert. "There are emerald chips scattered in the hazel."

Her heart thudded against her ribs and she felt a bit light-headed. "Don't," she murmured, clasping his hands with hers. "Someone could see us through the window."

He released her and stepped back. "As you wish, Miss Sims."

"It's not practical," she said, marching around the table to the much more suitable challis.

"Still . . ." His voice was low, just loud enough for her to hear. And to wonder what she would have looked like in the emerald velvet.

"Don't let me hold you up, Mr. Dundee." She

looked him square in the eye from the safety of the other side of the table. He wasn't going to rattle her spurs.

"You're not, Miss Sims." But he made no move to leave.

She unrolled the forest green challis, but after the emerald velvet, it looked so drab she couldn't bear the thought of wearing it. Turning to the fawn, she spread it on the table.

The curtain covering the doorway to the back swung away, and May emerged. "Caid, glad you decided to come in. Madame Fifi here has some boxes for you to load." Then she spotted Rowena. "Hello, Reena, so nice to see you again." She came around the table and fingered the fawn challis. "This would look lovely on you, my dear."

"Do you really think so?" Instinctively she knew she could believe May; she was one lady who didn't lie.

"Yes. Don't you agree, Caid?"

"I'm sure Miss Sims will look good in anything she chooses." His eyes met Reena's and she had the strangest feeling that he was picturing her wearing nothing at all. Reena looked away, flustered.

"And you will see it at the church-raising," May said, striding toward the door. "Now, let's go along. I want to introduce you to some of the town leaders. Good-bye, Reena."

Caid paused at the door. "I'll be seeing you, Reena." His eyes told her that was a promise.

*   *   *

"How did it go with Caid after I left?" Belle asked, as they left the dressmaker's two hours later. "What did he want? Besides your body, I mean."

"What are you talking about? He isn't interested in me." They were walking by the saddle shop and she inhaled deeply, loving the aroma of leather.

Belle stopped dead and pinned her with a narrow-eyed look. "Do you mean that?"

"Of course. Why are we stopping?"

"My God, you really don't know!" She began to walk along, shaking her head. "This is going to be a bigger job than I thought."

Rowena threw up her hands in disgust. "What are you talking about?"

"I am talking about you and Caid Dundee. Didn't you see how he changed when he spotted you? By the time you walked up—like a lady, I might add—to where he was sitting, he was buzzing like a bee around a flower."

"Well, he might be interested in me, but I'm not interested in him. He makes me feel sick."

"He what?"

"My stomach feels weird and I feel hot and a little light-headed and my heart pounds when I'm around him."

"You're not serious, are you?" Belle's eyebrows almost disappeared into her red curls and her mouth formed an O as she stared at Reena. "You are serious!"

"Why wouldn't I be?" She started up the steps to the hotel.

"Reena, we need to talk. Come with me." Belle

took her arm and led her over to the swing that looked out on Main Street and sat on it. She patted the cushion beside her. "Sit here."

"You look so serious. What's wrong?"

"Didn't you ever have any girl friends?"

"Uh-uh. I was always too busy at the farm. Besides, they were always talking about boys and babies and cooking. Dull stuff. Never anything interesting like breeding the latest bulls we'd imported, or who had the fastest horse." She shrugged her shoulders. "I was so bored the few times I went to women's meetings or quilting bees, I stopped going."

"Reena, I don't exactly know how to tell you this, but your feverishness and pounding heart are symptoms." Belle twisted her hands in her lap. "It's—"

Reena grabbed Belle's arm. "It's serious, isn't it? Go ahead. Tell me. I can take it."

"We-ll, y-you s-see," Belle quavered. Suddenly her face crumpled, and she clapped her hand to her mouth and turned away. Her shoulders shook.

Rowena patted Belle's back sympathetically. "It's all right, Belle. At least we got to meet and be friends."

"No!" Belle turned back and waved her hand frantically. "I'm not crying, you ninny," she said, between choked gasps. "I'm laughing! You're not ill."

Reena folded her hands primly in her lap and stared out at the street. "I'm glad I can make you laugh," she said quietly. No one had ever laughed at her before, and she was surprised to find that it hurt her pride and dignity and—Damn it, it just plain hurt.

"Oh, Reena, please don't be mad." Belle rested a hand on her arm, "I'm not laughing *at* you. It's just that I've never met anyone like you, and you're continually surprising me with what you know and don't know. I mean, you corrected Caid Dundee about Tacitus, but you don't know about—" She took a long breath. "Reena, I need to tell you about the birds and the bees."

"I know about the birds and the bees! After all, I've watched the stallions cover the mares all my life."

"It's a little bit different for men and women. You see . . .

". . . . And that's how it is for people," Belle finished, a few minutes later.

"I see." Rowena rested her elbow on the arm of the swing and cradled her chin in the palm of her hand. "If I understand you correctly, I get all hot and feverish because I'm in lust. I want Caid Dundee in my bed."

"No, Reena. You *don't* want him in your bed— at least, not yet. It's like learning to walk: you take tiny steps at first. You don't want to bite off more than you can chew—and you have a lot to learn."

Caid might be the most intriguing man she'd ever met, but the only steps she should take were *away* from him.

He was far too dangerous—and the worst man in the world for her to be attracted to.

Chapter 7

~~~~~oOo~~~~~

Rowena leaned against the corral fence behind the hotel stable, absently watching the few horses inside it.

What was she going to do about her growing attraction to Caid? He'd taken over her dreams. When she slept, she dreamed of his lips on hers, the feel of his fingers threading through her hair, the way his hands felt when he touched her, the way he awakened her senses.

Actually he'd taken over more than her dreams. Just remembering the look he'd given her at the dressmaker's could make her heart skip a beat. When he was in the dining room, she often glanced at him—even when she was serving other tables. Often—too often—their eyes met across the crowded room.

A horse nuzzled her fingers, reminding her where she was. And why.

She'd crept out to the stable early that morning to meet Jeff. Since it was Sunday no one was up yet, and she'd seen the sky lighten from leaden gray to sunrise gold to morning blue. But Jeff hadn't come.

She needed to warn him about Caid, and that the United States government knew about the Second Confederacy.

She glanced at the sun and decided Jeff wasn't coming. She turned to go back to the hotel, and met Caid's cool, speculative gaze. He lounged in the stable doorway, watching her. Gasping, she clasped her hand to her breast.

"Caid! You startled me." She consciously lowered her hand, and walked toward him. "I-I didn't hear you."

"I'm sure you didn't. Your attention was on the alley."

"I was waiting for a friend. H-have you been there long?"

His eyes were hooded, telling her nothing of his thoughts.

"Long enough." He put out his arm, blocking her way as she would have passed him.

Rowena gazed down at the bronzed arm revealed by his rolled up shirt-sleeve, and resisted the urge to run her fingers along it.

"Did he stand you up?" His voice was low—and tight with tension.

She looked up, wide-eyed. "Did who stand me up?" Oh God, did he know about Jeff? Did he know who she really was?

"Your lover." He crossed his arms over his chest.

He didn't know. He didn't know. The tension went out of her with a whoosh, leaving her limp as a cooked noodle. "Oh, yes . . . my lover," she murmured weakly. She tilted her head, trying to look sad. "He didn't know if he'd be able to get away today."

Reena watched him from beneath her lashes, but his austere features were completely devoid of any emotion and she couldn't tell what he was thinking.

"I have to get going. Belle has big plans for us for today's picnic."

"Have a good time," he said in a tone as bland as porridge.

Rowena and Belle watched the men swarming over the wooden framework of the church. Every man in town seemed to be there, either carrying lumber or holding it or hammering nails into it. Caid straddled a roof beam, his legs dangling on each side, and pounded away at a rafter. He reached into the chest pocket of his blue chambray shirt and took out more nails and continued.

"This will be fun today," Belle said.

"What?" Neither Jeff nor Robby had met her at the stable that morning, but at least there had been a note from them hidden in the hollow tree just outside town.

"He is one handsome devil, Reena," Belle said. "I don't blame you for being attracted to him."

"Who?" Rowena asked, feigning ignorance.

"Caid Dundee. Who else? And don't tell me you hadn't noticed him. He's already noticed you're here. And look at you. You've actually let me curl your hair, instead of just throwing it up on top of your head any which way. You're learning to walk like a lady. You're learning to bat your eyes and tilt your head shyly. You're even learning how useful a parasol can be. Now, in case you haven't noticed, there's only one person you're trying to impress: Caid Dundee."

"I am not!" She raised her chin and haughtily looked down her nose at Belle. "I am doing it for myself. Not Caid Dundee."

"And the moon is blue," Belle murmured. "He'll probably be coming over to the picnic area later and there'll be dancing after dark and if you two should happen to disappear into the woods and if anything should happen to happen . . ."

"With Caid? I couldn't do something like that." Nervously Reena fingered the tiny baby ring hanging from the old gold chain around her neck. "I just couldn't. It isn't in me."

"Why not? At least kiss him. Maybe he'll have bad breath or won't be worth a penny as a kisser. Maybe you'd get him out of your system with just a kiss. It's worth a try."

"I'll think about it." She hated to tell Belle that she already knew he was a great kisser.

A little boy about five years old dashed between them and kept going. He was dressed in a beautiful spotless white sailor suit.

"Who is *that?* How does his mother keep him so clean?"

"That's our darling Billy Hofsteader."

"Huh?" Rowena frowned at her, puzzled.

"His mother always calls him 'our darling Billy'— never 'Billy.' You have to feel sorry for the kid."

"Especially if she makes him wear white all the time."

"Yeah. I'm going on now. Come over to the picnic area when you're through looking and drooling."

"I am not!" Rowena protested absently, watching Caid. She'd never been so aware of anyone as she was of him. She'd had would-be suitors in the Colony. They'd been good Confederate men, but they'd done nothing for her heartbeat, and their kisses had ranged from forgettable to repulsive. Yet Caid could make her heart race with just a glance.

And his kiss . . . just the thought of feeling his lips on hers again made her heart sing. Damn! She should stay away from him.

He swung down off the roof beam and walked over to the water barrel. Filling the dipper, he lifted it to his lips as he scanned the site. His eyes met hers, and even across the people-filled area, she felt the intensity of his gaze. He drank the water and dipped out more. Finally he turned back to work.

Hours later Caid still hadn't come over to the picnic area, and Rowena was beginning to wonder if he would. She sat at a picnic table with Belle and two young cowboys, Mike and Bob. She knew Belle was enjoying their company, but they were boring her to tears. After fencing with a man like Caid, they seemed so shallow and young.

Too restless to sit still, Rowena got up and wandered over to watch the kids in the three-legged races. Even that didn't hold her interest, though. She spotted some young men bobbing for apples in a large galvanized tin washtub while their young women looked on.

"That's harder than it looks, Miss Reena," said one of the young cowboys who'd been at the picnic table with her.

"Really? But it looks so easy, Mike." Was that his name? He'd told her, why couldn't she remember it? Bobbing for apples had to be more fun than listening to him tell more stories.

He clutched his hat with one hand while he scratched the back of his neck with the other. "It's Bob, ma'am."

"Oh. Of course, Bob. I'm so sorry." Good Lord, what was wrong with her? She gave him her most brilliant smile and held out her hand. "Come on, let's see who can get an apple faster."

"You'll try, too? Aren't you afraid of getting your hair wet?"

"Pshaw! What's a little wet hair? It's for charity, isn't it?" At home she'd bobbed for apples lots of times. Always beat the boys, too.

He led her over to Mrs. Hofsteader, who was collecting coins. "We'll both try," he said confidently.

Mrs. Hofsteader's pince-nez glasses had slipped down her rather long nose. Now she looked Reena up and down with a distinct air of disapproval. "Are you sure, madame?"

"Mademoiselle," Reena corrected. Maybe Mrs. Hofsteader didn't know the second meaning of the word "madame."

"Well! Really!" Mrs. Hofsteader shuffled some coins around in her hand. "Young people nowadays," she muttered, seemingly under her breath, but loudly enough for Rowena to hear. "No respect for their betters."

"Elders," Rowena said in her sweetest voice. When Mrs. Hofsteader looked up, Rowena gave her a smile so full of sugar it should have choked her. "We're all happy to make sacrifices to raise money to build a church here in Lost Gold, aren't we, Mrs. Hofsteader?"

"Humph!" Mrs. Hofsteader straightened her bony shoulders. She busied herself stacking the coins she'd collected.

"I'll bet you a sawbuck I get the apple before you, Bob," Reena said.

"Huh?" Bob looked at her with the saucer-eyes of someone who couldn't believe what he'd just heard. "D-did you just bet me a sawbuck?"

"Sure did."

He paled. "A-are you sure, Miss Reena?"

"Damn tootin'." He actually gasped and she glanced away to keep from grinning. "It's for charity, isn't it?"

"Yes, ma'am, but. . . ."

She didn't wait to hear what he was going to say, just walked up to the tub, clasped her hands behind her back, and began trying to bite an apple. They were big apples, the hardest to catch.

The first one slid away. Across from her, Bob almost nabbed an apple, but it bobbed away. Still, he came close enough to scare Rowena.

If she didn't grab one quickly, she'd lose. A big red beauty floated past her nose, and she ducked her head and pinned the apple against the side of the washtub, so she could bite into it with a resounding crunch.

Easy as shooting ducks in a barrel, she thought. She came up with the big red apple clenched in her teeth and gleefully shook her head, flinging water out of her hair and eyes.

When she opened her eyes she saw Caid, barely an arm's length away, leaning against a cottonwood and watching her. His arms were crossed over his broad chest. She would have gulped, but couldn't with the apple in her mouth. Oh, Lord, why did he have to arrive now, when she looked like a suckling pig?

"Bleck!" She spat the apple out. It fell to the ground and, like a homing pigeon, rolled right to his feet. Maybe if she didn't look at the apple, it would disappear. She raised her chin and ignored it, looking Caid in the eye.

"Hello, Caid. I didn't know you were here." The curls that Belle had worked so hard on were plastered to her cheeks and forehead, dripping water down her face and neck. A rivulet ran down her nose and dripped off the end. Drip. Drip. Drip.

"The shell of the church is done and the roof is

on, so we've all called it a day and come over for some food and games." He reached in the back pocket of his pants and pulled out a linen hand-kerchief. "You look like you could use this."

"Really?" She took it and wiped her face. "I hadn't noticed."

His mouth twitched. He picked up the glistening red apple and turned it over to examine the punc-tures. "Hmm, sharp little teeth," he murmured, quirking one dark eyebrow at her as he ran his thumb over the fruit caressingly.

He stood close enough for her to smell the sweaty maleness of a man who'd spent the day do-ing physical labor. Normally she would have wrin-kled her nose at that scent, but on Caid, it was strangely sexy. She watched the slow, sensual movement of his thumb across the glistening red skin of the apple. What would his hand feel like, stroking her that same slow, sensual way?

"I believe this is yours," he murmured softly, holding it out to her.

As she took it, her fingers brushed his, making her aware of the warmth of his hand.

He leaned close and she tensed, unsure of his intentions.

His breath stirred the fine hairs along the nape of her neck. She shivered in the whisper-soft touch that was more whisper than touch. If she turned her head just a tiny bit his lips would be so close to hers, and. . . .

Her eyes met his and widened—for he was

thinking the same thing. She could read it in the darkness of his pupils.

Time stood still for a trembling heartbeat.

A lingering drop of water ran down the side of her throat and came to rest in the hollow where her pulse throbbed against the skin. Slowly, as if mesmerized by that single drop, he reached over and dipped it up on his finger. Then he licked off his finger while he watched her.

A frisson of icy heat went through her. She swallowed, and afraid of what she'd reveal if she met his gaze, focused on the dark curls visible in the open V of his shirt.

Suddenly his gaze moved beyond her. "Yes?" His tone was half-command, half-demand.

She remembered where they were and glanced over her shoulder. Bob watched them, his cheeks red with anger.

"She's with me," he gritted.

"Not anymore." Caid didn't raise his voice, but it had an unmistakable hard edge. "Miss Sims may have forgotten, but a week ago she agreed to come to the picnic with me."

A week ago she'd just met him. So much had happened since then. She looked from Bob, who was boring and safe, to Caid, who was intriguing and dangerous—so very dangerous.

Bob glared at Caid for several long seconds. Then he turned on his heel and stomped away.

Caid looked down at her expectantly.

"What?" she asked, puzzled.

"I'm waiting to see if I'm going to get another

tongue-lashing for rescuing you from another unwanted suitor."

This time she could think of better things to do with her tongue. "How do you know he was unwanted?"

He slowly inventoried her features with those too-knowing eyes. "I know."

The smoky promise in his eyes ignited an answering slow heat deep inside her. "Do you, Mr. Dundee?" she fenced. Was she so transparent?

He gave her a look that was like sun-warmed honey. "Would you like some ice cream, Miss Sims?" he asked.

"I'd love some, Mr. Dundee." Suddenly she was hungry.

He wrapped his large hand around her elbow and guided her across the picnic grounds, toward tables set deep in the shade beneath the cottonwoods. There young men cranked ice-cream freezers.

"What flavor would you like?"

"Peach." Papa and the twins had made peach ice cream to celebrate the first ripe peaches every year. "It's perfect for the end of summer. That's when the peaches are their ripest."

"And nothing is sweeter than a ripe peach." He lifted a still wet curl of blond hair off her cheek with his thumb. "Nothing."

He brought back two large bowls, one of peach ice cream, which he gave to her, and the other of strawberry. "Let's go someplace where we can talk without being interrupted."

"I don't know where—"

"I do." He led the way into the cottonwoods, until they were completely out of sight of the picnickers. Only the distant murmur of conversation, like a running stream, reminded them of the other people.

They settled on a fallen log. The ice cream was beginning to melt and Reena scraped at the soft edges with her spoon, while Caid plunged his spoon into the still-frozen center of his mound.

"What did you want to talk about, Caid?" she asked between spoonfuls. It was delicious, with big chunks of peaches and the tang of a bit of lemon.

"I—why don't we—"

His voice sounded oddly strangled and she looked up. He seemed fascinated by the movement of her tongue as she licked the back of her spoon.

Something made her tempt the devil. "Would you like a taste?" she asked, holding out a spoonful of peach ice cream.

Slowly, tantalizingly slowly, he licked the ice cream off her spoon. Reena felt a growing warmth deep within her.

"Try mine," he commanded, holding out a spoonful of strawberry ice cream.

Her gaze locked with his as she licked the spoon very slowly. The strawberries were wonderful. "Delicious," she sighed.

"Yes, they are," he murmured, studying her lips. Slowly he leaned forward until his mouth brushed hers.

China clinked as he dropped the bowl and raised

his hand to cup her cheek in his palm. He brushed his lips over hers in a tantalizing touch that was gone too soon. Finally he settled as lightly as a butterfly, promising much. His lips were icy, then warm. His tongue carried the tang of strawberries as he teased her. She leaned into him and teased back, enticed by his kiss, by the feel of his mouth on hers.

When he finally raised his lips from hers, she leaned back in the crook of his arm and gazed up at him through her lashes.

"Much better than bobbing for apples," he murmured, a tiny smile playing across his lips.

"Much," she agreed. Tingles of new sensations were flying along her nerve endings, and she wanted to sample more. Kissing Caid hadn't gotten a bit of the lust out of her system.

She glanced at the sun, already sinking behind the mountains. "Let's go back. I think they're going to have some dancing after dark."

"Dancing—I think I'd like that."

So would she. It would give her an excuse to go back into his arms. And she'd found she liked being in his arms—though how could she, when he was such a threat to her?

They walked back slowly, silently, watching the sky go from gold to crimson to violet.

Back at the picnic, men were lighting the Chinese lanterns strung across the grounds. Their colored shades shed a multihued glow over the crowd that gathered around two fiddlers. An accordion player joined the fiddlers and squeezed his instrument into shrill squawks as he warmed up.

Caid bowed over her hand. "May I have this dance, Miss Sims?"

How long had it been since she'd danced? "You may, Mr. Dundee."

He clasped her waist with his left hand and entwined the fingers of his right hand with hers. They were palm to palm and she could feel the calluses on his palm from long hours of holding leather reins. His long fingers curled over the back of her hand and she knew that even if she'd wanted to pull away, she couldn't.

The fiddlers broke into a foot-stomping polka and he whirled her around so fast her feet left the ground several times. Reena clung to his shoulders and laughed up at him as the world went by in a kaleidoscope of colors.

When the fiddlers slowed into the "Blue Danube Waltz," he drew her closer. Normally Rowena kept her arm stiff, so she could dance at arm's length with men she had no interest in. But that night she went into the circle of his arms willingly.

A young man she didn't know cut in on them. "May I have this dance, ma'am?" he said, looking at her as he tapped Caid on the shoulder. Caid didn't loosen his arms, just whirled her away.

Again the young man tapped him on the shoulder. This time Caid stopped and turned to look him straight in the face. "Get lost," he growled.

"But, sir, when I tap you on the shoulder you're

supposed to. . . ." The young man's protests died as he met Caid's determined glare. "I see," he muttered, looking crestfallen as he turned away.

"That wasn't nice," Rowena offered.

"I know," Caid admitted, entirely unconcerned.

The fiddlers slid into another of Strauss's lilting waltzes. He drew her closer, until they were knee-to-knee and hip-to-hip and breast-to-chest. They moved slowly, sensuously, against each other.

Caid lowered his head until his lips were close to her ear. "Do you like this?" he murmured.

"Yes," she whispered, closing her eyes and giving herself up to the magic of his arms.

They whirled around the perimeter of the dance area, gradually moving deeper and deeper into the shadows until they were alone under the trees and the fiddlers' music was softened by the soughing of the wind in the leaves.

Caid danced slower and slower, until they were merely swaying against each other.

"Caid," she murmured, turning her face up to his. Moonlight splashed through the leaves, leaving his strong features half-silvered, half-shadowed.

He didn't move for the longest time, as he gazed at her in the moonlight. Just when she thought he'd never move, never really kiss her, his lips crashed down on hers.

His earlier kiss had been full of promise, but this kiss was rough and hungry and demanding, and she met it with her own hunger and demand. He tasted her, teased her, and she tasted and teased and battled for supremacy.

Her heart thrummed against her ribs like a kettledrum. Her bones began to melt and she clung
tightly to his shoulders because she didn't know if
she could stand without him.

When he finally raised his head, they were both
breathing hard. Reena took a deep, shuddering
breath, still not believing the way her heart was
racing.

"Well, I guess that answers that question," she
murmured.

"What question?"

She merely turned her head slightly and leaned
against him, feeling how his heart was thudding
against his ribs. She smiled a secret smile, glad to
know that he was as deeply affected as she was.

He breathed deeply, as though savoring her
scent. "You smell of lilacs and cinnamon and. . . ."
He sniffed again. "You smell like springtime."

She felt as if they were speaking a second language beneath their words, a far more primitive
language. And it was exciting and enticing and exhilarating.

She'd never felt this way before.

Why Caid? What made him so different?

Chapter 8

❧⁓❧

"**W**ell, is he a good kisser?" Belle asked, as they got ready for bed later that night. She slipped into bed and drew the covers up to her chin.

"He's wonderful!" Reena lay down in her silk nightshift, folded her arms beneath her head, and gazed at the ceiling, dreamily.

"From the look on your face earlier, I'd say he was a hell of a kisser. Do you have anything to compare it with? I mean, besides dry, grandfatherly kisses on the cheek?"

"Yes—wet, repulsive, groping kisses by men with bad teeth and whiskey breath. His kisses are nothing like those."

"It sounds like you haven't had much selection to choose from. Not *all* other men are bad kissers."

"What's your point, Belle?" She glanced across

the narrow space between the two beds.

"He may be a great kisser, but that doesn't mean that he's Mr. Wonderful or even the right man for you," her friend warned. "You need to think about how he got to be such a good kisser: practice. Lots of practice."

"I realize that."

She didn't mention that he wasn't what he seemed. His family was obviously rich, so he didn't have to work for a living. Yet he did. And in the Wild Women Saloon she had seen him sip his whiskey, rather than gulp it down, as if he didn't want to drink enough for it to affect him. He was hard—as hard as her brothers, who were men with a mission, a cause to fight for. And his mission was to capture her brothers.

"Reena, you need to be careful, honey. This is the first man you've been attracted to. You don't want to get carried away building fantasies around him."

"Why would I do that?" Caid was flesh and blood and danger all rolled up into one.

"Maybe you wouldn't. But most women would. And he'd never live up to their fantasies."

"Don't worry. I'm too practical to do that." She rolled onto her side, and bending her arm, propped her head up on the palm of her hand. "Believe me he's the last man in the world to make me dream about happily ever after."

"I hope so," Belle said doubtfully. "Remember, you're a waitress in the hotel and he's rich. What if he's just amusing himself with you to pass the time? Which is not to say he is," she added quickly, "but there's always that possibility."

"I know," Reena admitted quietly. "You haven't said anything that I haven't already considered." It wasn't as if she had a lot of experience with men. "But I'm not the kind to turn back just because I don't know the road ahead. I always need to see what's around the next curve. To explore what I don't know. And Caid fits in that category."

Belle giggled softly. "You've got that right. But . . . be careful."

"I will. Now, let's go to sleep. Tomorrow morning will be here soon enough." Lying back, she folded her arms beneath her head again and watched leaf shadows dancing on the wall.

Their first kiss had only hinted at the pleasure that came from kissing. Today she'd tasted deeply. She hadn't realized how pleasurable kissing could be—until today.

She'd heard girls her age talking about it the few times she'd gone to quilting bees, but she hadn't paid any attention. She had thought they were just blathering on about nothing.

The window was open just enough to let the scent of roses drift up from the garden. She drew a deep breath and smiled, because the aroma wasn't half so enticing as Caid's scent of leather and lemon.

Or his kiss. His sensational, knock-out, I-want-to-taste-him-again kiss.

She'd always drawn back from the tobacco-stained mustaches and whiskey-sodden breath of the men who tried to kiss her. She had never kissed back. Until Caid.

She'd never wanted to. Until Caid.

She had never found it pleasurable. Until Caid.

She touched her lips, remembering the times when she'd heard women talking about pounding hearts and weak knees. She'd put it down to "womanly vapors." Even if it was fashionable for ladies to have fainting spells, she'd been too busy and level-headed to engage in such foolishness; she had even prided herself on being too healthy to fall victim to the "womanly weakness."

But now she had experienced the pounding heart, the breath thickening in her throat, her knees growing weak, and she knew those symptoms had nothing to do with weakness. They had to do with exhilaration and excitement and laughter and a thousand other things she couldn't even begin to name. And now that she had felt those glorious feelings, she wanted to experience them again.

With Caid.

But she couldn't. Not when he was her enemy.

Caid took a cigar out of his humidor, trimmed and lit it, then went out onto his balcony. The night air was crisp and he welcomed it. He needed it to cool his blood.

Kissing Reena had been all that he'd expected—and much more. *Never* had he felt the soul-stirring desire he'd felt when he had kissed Reena Sims.

She'd ignited a throbbing heat in him that still lingered. He'd always prided himself on being completely in control, on never letting his loins do his thinking for him. But with Reena, he was finding that control harder than ever before.

Just thinking about her, about how her breasts had felt against his chest, and how she'd felt in his arms was enough to make him glad he was alone at the moment. He leaned over the balcony railing and smiled ruefully. Reena had definitely jolted his self-control.

He took a long puff on his cigar. He had been right about her innocence. Except for his earlier kiss, he didn't think she'd ever been kissed—truly kissed. But she'd learned very quickly.

She was exciting and intriguing and mysterious.

Caid started to take another puff on his cigar, but he stilled as a thought flashed across his mind. Absently he took the cigar out of his mouth.

If Reena had never been truly kissed before, then it stood to reason that she didn't have a lover. Then who was the man she had met that first Sunday morning and waited for this Sunday?

If she was the Simpsons' spy, was he her contact? Could he be one of the Simpsons?

The next morning Rowena walked down Main Street on her way to Hofsteader's Mercantile.

For the first time in her life, she was beginning to understand the power of that elusive emotion called desire and she wanted to savor it.

The air swam with the aroma of apples and cinnamon wafting out of the bakery's open door and she waved to the woman behind the counter.

"Glorious day, isn't it?" Reena called.

She passed the vacant lots. Someday they'd have buildings and businesses, the way Lost Gold was growing. The door to the saddlery was open and she inhaled deeply.

She hummed a tune as she walked along.

As she neared the sheriff's office, she noticed he'd tacked up some new wanted posters on the bulletin board in front of his office. Curious, she idly glanced at the black and white drawings.

And her world fell apart.

Jeff and Robby Lee had told her there were wanted posters out for them; that was why she'd changed her name to Sims. But this was the first time she'd seen them.

Dizziness washed over her, and she swayed. She rested a hand on the bulletin board to steady herself and drew several deep breaths. She had to get a hold of herself; she couldn't afford to show any reaction in case anyone happened to be watching her.

She took several more deep breaths and stepped back, away from the board. Surreptitiously she glanced around, and tensed when she saw Caid coming toward her. Had he seen?

She smiled stiffly and waited for him to reach her. "Good morning, Caid."

"Good morning, Reena. Are you all right?"

"Y-yes. Why?"

"You seemed dizzy a moment ago and I wondered if you were feeling ill."

"No, I'm fine. It must have been your imagination."

Caid looked at the posters. "They're both very dangerous men."

"You know them?"

"Jefferson Davis Simpson and Robert Lee Simpson," Caid said, reading from the posters. "They're wanted for bank robbery, train robbery. And now murder."

"Murder?" Rowena gasped. "It doesn't say that here." She pointed at the fine print.

"The Sheriff told me; it happened last week. It'll be on the next wanted posters—if they're not caught before then."

"They do sound dangerous." Had she done anything that gave her away?

"They're ruthless," Caid said flatly. "They'll stop at nothing to get gold for their stupid Cause."

"Cause?" She hoped she sounded cooler than she felt. "What do you mean?"

"They're stealing gold to establish a Second Confederacy, like the one during the War Between the States. They're even training a Confederate Army." He went on in a contemptuous tone, "They don't even know enough about the world to know that time has passed them and their Second Confederacy by. That it's a lost cause."

"Why are you so angry?" She finally dared look at him, hoping none of her inner turmoil showed on her face.

"People like them and their father caused enough suffering during the war."

"Maybe they believe in what they're doing," she said, and realized how it sounded. "I'm not defending them; I'm just trying to see things from their side. Maybe they think they're fighting for their principles."

"Ha! They don't know the meaning of principles—or honor, either. There's absolutely no justification for stealing. None whatsoever. They're romantic fools who see only the world they want to see, not the world as it is."

He tightened his hands behind his back. Because if he wasn't careful, he could become a romantic fool over her—and given his suspicions, that could be the biggest mistake of his life.

"I can't believe we're back at this shop so quickly, Belle," Rowena said the following day, tipping the large round hatbox on its side to get through the door. "It seems as if once you buy one dress, you have to keep buying more and more stuff to go with it."

"A dark green felt cloche to cover your head and frame your face prettily in winter is not 'stuff,' Reena. Besides, we need some heavier-weight wool dresses than we bought last week for the winter. It's already cool in the mornings and evenings, and I can tell you it's going to get a lot colder."

"I admit, it's beginning to feel good to sleep beneath a blanket." Rowena slipped her handkerchief into the pocket of her dark blue dress. "Before we go back to the hotel, I need to go down to Hofsteader's Mercantile and get some thread. I was going to go there yesterday, but I got sidetracked."

Sandbagged was more like it. She'd been so flustered after seeing the wanted posters for Jeff and Robby Lee that she'd never gotten to Hofsteader's.

"What do you need from there? Especially after the way Mrs. Hofsteader treated you at the picnic."

"How did you hear about that?"

"Bob told Mike and me when he returned. Without you, I might add."

"Caid found me. I didn't go looking for him." She glanced at Belle. "I hope Bob wasn't hurt."

"No. He latched onto the Raleigh girl before the fiddlers started playing. And since she's a banker's daughter, she's a better catch than you, anyway."

"Good. I'm glad to know the only thing hurt was his pride. As for Hofsteader's, I need some thread because I ripped my skirt a couple of evenings ago when I caught my heel in the hem."

"Oh." Belle squinted at something down the street, past Rowena's shoulder. "I say, isn't that Caid Dundee coming out of Hofsteader's right now? What a coincidence!" She lifted an auburn eyebrow at Rowena. "You're learning, Reena."

"It *is* a coincidence." She glanced over her shoulder. "He's probably there with his aunt. At breakfast I heard her say she needed to stock up on supplies before they head back to the ranch."

Caid had a large hundred-pound sack of flour slung over his shoulder, but it could have been a picnic basket, for all its effect on him. He strode to the freight wagon parked in front of Hofsteader's and hoisted it over the side into the wagon box.

When he straightened, his blue chambray shirt had a white shoulder, and he brushed it off as he returned to the store.

Seeing him loading the wagon was an eye opener for Reena. She'd known he'd soon be leaving, but it hadn't really sunk in. Until now. She drew a quick breath, surprised by the sharp pang that washed over her. Soon he'd be gone—and she might never see him again.

"Maybe you're right," Belle conceded, as Caid's aunt came out with a basket of oranges. She placed the basket on the wagon seat, then turned to go back into Hofsteader's.

A sharp whinny from a flashy gold-colored horse with a white mane and tail drew the older woman's attention. She walked along the boardwalk toward him.

"Whose fancy horse and buggy is that?" Rowena asked, sensing trouble in the high-strung animal's behavior. He was stamping his hooves and sidling sideways at the slightest noise. "That's a beautiful horse, but he needs a good run. He's about to jump out of his skin, he's so raring to go. Whoever owns him should have been riding him more. He's—"

Shots rang out as two cowboys unloaded their revolvers into the air in front of the Seen-the-Elephant Saloon. The golden horse reared in his traces, neighing in fright.

May was only a couple of steps away and she lunged for his reins. More shots boomed down Main Street as a third cowboy joined the other two.

It was too much for the horse and he leaped forward in a dead run. When the buggy lurched forward, the corner caught May in the side and knocked her off her feet. She tumbled into the thick dust beside the boardwalk.

"Belle, that horse! He knocked Caid's aunt down."

Head flat, ears laid back, the horse galloped straight toward them, the buggy bouncing along behind. The loose reins flapped against his back, scaring him even more.

Reena glimpsed something wedged onto a corner of the leather seat. Then she realized it was a young boy, hanging on to the buggy for dear life. His face was white and his eyes huge.

"My God, there's a child in there!" Rowena dropped her hatbox and dashed into the street.

The horse came straight toward her, wall-eyed with fright. The buggy hit a rut and bounced hard, and a front wheel came off, dropping the front corner. The horse's rear hoof banged against the dragging buggy, adding to his terror.

A man ran into the street and tried to grab the reins, but he missed.

Reena glanced behind her. There was no one else between the horse and the end of town. If she didn't stop him, the horse would keep running, out of town and possibly for miles—dragging the buggy until it broke up.

She was the only one with a chance of stopping the crazed animal before the buggy overturned and the little boy got hurt. The buggy's axle dragged through the thick, ankle-deep dust, raising a cloud of dust and slowing the horse a bit.

Was it enough?

She'd have only one chance to stop him.

As the horse dashed toward her, Reena began to run parallel to his path, and when he passed her, she grabbed his loose left rein and jerked his head around as much as she could. He screamed in her ear, but he slowed. She raced alongside, pulling hard on the rein and keeping his head turned.

In her other hand she clutched her lifted skirt, expecting at any second to trip over it or be jerked off her feet. Somehow she managed to keep up with the horse as he slowed more and more. Finally his heel banged the buggy, he stumbled, and came to a trembling halt.

The golden horse was snorting and trembling and blowing white foam all over her, but he was stopped. Steam rose from his back. Reena was too winded to do anything but rest her head against his sweat-darkened neck and take deep breaths.

She was trembling so badly she didn't know if her legs would hold her, and she grabbed a handful of white mane to hang onto. She heard people shouting . . . running footsteps. A boy crying. Caid's commanding voice as he ordered someone to take care of the boy.

Then he was beside her, slipping his arm around her waist and holding her tightly to his side. "Are you all right?" His lips brushed her ear.

"I think so." But now that it was over, her legs were going soft and rubbery.

"Lean against me. I've got you. I won't let you fall." His voice was deep and soothing and wrapped around her like a warm quilt.

She sagged against him. Caid was there. Everything would be all right. He would see to it.

"Let go of the horse, Reena. You can let go now. I've got you."

"W-what?" Opening her eyes, she saw that her right hand was still tangled in the horse's mane. She tried to let go, but her fingers wouldn't work. "I can't, Caid," she whispered. "My hand's numb."

"Just relax." Keeping her wrapped against him with one arm, he massaged her fingers and gently pulled them loose from her death grip on the horse's mane. "You're all right," he murmured. "You did what no one else in this whole town could do, Reena. You took a hell of a risk and saved that little boy."

People were running up from all sides, staring at Caid and her. She glimpsed Belle at the edge of the crowd, her eyes big and her mouth a round O. Reena hid her face against Caid's chest. He stroked her back and murmured soft words. Slowly she began to feel strength flowing back into her arms and legs, and knew it was his strength.

Finally she raised her head. "I'm fine now." But she was surprised at how faint she sounded.

"Not yet, but you're getting there."

"Really, I'm fine." She pushed away from him, albeit weakly. "See? I can stand by myself."

He had a white smudge of flour on his light blue shirt, and without thinking, she reached up and brushed it off. He raised a questioning eyebrow at her. "You still had flour on you."

He smiled then and she wondered if she'd melt in his warm regard. "I'm not worried about wearing flour. I'm worried about you, lady." Townspeople crowded around them, but he had eyes only for her.

"Mr. Dundee, Mr. Dundee!" Mrs. Hofsteader, carrying a crying little boy, pushed Reena out of her way, almost knocking her over. "Thank you so much for saving our darling Billy."

Caid hurriedly backed up a step and raised his hand, as if to ward the woman off. "Wait, Mrs. Hofsteader—"

"Thank you. Thank you." The woman grasped Caid's hand in hers and pumped it up and down. "You saved our darling Billy."

"You've got the wrong person, Mrs. Hofsteader. I didn't save your son."

"You didn't?" Mrs. Hofsteader stopped pumping his hand and let it drop. Her eyes grew round with surprise. "Who, then?"

"Miss Sims." He gestured at Reena. "I saw what happened. There was no one between Miss Sims and the end of town to stop your horse. If she hadn't had the presence of mind to run out and catch him, he'd still be running—and probably dragging an overturned buggy."

Mrs. Hofsteader opened and closed her mouth several times, like a fish gasping for air, before she managed to speak. "You saved our darling Billy?" she asked Rowena in a tight voice.

"I just stopped the horse, that's all."

"Mama, mama," Billy cried, wrapping his arms around his mother's neck.

"You're all right, darling," she soothed him. "Mama's got you." She walked away, her head close to his, whispering to him, then paused and turned. "Thank you, Miss Sims, I owe you a great deal this day." Her eyes met Reena's. "And I won't forget what you did."

Caid turned to the townspeople still clustered around. "Will someone please take care of the horse?"

"Happy to, suh." The blacksmith led the horse off and the crowd drifted away, leaving them standing alone in the middle of the street.

"Caid, the buggy struck your aunt," Reena exclaimed, tugging at his sleeve. "Did you see her?"

"I checked her, then I left her in Tanner's capable hands when I saw you run out into the horse's path."

"Oh." He'd left his aunt to see that she was all right. That was more than mere politeness.

He shook his head. "That was a damn fool stunt, Reena," he growled, "and I'm damn proud of you."

His regard sent a comforting wave of warmth through her, like a spoonful of warm honey did when she had a sore throat. All her life she'd relied on herself, never asking for help, never receiving it. But that afternoon had been different.

She had leaned on him and he had taken care of her.

She could depend on Caid.

It was a feeling she had never had in her life, and she relished it.

Chapter 9

~~~~~

"**C**ome on, let's get out of the middle of the street before some other horse runs us down." Caid wrapped his arm around her shoulders. His fingers rested in the hollow of her shoulder and he could feel how fast her heart was still beating. His was, too—after the scare she'd given him.

When he'd been kneeling at May's side, and looked up and saw Reena run into the street, directly into the horse's path, a surge of fear had washed over him unlike any he'd ever felt.

He'd left May in Tanner's care and raced after the horse, terrified that he'd find Reena's smashed and broken body.

Instead, he'd found her standing there, holding the horse, as calm as if she were sitting in church listening to a minister. There hadn't even been a

121

scratch on her. Just a few smudges of dirt on her face.

At first he didn't know whether to yell at her for running into the horse's way or enfold her in his arms. But when he looked into her eyes and saw her shock, his anger had dissolved into concern. That was when he had wrapped his arms around her and held her and soothed her.

And he wanted to go on protecting and cherishing her. It felt so right to have her turn to him and lean on him.

When they halted beside the road, he put his fingers in his mouth and whistled for Diablo.

"What are you doing?"

"Getting my horse," he replied, as Diablo trotted up to them. "I thought you'd prefer to ride instead of walking back to the hotel." When she'd sagged against him earlier, he'd wanted to swing her up in his arms and carry her away to a place where they were alone. And he still did.

"Thank you, Caid." She smoothed her hand back over her hair, trying to get it out of her eyes.

Caid tapped Diablo's front leg and said "Bow." The horse bent his forelegs and went down on his knees.

"Good trick," Reena said admiringly.

"It's come in handy a time or two." Caid gestured her forward and grasped her tiny waist. "Here you go."

She gripped his shoulders tightly as he lifted her sideways onto the saddle, and then gripped the horn as the horse lurched to his feet.

Caid rested his hand on the horn and swung up behind her. He gathered the reins and wrapped his arm around her waist, then drew her against him. "You don't need to worry about falling off. I won't let you." He clucked to the horse and they set off at a sedate walk.

She looked at him over her shoulder. "Me, fall off? I was born on a horse, Mr. Dundee. I don't fall off."

"I'll still keep my arms around you, Miss Sims." But he was glad to see that she was returning to her feisty self. And as they rode along Main Street, Caid was pleased by the number of townspeople who waved at Reena in recognition of her heroism.

"Thanks," one called.

"Good work," yelled another.

"You can stop my horse anytime, Miss Reena," a cowboy shouted from the saddle shop.

Rowena ducked her head, as if embarrassed by the attention, and he tightened his arms around her. He could feel her ribs rising against his chest as she took a deep breath. He enjoyed holding her, feeling her subtle movements as she swayed with the horse's walk.

They were coming up to the hotel but Caid wanted to keep going, far out of town, until they were truly alone. He reined Diablo in at the hitching rail and stepped off, then reached up for her and lifted Reena off.

She still looked a little pale. "Are you all right?" he asked, reluctant to let her out of his arms.

"I'm fine." She squeezed his arm, gently but definitely. "Really, I'm fine."

"If you're sure?" Damn! He wanted her back in his arms.

"I am." She backed away, watching him. Then she was engulfed by Lowry girls and turned away as they flocked around her, all talking at once.

Caid mounted Diablo. She turned at the top of the steps and her hazel eyes met his once more, and he wondered what she would do if he held his arms out to her. Then he nudged Diablo into a trot and didn't look back.

Trying to answer everyone's questions, Rowena edged her way up across the veranda and into the lobby. There Miss Abigail called her a heroine and a credit to Fred Lowry, and told her to take the evening off. But Rowena insisted on working her normal shift.

It was after nine before the dining room closed. Rowena hung back as the other Lowry girls headed upstairs, where she knew they would crowd into her room with more questions. Craving silence and solitude, she slipped across the rear of the empty lobby to the library.

Its entrance was hidden by the sweeping staircase that curved up to the second floor. Although well stocked, it was undoubtedly the least-used room in the whole hotel. She'd never seen anyone in it, so it had become her refuge in the hurly-burly of the large hotel and restaurant.

The library was dark. Someone had started a fire in the fireplace earlier, but it had died down to a single log on a bed of red embers. The gaslights were turned down. They were the safest, newest model available and she turned up several of the wall sconces, still surprised by the way the dim flame would grow bright and strong.

At the Colony in Mexico they were still using oil lamps, although her father had talked of building a gas plant. As usual, nothing had come of it, because Papa said what was the use of investing in houses they would leave as soon as they took over Arizona for the Second Confederacy.

She exhaled a long sigh. Tonight she didn't want to think about anything. She felt drained by the events of the past few days.

Reena browsed the shelves, crowded with new books that no one else had read. Selecting a book she knew would take her into a different world, she curled up in a corner of the high-backed sofa which, along with flanking wing chairs, faced the fireplace.

During the evening a surprisingly chill wind had begun to blow from the north, and she welcomed the warmth radiating from the fire. The flames were quiet except for occasional popping sounds.

Reena read the same page three times before she gave up. The feelings Caid Dundee had stirred in her that afternoon were entirely new to her. It wasn't that she became weak when he was near; quite the contrary, just knowing that he was there, that she could rely on him, somehow made her stronger. It was as if she drew strength from his strength.

Reena pulled off the snood that restrained her hair and raked her fingers through the long strands, loosening her curls. It was time to face facts, she told herself.

Today had changed her. Forever.

For when she'd needed someone, she'd turned to Caid—and he'd been there for her. And when he wrapped his arms around her she had felt so safe, as if he would protect her from everything.

Reena stiffened when the door opened behind her, but didn't move. As soon as whoever it was saw that this was a library, they'd skedaddle.

Right on schedule, the door closed. She smiled, glad to be alone again. But a footfall on the thick Oriental carpet blew that thought away.

Unwilling to give up her solitude, she stayed in her niche in the corner of the high-backed sofa. To her surprise, Caid strode past the sofa without glancing at it. He sprawled in one of the tall wing chairs that faced the fire and stretched out his long legs. He rested his brandy snifter on the arm of the chair and stared deep into the fire.

Absently he swirled the dark gold liquid in the snifter, then lifted it to his lips. He took only a sip before putting the snifter down.

Not knowing what to do, she stayed silent. He'd probably leave soon without ever knowing she was in the room. A whiff of the rich, sweet scent of the brandy wafted by her. The log burned through and split in a shower of sparks.

Caid rose and placed his glass on the wooden mantel. Picking up three chunks of firewood from the pile at hearthside, he arranged them on the coals.

Casually he leaned an elbow on the mantel and propped one boot against the hearth as he continued to stare into the flames.

What could he be thinking about with such concentration? Should she say something? But caution kept her quiet.

Finally, when the wood had caught and was blazing cheerily, he picked up his brandy and turned around. Reena had to give him credit; he managed to control his start of surprise. But she saw the flash in his eyes.

"Well, well, what do we have here?"

"*We?*" Reena leaned out of her niche and looked around the room. "I only see you."

"How long have you been there?" It was phrased as a question, but Reena knew it was really a demand.

Her chin went up. "Since before you interrupted my solitude."

He raised a dark eyebrow. "I see." His gaze went to the open book in her lap. "What are you reading?"

She had the feeling that he'd changed the subject on purpose. "This?" She closed the book and clasped it in her hands as she stood, wanting to be on equal footing with him, not looking up. "Just one of Scott's novels."

"You like Sir Walter? With his tales of heroes and maidens-in-distress and derring-do in the days of knights and chivalry?"

She tilted her head. "What's wrong with that? His stories are enthralling."

"But they're just fantasies. There *are* no heroes anymore. Now, take Mr. Verne: he writes about worlds that can be."

"Ugh. *You* take him. He's cold and in love with machines, like that submarine."

"You've read *Twenty Thousand Leagues Under the Sea*?" he asked in surprise.

"No, I couldn't finish it. He painted a picture of such a hard, cold, mechanical world, with nothing warm or soft in it. It wasn't a world I wanted to visit."

"Yes, a controlled world."

"You sound as if you admire that world. But it had no humanity in it. No room for human foibles and mistakes."

He eyed her over the rim of his snifter as he lifted it to his lips. "Interesting view." He put the glass down on the mantel. "I came down to get a book for May."

"Is she all right?"

"A little bruised, especially her arm. But nothing's broken." He paced toward her, and her awareness rose the closer he came.

"I'm so glad. It was brave of her to try to stop that horse." She wanted to go back into his arms, to feel his heart beating beneath her ear and his arms around her.

"She thinks the same of you." He stopped, so close he could have touched her. But he didn't.

"But she risked a lot more—after all, she's so—"

Rowena searched for something to say beside old. Caid's aunt didn't act old, but her age would have made any broken bones a big problem.

"So much older?"

Reena nodded. Tension crackled between them. Why didn't he touch her?

"She's resting comfortably now. In fact, she wants something to read by Dickens."

"Bah! I can't stand his stories." A lock of his dark hair hung down over his forehead and she wanted to brush it back.

Caid smiled. "Now, there I agree with you. Do you think I should take her Tacitus instead?" he asked innocently.

Rowena stiffened, then she saw the twinkle in his startling blue eyes. "Sure, if you think she'll enjoy him."

"Probably not as much as you." He walked over to the bookshelves and scanned their contents. "Do you have any suggestions?"

"No. All Dickens is equally boring to me." Moving to his side, she selected another novel by Scott and held it out to him. "Here, take her Dickens and this and see which she reads."

He trailed his fingers over the back of her hand as he took the book, and her heart did a little thumpity-thump.

"What about you? Still all right, or have you stiffened up?" His deep voice rumbled through her.

"My arm's a little sore, that's all." Was he going to kiss her?

"Reena, I—" As if remembering where he was,

he shook his head, and glanced at the books in his hand. "I'll tell May you sent the book."

What would Reena have done if he'd swept her up in his arms and laid her on the sofa? Caid wondered, as he walked upstairs. He'd wanted to, so badly.

He hadn't needed an encounter with her to remind him of what had happened that afternoon. The overwhelming fear he'd felt had told him what he didn't want to know, what he could no longer deny.

He was deeply attracted to Reena Sims—on many levels, including fencing with her, probing her bright mind, and being surprised by what he found.

Everything about her fascinated him. She was quick-witted and not afraid to show it, unlike most women he'd met. He found that as refreshing as lemonade on a hot summer day and she was the same combination of sweet and tart.

He'd discovered how astonishingly good it was to hold her and protect and cherish her. He wanted to be there whenever she needed him.

Her glorious crown of golden curls beckoned to his fingers. Normally he preferred brunettes over blondes, but in her case he'd make an exception. She was slim rather than curvy, again a change for him, but every time he thought of the surprise of finding out the boy he'd noticed was a girl, he smiled.

Tomorrow he would use May's injured arm to

convince Reena to come out to May's ranch with
him. If she *was* the spy he'd come looking for, he
could keep an eye on her there and keep her from
passing information to the Simpsons.

Wanting her at the ranch had nothing to do with
his deep-down, soul-stirring desire for her, he as-
sured himself.

The next morning, Reena was clearing off an
empty table when she spied Caid and May standing in the doorway. The white bandage on the
older woman's arm and hand contrasted sharply
with her brown dress.

"This way, please." Reena led them to a table
beside a window where they could look out on the
sunny veranda and the garden beyond.

May walked slowly, leaning heavily on Caid's
arm. "Good morning, Reena," she said with a
cheery smile. But she sank into the chair as if glad
to be sitting.

"Good morning. How's your arm?" Reena
snapped open a linen napkin and draped it over
the older woman's lap.

"Tolerable. Aches a little, but I can live with it.
A cup of coffee would do a lot for those aches."

"Coming right up." Reena hastened to the serving station and picked up one of the coffeepots kept
over warmers. Turning, she found her way blocked
by Caid's broad chest, attired in a ruffled white
shirt and a black jacket. She wasn't taken in one bit
by the ruffles. Caid was as hard and unyielding as
the mountains visible through the windows.

"How's your arm?" Caid's low voice vibrated through her.

"Fine." Slowly she looked up, past the neatly buttoned shirt to the steady throbbing of his blood at the base of his throat. She wanted to touch it, to feel his life force pulsing against her fingers.

"I'm glad." His Adam's apple moved as he swallowed. "May was hurt more badly than she lets on."

"I can see that."

"I wanted to be sure you understood." He glanced over his shoulder at May. "You see, she has a proposition for you."

Rowena blinked. "She has a proposition for me?" Why didn't *he*? Good lord, where had that thought come from?

"Yes. I'll let her tell you about it." He stepped out of her way, and gestured for her to precede him back to the table.

She filled May's cup, then Caid's.

"Bring a plate and service for yourself," May said. "And sit down. I want to talk to you."

"I'd love to, May, but I can't. I'm working."

"Don't worry, I already talked to Miss Nightingale."

"Miss Abigail?"

"Whatever her name is. Now, bring yourself a plate of breakfast and a cup of coffee and sit down."

Reena complied, then sat with her hands in her lap.

Caid cleared his throat. "May wants to ask a favor of you."

"Go ahead. You can eat while we're talking." May leaned back in her chair and looked around at the almost empty dining room. "You think they'd object if I lit up a stogie?"

"You?" Reena smiled, both astounded and delighted. "I don't think they'd have the nerve to say anything."

May pulled a long cigar out of her handbag. "Caid, will you do the honors? I can't light it with one hand."

"My pleasure." Caid snipped off the end, stuck it in his mouth, and took a sulfur match from the metal container May carried. He struck it on the sole of his boot, then lit the cigar and puffed several times until the end glowed cherry red. "Here you go," he said, handing it back to May.

"Thanks." May took a slow puff, then blew a perfect smoke ring toward the ceiling. "You don't inhale with these," she explained.

Miss Abigail and the chef came running out of the kitchen. Miss Abigail's mouth became an O as May blew another smoke ring toward the crystal chandelier. The chef started toward them, but Miss Abigail grabbed his arm and stopped him. He glared at May the whole time Miss Abigail was shoving him back toward the kitchen.

"You know, Reena, it's my right arm and hand that I injured. The hand I use to cook with. I've got a herd of hungry cowpokes at home who will be looking forward to my home cooking, and I won't

be able to do it for a few weeks." She waved her
hand when she spoke, flicking ashes all over the
table. "I wondered if you would consider coming
out to my ranch and cooking for Caid and the boys
until I'm able."

"But my job—"

"I already talked to that Abigail woman and she
said it was all right with her. Besides, it'll only be
for a couple of weeks. Your job will be here when
you return."

"What about you, Caid? You've been quiet. What
do you think?"

If she went with them, she could keep an eye on
him. And no matter what kind of threat he pre-
sented to the Cause, she had found that his arms
were the right place for her.

"I think you should come. May needs you."

She'd rather he needed her. "So you want me to
come out to your ranch?" She rubbed her thumb
over the weave of the linen tablecloth. She would
leave a note for Jeff in the hollow tree outside town
where they'd agreed to leave messages. "Yes. Then
I'll be glad to help out."

"Good, dear." May stubbed her cigar out in the
middle of her egg-crusted plate. "I'm glad. We'll
leave tomorrow, so have your valise packed and in
the lobby early."

Reena walked along the second-floor hallway
with the extra blankets May had requested. She noticed that Caid's door was ajar, and as she passed,
she heard two words that stopped her in her tracks.

"Waddell Simpson," May was saying. "Many years ago Jeter introduced my Sydney and me to that wretched old man. He lives in Mexico in a Confederate colony, you know. He once threatened to kill my Sydney because he wouldn't join the Cause. He even called my Sydney a traitor to all the South stood for."

"When I was in Savannah, I heard rumors of a Confederate plot to take over Arizona," Caid replied. "I wondered if you'd heard anything about this."

Reena flattened against the wall beside the door, determined to hear everything she could.

"Pshaw, Caid. For twenty years they've been talking about the Confederacy rising again—and for twenty years nothing has happened."

"I'm afraid the rumors are a little more specific this time. Simpson and his sons intend to take over Arizona."

"You're worried, aren't you? I'll talk to Jeter as soon as we get back to the ranch. He might know more, since he's a Southerner and his son is a hotheaded firebrand."

"I want to know everything he knows. I think that when it comes to the Simpsons, where there's smoke, there's fire. And I'm going to put it out."

"Well, I'll be a cross-eyed goat! You're no dilettante, after all. You work for the government, don't you?"

Voices on the stairway at the end of the hall carried to Reena and she hastily turned away and continued along the hall to May's room. She used her passkey to get in and spread the extra blankets on the bed.

As she was ready to leave, she heard Caid and May on the other side of the door.

"Does your mother know what you do?" she heard May ask. "How about the senator?"

"No, and you won't tell them. My father is a senator. First, last, and always, a senator."

Reena took a deep breath and opened the door. May and Caid both turned to her, startled. "Oh, May, I wondered where you were," she said, feigning surprise. "I just spread those extra blankets you wanted on your bed." She slipped past them. "Good night."

" 'Night," May called. "See you in the morning."

"I'll be there." Reena didn't look back.

Caid sounded as if he knew Papa and the twins and May had said she knew Papa. Rowena paused at the top of the stairs, frowning. May said Papa had threatened her husband, but that wasn't the Papa she knew. May had to be mistaken about that.

In the meantime she had to get word to her brothers. She would get up extra early to leave the message for them in the hollow tree. When she didn't meet them on Sunday, they'd look there.

And she wouldn't give in to the heart-stopping desire she felt for Caid. She couldn't!

Chapter 10

$\sim\!\!\mathcal{O}\mathcal{O}\!\!\sim$

Caid walked down to the Ranchers' Mercantile Bank the next morning. Main Street was deserted except for a few men walking along and a drunken cowboy sleeping underneath the chairs in front of the Wild Women Saloon.

He'd strapped on his gun and holster that morning and the revolver's weight at his hip felt comfortable.

As he walked along, he felt that tingle along the back of the neck that told him someone was following him. He paused to pull a cigar out of the case in his inside chest pocket. He turned, ostensibly to draw the sulfur match along a porch post, and looked behind him.

No one was there. But he was sure someone *had* been. Was he just getting jumpy, seeing spies where there were none? Was he being overly suspicious—

of everyone? He shook out the match, put his cigar back in the case, and continued his stroll on Main Street.

President Cleveland had personally asked him to take this assignment, since Caid had known the Simpsons when he was growing up. They had run away to Mexico years ago, but he still remembered what they looked like. Although Waddell Simpson might now have white hair and stooped shoulders, his eyes would still be as mean. And the Simpson boys had already begun to look like their father when he'd known them so long ago.

As he approached the bank, he noticed two heavily muscled horses tied to the hitching rail in front. They were trail horses, in fine shape, ready to cover lots of miles fast. And tied loosely—ready for a quick getaway.

Although he didn't glance through the bank window, his strides slowed and out of the corner of his eye he saw the rigid, tense way the banker and the teller stood. And he saw a masked man wave a revolver.

He glanced up and down the street as he came to the passageway next to the bank. He didn't see anyone suspicious looking, so he ducked down it. In the alley behind the bank, he tried the rear door, softly, carefully. It was unlocked.

Drawing his gun, he slipped in and leaned back against the door, listening to the conversation that came down the short hallway from the front.

"I'll take all the gold, suh. Not just what you've got out here."

"I-I don't know what you mean." Raleigh's voice had a pronounced quaver. He must have been puffing on one of his cheap cigars, because Caid could smell its coarse stench all the way down the hall.

"The hell you don't, suh. Now we'll all just go on down the hall to your vault and empty it out. You too, Mister Teller. We wouldn't want to leave you up here to give the alarm."

Damn! Of course they'd want to empty the vault. He scanned the hallway. There was only one place for him to hide. Opening the door, he backed into Raleigh's office, which reeked of cheap cigars and cheaper perfume. He left the door ajar so he could see what was going on in the hall. Caid circled the huge desk, noting the open file folder full of papers on it, but there was nothing he could use to create a diversion.

Silently, he returned to the door and watched. The gray-haired teller came first, looking scared as a rabbit. Then Raleigh came into sight, walking jerkily. Behind him came the man he'd seen earlier. A bandanna masked the lower half of his face.

He wore a crushed gray Stetson that had seen years of wear. But stuck in his hatband was a jaunty gold ostrich feather that fairly shouted, "Look at me." Even without the dark brown hair that brushed the man's shoulders, Caid would have known him: Jefferson Davis Simpson.

And he held his revolver carelessly.

"Open it." Simpson waved at the vault with his gun.

Raleigh reached into his back pocket.

"Freeze!"

"I-I'm just getting my handkerchief. I-I-I think I'm going to—*a*—*a*—*achoo!*" He finished wiping his nose and pushed the handkerchief back into his pocket. "There's nothing in the vault. Nothing at all."

"Shut up and open it," Simpson snarled.

"Yes, sir. Right away." He pulled the handkerchief back out and wiped his forehead. "But I—I—"

"What the hell is it now?"

"I don't have the combination. It's in my desk drawer. In my office."

Caid eased behind the door and waited. He was beginning to understand Simpson's impatience with Raleigh. The man was as incompetent as they came.

The door swung open and around in front of him, hiding him from the two men as they entered the room. He heard the rustle of clothing and a grunt and knew Simpson had poked Raleigh with his gun.

"Get the damn combination."

A drawer scraped as it opened.

Caid kicked the door shut and launched himself at Simpson, who was half-turned toward him. Caid barreled into him and knocked him across the desk, scattering papers everywhere. Beyond Simpson, he glimpsed Raleigh, standing, with his mouth open.

Simpson rolled over and landed on his feet behind the desk, coming up with his fists raised. Caid leaped to meet him with a fist to his nose. Simpson's hazel eyes flared, and for a moment Caid had the feeling he'd seen those eyes somewhere before.

Then Simpson landed a blow to his temple. Caid shook his head and ducked a second blow. He threw a fist into Simpson's stomach, doubling him over. As he moved in closer to knock him out, the boom of a revolver filled the room, and a bullet whizzed by his head and plowed into the woodwork.

"Freeze, cowboy!" The gruff voice came from behind him. "Brother, get over here."

Caid turned slowly as Simpson edged past him and scooted out the door. Robby Lee, the other Simpson twin, pointed his revolver directly at him—and he held his revolver very seriously. A deadliness in his hazel eyes told Caid that if he moved, he was a dead man.

"Get the horses, Jeff," he ordered, as he backed out the door, dragging the white-faced teller with his left hand. His right kept the gun aimed unwaveringly at Caid. "If either of you goes for the sheriff before we get out of town, your buddy here gets it."

Caid waited until he heard the front door of the bank open and slam, and the hollow thud of boots on the boardwalk outside, then he raced down the hall.

He banged through the double doors as the Simpsons whirled their horses around and galloped away. Caid ran out into the middle of Main Street and took careful two-handed aim. The few men on the street dived to the right and left to give him a clear shot. He unloaded his revolver, but the Simpsons were out of range by the time they galloped past the hotel.

He muttered a couple of curses under his breath as he holstered his gun and turned back to the bank. The teller slumped against the door, staring at him with a bug-eyed look.

"You all right?" Caid took the steps with one stride and reached the old man.

"Yeah." He wiped a shaking hand over his forehead. "I'm fine."

Reena carried her caramel-brown valise out onto the hotel veranda and set it down. She smoothed her palms down the bodice of her new apple-green dress and took a deep breath of crisp morning air.

Mrs. Hofsteader was coming up the steps and Reena nodded to her. "Hello, Mrs. Hof—"

They both turned as shots rang out down the street. Reena ran to the white railing and leaned out over it, trying to see what was going on.

Two men on horseback rode hell-bent-for-leather straight at her. They leaned low over their horses' necks to present smaller targets.

"Oh, my God!" Reena clutched her throat in fear as she recognized her brothers. Bullets zinged around them and sent up dust spurts in the street. Holding tightly to the veranda rail, terrified for their safety, she watched them gallop past.

Someone was shooting at Jeff and Robby!

Horrified, she backed away from the rail and sat down heavily on a rocker.

"Are you all right, Miss Sims?" Mrs. Hofsteader asked.

She nodded, unable to trust her voice. She gazed at her hands, clenched tightly in her lap.

Someone was shooting at Jeff D and Robby Lee!

"Reena? Answer me!"

"W-what?" She blinked owlishly. Caid hunkered down in front of her, his hands on her arms, shaking her, gently. How long had he been there? How long had he been shaking her?

Had he seen her brothers gallop past? She focused on her hands, still tightly clenched in her lap.

"What's the matter?" He gently brushed several curls off her forehead. "You're so white, you'd make a sheet look pink."

She tried to clear her mind. She couldn't afford to make a mistake now. "Those men . . . being shot at. I've never seen anything like that before."

"They were bank robbers." He frowned and shook his head. "I tried, but didn't wing either of them."

"You!" She knew her eyes had saucered with shock, but she couldn't help it. Oh, Lord, he could have killed one of her brothers. One of her own brothers!

"It's all right." He patted her hand reassuringly. "The sheriff's getting together a posse to go after them."

Jeff D and Robby were still in danger! What could she do to help them? "Are you going, too?"

"No. The sheriff's got enough men; he doesn't

need me. So we'll just go on with what we were doing."

She blinked, trying to think clearly through the terror buffeting her. What had they been doing?

"Let's get May and get going." He clasped her hands in his and drew her up out of the chair. His brow furrowed and he looked down at them. "Your hands are ice cold."

"Are they?" She pulled them free. "It must be the shock. That's all."

He clasped them again, and the warmth in his hands seeped into hers. "Are you sure you're all right?"

"I'll be fine." She pulled free and walked to the railing, praying that she wouldn't sway or faint. She had to be strong, for the twins. They needed her. She couldn't give herself away. "Let's get May and be on our way." She tried to speak briskly, confidently, but her voice quavered.

She turned, and for the first time noticed the holster riding low on his hip, its bottom secured with leather strips tied around his leg. They were not the gun and holster of someone playing around.

His gaze swept her from head to toe, openly assessing her. But she couldn't afford for him to get suspicious now.

She flicked her tongue over her dry lips. "My valise is already here; I'm ready to go."

He nodded sharply. "Why don't you bring May down; I'll get the wagon and bring it around."

By the time Reena collected May and returned to

the veranda, Caid had driven the wagon to the front of the hotel.

"Where's Tanner?" Reena asked, glancing around.

"He's decided to stay in town." He helped May up onto the high wagon seat, taking care that she didn't bang her bandaged arm. "Now you," he said, turning to Reena.

Not wanting him to know that her hands were still ice cold, she lifted her skirt up out of the way, braced her foot on the wheel hub that served as a step, and reached up to grab the wagon box with her other hand. But the skirt was hobbling her, and she couldn't get her leg up over the high side into the wagon box.

Caid's large hands settled around her waist and he lifted her up the last few inches. Reena stepped into the wagon box and settled on the seat.

"Thanks." She adjusted her skirt, picked up the reins, and nodded. "Let's go."

"Uh-uh; I don't trust you with that team. You're still looking too shaken. I'll drive."

"No! I'm plenty strong enough, and fully recovered now." That was all she needed: him sitting beside her, hip to hip, thigh to thigh.

"I want to drive." He led a prancing Diablo to the back of the wagon and tied him there, then returned to step up into the box.

Reena moved over against May as much as she could to put some space between her and Caid, but it was a vain effort. His thigh was pressed against the length of hers, and she could feel his heat through his sturdy blue denim pants, through her skirt and petticoats, all the way to her flesh. And she didn't want to.

Caid clucked to the horses and snapped the reins, and they leaned forward into their collars, getting the wagon rolling. Whenever he moved his left hand, his elbow brushed her side. Reena unobtrusively tried to move over more, but May was as immovable as a boulder.

"Caid," May said, leaning forward to peer around Reena, "I can't wait to hear all about the bank robbery. I hear you foiled it."

"It must have happened just before I walked in, because they didn't have time to get any gold this time. That's all."

"Come on, Caid, there's got to be more to it than that. It's miles to my ranch, so you might as well tell us the whole story. Right, Reena?"

"Maybe Caid doesn't want to talk about it." Rowena suggested. She didn't want to hear all the gory details. Not when it was Jeff D and Robby Lee he had been shooting at.

Caid shot her a speculative glance. "You still look shaken. Maybe *you* don't want to hear about it."

"Pshaw! What are you talking about? Of course she wants to hear about it. We're glad you were able to stop them, aren't we, Reena? Did you wing either?"

"I don't think so."

"So, which way did they go?"

"Toward your ranch again."

"Again!" Reena turned to the older woman with horror. "Have they been to your ranch? Have you seen them?"

"I don't know. Sometimes strange riders stop by." May shifted restlessly on the wooden bench. "Damn, this seat gets harder every year. The sheriff's chased them toward my ranch before. But he always loses them."

"Sheriff Huddle has already gathered a posse and gone after them." Caid nodded at a dust cloud on the horizon in front of them. "That's probably them now."

Reena kept looking from one to the other as they talked over her head. "I don't understand. Why would they always head in the same direction?"

"The sheriff thinks the Simpsons have a hideout somewhere in the narrow finger canyons that run down from the mountains and mesas toward the Grand Canyon. He's always lost them in there."

"The S-Simpsons? The men whose pictures were on the posters? How do you know it was them?"

"I recognized them. After all, there aren't many outlaws who are twins."

"They're twins?" Reena feigned surprise and hoped she sounded believable.

Caid shot her a sharp look. "Uh-huh. Besides, the one named after Jefferson Davis wears a yellow ostrich feather in his gray hat. I guess he wants everyone to remember that he's a Johnny Reb."

"That doesn't sound very smart to me." And it didn't. She'd never thought about that yellow feather before. It had always been a part of Jeff D's hat. She'd have to talk to him, tell him how stupid it was to wear it.

"It isn't. But they're unwavering fanatics. Them and their father. And they have a sister."

"Is she an outlaw, too?" She was pressed tightly against him. Could he feel the way her heart was pounding?

"Not that I know of. But with a family of fanatics like that, you never know."

Reena wanted to scream at him that she wasn't a fanatic.

He snapped the reins again, urging the horses into a trot. The wagon jounced and jolted over the ruts and the barrels in back rolled back and forth, squeaking as they rubbed against each other. The horses' harnesses jingled and the wagon rattled and squeaked until it was impossible for them to talk. Which was fine with Reena.

Reena watched the dusty track ahead as she went over what Caid had revealed. He knew more about the twins than she'd realized. She stole a glance at him from beneath her lashes. But how did he know about her? There weren't any wanted posters for her.

Absently she reached up to finger the ring on the gold chain around her neck. *It wasn't there.*

She ran her finger down her throat, thinking she'd missed it. She hadn't. Then she remembered that the chain had broken last night while she was washing her hair and Belle had offered to get it repaired while she was gone.

"Anything wrong?" Caid asked.

He must have felt her tense, they were all sitting so close together. "It's nothing. I—I just forgot something."

"Important?"

"No." Only to her.

She'd gotten the ring from the dark-haired boy. She'd never known his name, only that he and his parents often visited them when they lived at the plantation in South Carolina. He'd given her the ring and told her it was because she was special. He'd made her feel special, too, not teasing her unmercifully, like her brothers, and he'd even let her sit on the saddle in front of him.

Then the war had ended. Papa had picked up the whole family, lock, stock, and barrels—full of flour and china—and moved to Mexico.

She had never seen the dark-haired boy again.

"How are you doing, May?" she asked, pushing her memories away.

"Fine. Fine."

Caid inhaled deeply, inhaling Reena's lilac scent. When he'd climbed up to drive, he hadn't realized how hard it was going to be with Reena sitting beside him, pressed against him.

He could feel it every time she tensed or relaxed. Actually, she hadn't relaxed at all, just gone between tense and very tense. She'd tried to scoot over against May a couple of times and put some distance between them, but there hadn't been enough room.

At first he'd been glad. But now his blood was rushing through his veins like hot lava, and he wanted to drop the reins and kiss her until she was as mindless with need and desire as he was.

"How much farther to your ranch, May?" he growled.

"Eight or nine hours, I'd say."

"That far, eh?" *Get a grip on yourself, Dundee!*

He unconsciously tightened his grip on the reins, and the horses came to a sudden stop in the shade of a grove of junipers.

"Why are we stopping?" Reena asked, with that breathless little catch in her voice that told him how aware she was of him.

"It's time for lunch," he said, jumping down. "And this is a good place."

He helped Reena and May down, then walked to the back and jerked Diablo's reins free and swung up on him.

"Where are you going?" May asked.

"Scout the trail ahead." Diablo pranced under him, ready to run. "You two go ahead and eat."

"The trail's fine. You don't have to do that."

"Diablo needs a run." And so did he. He nudged Diablo with his heel and gave him his head.

"I wonder what's wrong with *him*," May said, watching him ride away in a roostertail of dust.

"I can't imagine," Reena said, hoping he'd been as uncomfortable as she was. Lordy, sitting hip-to-hip with him had been tense. She opened up the wicker picnic basket the chef had packed for them. "Here, May, have a sandwich."

Reena had already packed the basket back in the wagon by the time Caid returned. He and Diablo were breathing hard when he reined in.

"We're ready to go on, Caid. I kept out a sandwich for you."

"Good. Don't want to waste any time." He handed May up onto the seat, then Reena. "You're looking a lot better this afternoon, Reena. Do you think you could drive those horses?" He didn't think he could take another five hours with her pressed against his side. He wanted her too badly.

"Sure can, Caid." So, he'd been as bothered as she. Good! "Here's your sandwich."

Hours later, the sun was already setting when Reena drove the horses through the ranch gate. Recognizing that they were close to shelter and feed, they began to trot faster toward the distant cluster of ranch buildings.

There was a barn, a bunkhouse, another building, and a ranch house. A windmill turned in the wind, squeaking with every rotation as it pumped water for the house and stock. Reena sighed, glad that they were finally there.

Caid rode beside the wagon on Diablo. She glanced at his hard profile. As if he sensed her scrutiny, he turned his head and his eyes met hers. Reena's heart gave a great somersault against her ribs, and she knew.

In spite of everything, she still wanted to feel his lips on hers, his hands on her, his body on hers.

How could she want her enemy?

Chapter 11

Although she had a lot to do, the next day dragged on endlessly, and Reena knew it was because she hadn't seen Caid since breakfast. In the late afternoon she walked out on the ranch house's rear porch and stopped short.

Caid was at the woodpile. He tapped a wedge into a piece of tree trunk which was way too large to go in the fireplace or stove. His blue work shirt drew taut across his wide shoulders when he picked up the heavy sledgehammer and swung it. His ringing blow drove the wedge deeper into the wood.

Again his shirt drew taut, again a ringing blow drove the wedge deeper. Then another. And another. Finally the wood split into halves.

Caid took off his shirt and flung it to the side, then picked up the ax and began to chop the large pieces into stove-sized chunks. The rhythmic play of muscles across his bronze back and shoulders, the tensing and curling and extending, fascinated Reena. She had seen her brothers and other men chop wood countless times, but never had it been so completely engrossing.

"Damn," she muttered, "Belle's right. I *am* in lust."

As if he sensed her, Caid looked up and saw her. Propping the ax against his boot, he leaned on it and took deep breaths while wisps of steam curled up from his broad shoulders in the nippy autumn air. Reena felt like a deer caught in the glare of a lantern at night. Then Caid picked up his ax and turned back to the wood, releasing her.

She marched out to the root cellar, leaned down, and flipped open the wooden door. She hesitated on the top step, trying to make herself descend into the cavelike darkness.

"Why are you staring down the stairs instead of going down them? And where's your lantern?" Caid asked from right behind her.

"I—" She stared into the dark hole . . . remembering. "During the War, Mama and I would hide in a tiny dark hole whenever the Yankees came," she said faintly. "And I was always terrified Papa wouldn't come back for us."

"Reena?" Caid's voice was soothing as he gently grasped her shoulders and turned her away from the steps. "You don't ever have to go back in the dark hole again."

She shook her head, trying to clear away the im-

ages that still haunted her. "I've never told anyone," she whispered.

He gently kneaded the tight muscles in her
shoulders. "It's not your burden alone anymore.
Feeling better?"

She nodded, too embarrassed to look him in the
eye.

"Here, I'll go down. I don't need a lantern." He
glanced at her. "No bowl? Give me that apron
you're wearing."

She untied the half-apron from around her waist
and held it out to him, and he tied it around himself. On any other man, it would have been laugh-
able—but Caid's masculinity wasn't even dented.

"What do you need?" he asked, as he descended
the steps.

"Carrots and potatoes and a couple of heads of
cabbage, and see if there's any canned fruit on the
shelves."

She hovered over the hole, listening to him
knocking into things in the dark, embarrassed yet
thankful. Finally he came up the stairs with her
apron full of enough vegetables to feed an army.
He untied the apron with one hand and handed it
to her.

She held it by both ties so it was still bowl
shaped. "Caid, I can't tell you how much I appre-
ciate your—"

"Don't mention it. We all have dark places where
we don't want to go. Sometimes they're physical,
sometimes they're mental, but we all have them.
And in this case, it was easy for me to go there.

There might be a place where you can go that I can't or won't."

Reena studied his silver-blue eyes. "You don't have dark places. You're too strong."

"Yes, I do. You just don't know what they are."

Reena was surprised he'd admitted a weakness. Having weaknesses wasn't allowed in the Simpson family. That was why she'd never told another living soul about her terror.

"Thank you, Caid. You've helped more than you'll ever know." And she wanted to go back into the warmth and safety of his arms.

Instead, she went back inside, sat at the table, and began to peel the potatoes. She tossed the first one into a pot of cold water so it didn't darken, then went on to the next. By the third potato, she'd risen and walked to the window. *Just to make sure he's all right*, she reassured herself. After all, working with an ax was dangerous.

Caid smiled warmly at her and waved, and she quickly returned to her potatoes. Afterward Reena found herself another chore. She was *not* going to moon after him—he might be an attractive man, but he was still dangerous.

Caid walked into the kitchen with an armload of firewood and stacked it beside the stove. He couldn't forget the look of stark terror on Reena's face when she'd been looking down those steps, and her voice had been so faint, so distant, he'd barely been able to make out her words. She had been a very young child during the war, but she must have gone through some hellish times.

Yet she'd grown up into a feisty, independent, strong woman. Those were the qualities he admired in her, that made her who she was.

And where was she now? he wondered. The kitchen was empty. Had she been more upset than she'd let on?

When he walked into the living room, he stopped short, surprised to see Reena sweeping the ashes out of the fireplace. Smiling, he leaned in the doorway and contemplated her nicely rounded backside.

"Cinderella, I presume."

Reena gasped. Which made her inhale ashes. Which made her cough, stirring up even more ashes. "Oh!" She reared back, trying to get out of the gray cloud, and hit her head on the fireplace. "Ow!"

Caid strode across the room and, grasping her around the waist, pulled her free of the swirling ashes.

"Don't open your eyes," he commanded, setting her upright. She grasped his arm with both hands and bent forward, coughing and choking at the same time.

"You'll be all right." He rubbed her back gently as spasm after spasm rocked her. "That's it, cough until you don't need to."

"I—"

Her head was bent, exposing the nape of her neck, and the need to kiss it flamed through him. He brushed his lips across it.

Gradually her paroxysms faded until she was quiet.

"Don't open your eyes yet. I'm taking you into the kitchen so we can use a wet cloth to get the ashes out of your eyes."

Wrapping his arm around her back, he guided her to the kitchen sink. He primed the pump and pumped a few times until the stream of water filled the sink.

"This is going to be cold, so be prepared." He dipped the corner of the dish towel in and wrung it out, then tilted her head up. Tears had left two white trails in the gray ashes. Gently he dabbed at the ashes, removing them from her long brown eyelashes. He tried not to notice the way the curve of her breast brushed his arm.

She was depending on him, trusting him. A wave of protectiveness swelled inside him and he swallowed heavily, suddenly wanting the moment to last forever.

"Almost done." Her skin felt like silk. "There, try opening your eyes now."

She blinked several times, then opened her hazel eyes so wide he could see the flecks of emerald in her irises. She gazed up at him—a wide-eyed innocent.

"I made an ash of myself, didn't I?" she said.

Caid choked, surprised. But even as he was chuckling, his blood was pulsing like it had when he lost his virginity when he was fourteen.

Never had he felt such an awareness of a woman as he felt at that moment—and it was more than physical. He wanted to explore her mind, to know everything about her.

He wanted to touch and stroke and kiss her—all over. And then do it again.

Her hair was pinned up off her neck and her pulse throbbed against the delicate snowy skin at the base of her throat. Desire swept through him, like hot lava boiling beneath the surface of a volcano.

Damn, how he wanted to make love to her! To sink into her warmth and—*never mind, Dundee. Take a cold shower*.

Footsteps in the hall made him look up.

"Sure do smell good in here," May said, as she came around the corner. Her eyes widened at the sight of the two of them. "Why didn't you say something, Caid? I didn't have to come in here."

Caid smiled. "You're not interrupting anything, May."

"No, you're not," Reena seconded. "I just took a bath in ashes and Caid was getting them out of my eyes."

"So, I'm not interrupting anything. Well, why not? Can't you two see what's right in front of your noses?" She shook her head in disgust and walked away.

Reena served roast beef and mashed potatoes that night. The kitchen was filled with the aromas of beef and the cherry cobbler she'd made for dessert. The cowhands clattered in, talking and laughing and spreading dust with each step they took.

They'd washed out on the porch and their faces had a pink, well-scrubbed look.

Chairs scraped and creaked as they took their places around the table. Reena couldn't remember all their names yet. She recognized Curly, the youngest, who had straight blond hair, and Vinegar, who seemed as wrinkled and old as the mountains. They were hungry and served themselves.

"Whooee! Miss May, this here lady can shore cook, ma'am," Curly said, as he pushed a third slice of roast beef onto his plate.

"You telling me you like her cooking better than mine?" May challenged.

"Yes, ma'am." Six voices spoke as one.

May grinned. "Eat up while you can. Reena is only staying until I'm healed. Then it's back to my beans."

A chorus of groans greeted her announcement, then silence fell over the table except for the clink of utensils against the thick pottery plates.

"May, I'd like to ride over and meet Jeter tomorrow." Caid said, as he forked two slices of roast beef onto his plate. "Would you draw me a map how to get to his place?"

"Map, nothing! I'll ride over with you. Haven't seen old Jeter in a couple of weeks now."

"Looks like you're gonna see him sooner than you thought," Curly said, pointing at the window with his meat-laden fork. "He's coming through the gate now. Looks like he's got Seth with him, too."

"Seth?" Reena asked with a sinking feeling.

Could he be the obnoxious cowboy from the restaurant?

"His son," May replied. "A real firebrand and a load of trouble for his papa, if you ask me. That Seth boy is something else. Better put two more plates at the table, Reena. They'll be starved enough from the ride over to eat a whole side of beef by themselves."

Reena watched through the window over the sink as the two men reined in their horses at the hitching post just beyond the white-picket fence that surrounded the house and May's few rose-bushes. Caid joined her there, under the guise of getting down two more plates off the high shelves.

"He was so drunk, he may not remember anything," he murmured.

"Not that drunk." She got out more silverware.

Jeter Biggs dismounted and strode through the swinging gate without looking back to see if his son was coming. Short, scrawny, and bow-legged, he reminded Reena of a bantam rooster, just spoiling for a fight.

He banged through the door without knocking.

"Thought I'd find you all feeding your gullets," he said. "Although I must say it smells a lot better than usual in here, May."

"I got me a new cook, Jeter." May nodded at Reena. "Why don't you take a load off your feet, old man, and set a spell? We've already put out some extra plates."

"Don't mind if I do. Don't mind if I do." He slid into an open seat at the table and immediately forked three slices of roast beef onto his plate.

"How did you know I was back?" May asked.

"Sheriff stopped by with his posse this morning."

"Did he get 'em?"

"Nope. Lost them again in those damn canyons where we're always losing cattle. Which reminds me, that's why I came over to see you, old woman."

"To call me an old woman?" May teased

"No, I came because I reckon we're going to have an early winter and I want to bring the cattle down out of the high country."

"What makes you say that, Jeter?" Caid cut a piece of roast beef and began to chew. He slanted an approving glance at Reena that told her he liked the beef.

"Have you noticed how thick the horses' coats are already? And it's only early October. The geese headed south a week ago." Jeter rubbed the back of his hip. "And my rheumatiz is acting up something terrible."

"I've got some liniment for your 'rheumatiz,'" May offered.

"You stay away from me with that stuff, woman. It'll take the paint off a barn. Hell, I wouldn't wish your liniment on a marauding bear."

"It was good enough for my husband," May shot back.

"And he up and died, didn't he? Had to take that way out to get away from your liniment."

It was the banter of two people who'd known and liked each other for many years, Reena realized, as she glanced from one to the other. "Do I hear wedding bells?"

May snorted. "Hell's bells, more likely. I like my freedom. Besides, he'd have to stand on a box to kiss me."

"Woman doesn't have any sense, anyway," Jeter said to Caid. "Do you be her nephew from back East?"

"Yes. And I'm glad to know she's got a neighbor like you. May said you kept an eye on the ranch while she was gone."

"I did, and—" He broke off as the porch door banged open and hit the wood frame with a resounding crash.

"Hey, Pa, I—" Seth's words died in his throat as he stared at Reena. "Well, well. What do we have here? My little desert thistle?"

May cast a speculative glance at him. "Do you two know each other?"

"Just in passing." Reena explained. "From my work."

"Not my fault, that," Seth growled. "I was willing and able. Very able."

Reena bit her tongue to keep from saying anything.

"Shut up and sit down, son," Jeter said. "This is mighty fine cooking tonight. A lot better than May's, so don't waste your time jawing when you could be eating."

Seth looked around the table for an empty seat, and spied Caid. "You!"

May rolled her eyes. "Don't tell me you two know each other, too!"

"We haven't been formally introduced," Caid said noncommittally. He pushed away from the table and walked over to the stove. Using a folded towel, he grabbed the dented gallon coffeepot that sat on a back burner and went around the table, pouring coffee for everyone.

Everyone murmured thank you except Seth.

To Reena's surprise, Jeter looked up from the slice of roast beef he was demolishing. "Where's your manners, boy?"

To her greater surprise, Seth mumbled something that sounded like thank you.

"Anyway, I think we ought to combine our hands and get the cattle down out of the mountains," Jeter continued. "And I think we better do it right quick. I can just about smell snow on the air."

"May and I were just talking about a roundup, Jeter," Caid said, putting the coffeepot back on the stove. "We'll be ready to go in a couple of days."

Reena moved her fork around in her mashed potatoes and kept her eyes on her plate. She knew he was going to use the roundup as cover while he searched for her brothers' hideout.

"Fine. Fine. Pass down that cherry cobbler you're trying to hide on top of the stove. Damn small bowl for cobbler that smells so good," Jeter added, pointing at the soup bowl Reena had placed beside each plate for the desert. "We'll comb the south side of the mountains if you'll comb the north side. We'll sort out the animals after we've got them down out of the high country. How's that?"

Caid nodded. "Fine with us."

Jeter broke the flaky crust of the cobbler, then tilted it and spooned it out until his bowl was full.

"Take yourself some cobbler, why don't you, Jeter?" May jibed.

"Damn right I will, woman," he said, pouring cream over the cherry-red mound in his bowl. "It's got to be a sight better than those poison apples you make."

Caid reached into his chest pocket and pulled out a cheroot, leaned back in his chair at the head of the table, and surveyed the men who would be going on the roundup. Which ones were workers and which ones slackers? Which ones could he trust?

"Surprised you haven't lit up, too, May," Jeter said, looking up from his second helping of cobbler. His lips were stained so red, he looked like he was wearing lip rouge.

"I was just about to, old man. Send one of those down here to me, Caid."

After that the conversation swirled back and forth as the cowhands talked about what had happened at previous roundups. Caid ignored the glares Seth sent his way. He'd taken care of Seth once, and if he had to, he'd do it again.

Seth joined the cowhands as they trekked back to the bunkhouse, but Jeter decided to stay in May's remaining spare bedroom. Two of the hands whose evening it was to do the dishes grumbled, but began to clean up. May and Jeter disappeared into the parlor to play a game of checkers and heckle each other.

Caid walked out on the back porch and contemplated the stars sparkling in the velvet darkness.

What was he going to do about Reena if they all went out on roundup? She had come out to May's to cook for the hands, but he wanted her where he could keep an eye on her. If she was the Simpsons' spy, she might know where their hideout was.

He wished he knew whether she was innocent or not. It was beginning to drive him crazy.

The screen door's hinge squeaked softly as someone joined him on the porch. He took another puff of his cigar, but didn't turn around. He didn't have to. He knew who it was, even before he caught a whiff of her scent.

"If I can drive a wagon, I can drive a chuckwagon," she said, as though answering his question. "A roundup is darn hard work and the hands will need good meals while they're out." She paused. "Or you *will* have a mutiny on your hands."

He blew out the smoke. "We'll check the chuckwagon tomorrow. Did you bring any boy's clothing?"

"Of course."

He rubbed his cigar out on the wooden railing, then tossed it into the rose bushes. "Come here," he said, reaching back and snagging her wrist without looking. He pulled her in front of him, then pointed at the velvet black sky. "See that bright star? Sight along my arm." He pointed.

"That extra-bright star? I see it."

"That's a comet. It won't be there next year." He slid his hands around her waist and laced his fingers together.

She rested her hands on his and leaned back against him. "It's so beautiful out here."

"Yes." He could feel the beat of her heart. He nuzzled the side of her throat and dropped a tiny kiss on her shoulder. It felt so good to hold her. What would it be like making love to her?

"Oh, look! A shooting star!" She pointed as it flamed across the night sky.

"Did you make a wish?" he asked, as it disappeared.

She looked up at him over her shoulder and he felt a fierce jolt of pleasure. "Yes."

"What did you wish for?" he murmured, knowing what he wished for.

"It won't come true if I tell you."

Caid brushed a soft kiss onto the sensitive spot behind her ear. He moved his hands up over her breasts and cupped their fullness through her dress.

"Did you make a wish, Caid?" she asked, in a throaty voice that made him want to pick her up and carry her off to bed.

"Yes." About her.

He'd stayed away from the ranch house all day in order to stay away from Reena. And he'd still spent the whole day wanting her.

How had she become such an important part of his life?

Chapter 12

Being around Caid all the time was going to be more difficult than she'd realized, Reena thought the next morning. When they were in the same room, her attention focused on him, not on what she was doing—earlier, she'd almost poured salt into her coffee instead of sugar. If Caid hadn't reached across the table and stopped her, she'd have had a heck of a surprise.

She'd laughed it off, but she knew what had happened. Caid. And she hadn't even been watching him. In fact, she made it a point not to look at him—besides, she didn't need to. The way his blue-gray eyes could turn intent and piercing, the way his sensual, full lips could grim into a thin line, the way his powerful hands could be hard or gentle, were indelibly imprinted on her mind.

She watched him through the kitchen window as

he led the ranch hands toward the corral. They'd
drunk another gallon of coffee and inhaled more
pancakes than she could count, but now they were
saddling up.

"Reena," May said from the doorway. "I've decided to go back to Jeter's ranch with him. He
needs someone to supervise the stocking of his
chuckwagon, and I know that between you and
Caid, you'll know what to stock in mine."

"Are you sure you're up to it, May? After all, that
was a pretty hard trip we had."

"I'm fine." She glanced over her shoulder, saw
that Jeter was outside, and added in a whisper,
"Besides, it's good to heckle Jeter a bit. He needs
it."

Reena smiled. "I see. Well, have a good time."

"I will."

Reena did the breakfast dishes as she watched
them ride away. Then Caid and the hands rode off
in the opposite direction. She was alone.

After the dishes were done, she'd do a little riding on her own and see if she could spot any familiar landmarks that would help her find the
hideout. She set beans to soak for dinner, then
changed into her boots, baggy pants, and a flannel
plaid shirt, and headed for the corral.

There was no one in the barn, so she lifted a
coiled lariat off a hook and went out to the horses
in the corral. She climbed up the log rails and sat
on the top one, studying the animals. The cowhands had lassoed and saddled the good horses
earlier. They'd left a jughead bay, an old white

horse who was a sack of bones, a swaybacked chestnut, and a strawberry roan who didn't have any obvious defects.

The roan, who was standing alone, limped away, trying to blend in with the other horses. She dropped into the corral, shook out the rope, and swung it over her head several times until the loop opened, then dropped it over the roan's head. As soon as she did, he began bucking, but it was already too late. She had him.

"Easy, boy," she said. Slowly, hand over hand, she walked up the rope to him, murmuring soothingly. He snorted when she reached him, but stood quietly. She reached up to rub him behind the ears. "Good boy. You tried the old sore leg trick, but it didn't work."

Behind her, someone clapped slowly. She whirled. "Good roping," Caid said, "especially for someone who grew up on a farm."

"Can't people on farms know how to rope?" She led the horse toward the gate. "Why are you always so suspicious of everyone?"

"Am I?" He slid the wooden latch back and opened the gate just wide enough for her to lead the gelding out.

"Yes. You are." She led the horse toward the barn and tethered him near the door.

"Where were you going with that horse?"

"To catch up with you and the rest of the hands," she said, running a currycomb over his back where the saddle blanket would lie. "And since you're here, you can put the saddle on him."

"I've got the hands riding the fences in the near pastures, so that they're in good shape when we bring the cattle in. If you want to spend the day tightening barbed wire, we can do that, or we can check the chuckwagon and supplies instead."

Resting the currycomb on the roan, she glanced at Caid over her shoulder. "Is that why you came back?" He wasn't suspicious of her, then. Good, that would make it easier for her to slip away on the roundup.

"Of course." He wasn't going to admit to either of the real reasons he'd come back, that he was suspicious of her, and that he wanted her. With every particle of his being, he wanted her.

"Then let's have at it." She led the horse back to the corral.

"Let's start with the cellar," Caid said, as he opened the gate for her.

An hour later Reena sat on the top step of the root cellar, peering down into the darkness. "All right, Caid, I need a bucket of carrots, and two of potatoes."

"Here, I'll hold the tin," she said, when he came up the stairs. Kneeling, she flipped back the lid and he tumbled the potatoes into the storage container. As they bent over the tin, their shoulders and hands brushed several times. Reena glanced at Caid, but he didn't appear to have noticed.

Caid took the steps back down into the darkness two at a time and told himself to ignore her light fragrance, to ignore the way more and more tendrils of hair were curling around her face, and how full and soft and made for kissing her lips were.

He brought up a bucket of carrots and tipped them into the next tin. A few missed and landed on the ground. They both dived for them, and Caid wound up partially on top of Reena.

He felt her go very still beneath him. "Sorry, Reena." He hastily slid off her and slanted her a rueful smile. "You'd think those carrots were made of gold."

"Right now, they're squash," she said dryly, reaching beneath her bosom and pulling the carrots out.

He didn't know whether to laugh or kiss her senseless.

Rolling away from her, he got to his feet and held out his hand to help her up.

They gazed at each other.

His long fingers circled her wrist loosely and he considered pulling her into his arms.

Damn it! What was he doing? Was he nineteen again, letting his rod do his thinking for him? Never had he flamed with such desire for a woman. Just the thought of making love to her, of stroking his hand down the delicate curve of her back, of palming her breasts and teasing her nipples with his fingers and mouth, of sinking into her welcoming warmth so deeply he might never come back, sent a tidal wave of heat rushing through him.

"No!" he muttered, in answer to the fire in his loins. Turning, he stalked away. It was a good thing

May had a pond nearby. He'd used it a lot in the few days he'd been there.

Reena ran after him. "Caid? What's the matter?"

"Leave me alone, Reena," he gritted.

"Maybe I can help."

He whirled. "Oh, you can help, all right! You can—" He took a deep calming breath that did nothing to calm him. "Go back to the house."

He saw realization dawn in her eyes, followed a second later by a flush that stained her cheeks a delectable shade of pink. "Oh." She turned and walked away without looking back.

How many more times did he have the strength to say no to his body and his mind? Because something told him sleeping with her would only be the tip of the iceberg.

Reena watched Caid saddle Diablo and ride away. As the beat of the horse's hooves faded, she went inside the house to finish gathering the supplies. It was mid-afternoon when she finally carried the last flour sack out to the porch.

Since Caid still wasn't back, she decided to go for a quick ride to see if she could spot his trail. Or maybe she'd see something familiar that would lead her to the hideout. She quickly lassoed the horse she'd caught earlier, bridled him, and swung up on his bare back.

Soon Reena was crossing gently rolling red earth, sprinkled with clumps of gray-green bunch grass. She could see for miles, but didn't spot anything that looked familiar. Pushing further on, she followed a trail that wound through the woods and across streams several times, but didn't find any tracks.

She finally turned back, and was guiding her horse along the base of a boulder-strewn slope when she spied a rattlesnake sunning on a boulder beside the trail.

The horse saw it too, and shied and leaped sideways, throwing her.

Reena didn't have time to roll into a ball and she landed hard, in a sprawling heap that knocked the wind out of her. She scrambled to her feet as fast as she could, and saw with relief that she wasn't in striking distance of the snake. But her horse was a rapidly disappearing dust cloud, as he hightailed it for home.

"Damn! It's going to be a long walk back." Brushing dust off her tan pants, Reena began walking fast. Though the trail would lead her back to May's ranch, the sun would be down in another hour and she wouldn't be able to see the trail in the dark.

Rena got across one stream by stepping on stones, but a slippery rock in the second stream resulted in a soaking. She trudged on in her wet clothes. Once the sun dropped below the horizon, the air began to chill and she shivered and rubbed her hands over her upper arms, trying to get warm.

Soon it was pitch black out and she knew she was in trouble. Bad trouble. She didn't know how far it was to the ranch, and her cold wet clothes were sucking the heat out of her with every step. If she didn't find shelter soon . . .

How could she have been so stupid to go riding so completely unprepared? She didn't even have any matches with her.

Reena didn't know how long she'd been walking, or how many streams she'd fallen in, but she was shivering badly when she heard the thud of hooves.

"Hey!" she yelled. "Over here."

"Reena!" Caid's voice came out of the darkness. "Keep talking."

"Keep coming and I'll keep talking." She saw the flicker of a torch through the trees. "Over here, Caid."

Finally he appeared out of the darkness and trees, holding a torch high. "Are you all right?" he asked, jumping down.

Beyond him Curly and another cowhand rode out of the trees, holding up flaming torches to give them light.

"I'm j-just c-cold," she gasped through her chattering teeth.

"We'll take care of that right away," he said, pulling a sheepskin jacket from behind his saddle and wrapping it around her shoulders. "Come on, let's get you back to the house." He helped her up on Diablo, then swung up behind her.

Turning Diablo toward home, he urged him into a canter.

"Oh, Caid, I'm so glad to see you." She looked up at his craggy features in the torchlight. "How did you know I needed help?"

"A riderless horse and no cook pretty much told the story." He rubbed her shoulders vigorously through the jacket, trying to warm her.

"I was in big trouble. Thank you for looking for me."

"Hey, the hands would have mutinied if I'd lost the cook." He gazed down at her with a twinkle in his eye. "And I would have missed you, too," he added, suddenly serious. "Now just save your strength. We'll be back at the house soon."

Reena could hear Curly and the other cowhand pounding along behind them. The wind made her wet clothes even icier, and soon she was shivering so badly she couldn't talk. Only Caid's arms around her kept her from falling off.

Diablo leaped the white picket fence and clattered to a halt at the house. Caid dismounted, swept Reena back into his arms and carried her inside, through the kitchen and down the hall to her bedroom.

"While we were looking for you, a couple of the hands were heating water," he explained as he kicked the bedroom door shut behind them. "You've got a hot bath waiting."

"Put me down. I'm all right." She pushed at his chest weakly.

He stood her on her feet, but watched her carefully.

Reena tried to smile, although she had a feeling it was really a grimace. "I'm okay, now."

"Sit down and let me get those boots off you."

She did, knowing that she didn't have the

strength to wrestle them off herself. Caid straddled her leg, grasping her boot in his hands, and working it back and forth until he could slide it off her. Then he did the other boot.

"You'll be a lot better after you get out of those clothes and into that bath." He gestured at the gently steaming tub sitting in the middle of the room.

"That's what I'm doing." She was shivering violently as she plucked at her shirt buttons, but her numb fingers couldn't get them unbuttoned.

"Here, let me do it." Caid gently pushed her hands away and unbuttoned her shirt. He peeled it off her and dropped it. Her nipples had hardened to tight buds in the wet cold. Embarrassment rippled through Reena along with her shiver, and she tried to cover her breasts.

Caid opened a warm, dry towel and draped it over her shoulders and breasts. Then he unbuckled her water-swollen belt, and got her pants unbuttoned, too.

"I'll take it from here," Reena said, resting her hands on his.

Caid studied her for a moment. "Do you want me to help you get into the bath?"

"No. I'll be all right now." She stood up, to show him she could. "See?"

"Get in the water then, and I'll bring you something hot to warm your insides."

As soon as the door closed behind him, she peeled off her soaked pants and stepped into the water. It was soothingly hot as she slid down into it.

A few minutes later Caid walked in with a mug

of hot chocolate laced with coffee. "Here," he said, kneeling beside the tub and handing it to her. He ignored her nakedness as if it didn't matter, and she knew it was so she wouldn't be embarrassed.

"Thanks, Caid. You're spoiling me." She sipped the hot drink and was amazed at the way it restored her.

"You deserve some spoiling, after what you went through." He paused in the doorway. "The hands have gone back to the bunkhouse, so when you get out of the tub, come sit by the fire in the parlor if you want to."

Reena finished rinsing her hair and stepped out of the tub, finally feeling warm again.

She slipped her garnet silk dressing gown over her silk chemise, then went out to the living room to let her hair dry. Scooting the footstool close to the fireplace, she sat down and began to brush her hair.

She didn't know how many strokes she'd done when she heard Caid's bootsteps come into the room, and she looked up.

A wild singing began in her blood.

"I'll brush your hair for you." He held out his hand.

"I can do it."

"Sometimes, Reena, it's better when you let someone else do it." His promise wrapped around her, as warm as a June afternoon.

She laid the brush in his hand, and he pulled a chair up behind her. He held a section of her long tresses in his hand and started at the bottom, gradually making his strokes longer and longer as he smoothed away the wet tangles. When that section was completely smooth and shiny, he moved on to the next. The whisper of his fingers sent delicious shivers rippling up and down her spine.

She leaned back against his knees, enjoying the contact. When she turned sideways for him, she rested her arm across his knees.

Silence cocooned them.

A log popped in the fireplace and she jumped.

Caid hesitated. "Did I hurt you?"

"No. Don't stop." She arched back against his hand.

He kissed the nape of her neck, sending a wash of pleasure over her. "Stand up and I'll finish."

She suddenly turned and leaned against him, wrapping her arms around his waist, listening to the beat of his heart.

"What are you doing?" he asked, his voice rumbling through her as he spread his big hands over her shoulder blades.

"I'm deciding if I like the way you feel against me."

She felt him stop breathing. "And *do* you?"

Reena smiled up at him. "I'm not sure. Why don't you do something to help me make up my mind."

He smiled and kissed her. "How's that?" he asked against her mouth.

"Nice. How about another sample?" She leaned

back in his arms, wanting his mouth on hers. His eyes glittered with flame and fire.

She closed her eyes, waiting for his kiss, wanting his kiss. She waited. And waited. She opened her eyes—

And his mouth crashed down on hers, demanding everything. Drinking passion from her lips. She met him and dueled his tongue, parrying and feinting back and forth, touching and tasting . . . until she surrendered and gave herself up to pure pleasure.

When he raised his head and gazed down at her, she was light-headed and breathless.

She clasped his cheeks with her hands. "What are you doing to me, Caid Dundee?"

"Don't you know?" His voice was warm honey, flowing over her and coating her in sunshine. "I'm seducing you."

His mouth ravished hers once more, and when they finally came up for air, she was breathless and giddy with need. He swung her up in his arms, and Reena locked her arms around his neck. She could feel the sinews in his neck flexing as he carried her down the hall to his bedroom. He released her legs and let them slide down him so she could stand.

He turned down the oil lamp on the nightstand until it gave off a dim golden glow.

He returned to her and slid his hands down her back in a slow, sensuous slide. "I can still stop," he murmured in her ear, "if you want to."

She unbuttoned the top button on his shirt, then

the next and the next, spreading the soft flannel back and trailing her fingers through the dark hair curling over his chest. He shivered beneath her gentle touches.

"Two can play that game, you know."

His fingers brushed her chin lightly as he unbuttoned the top button on her silk dressing gown, and her pulse drummed in her ears. His fingers went to the next, and the next and then there were no more buttons and he was pushing it back over her shoulders until it rustled down to pool at her feet.

Reena trembled in the fire of his gaze.

"All right. Your turn. I'm all yours."

She planted tiny kisses among the dark curls. "Do you like this?"

"Too much." He drew a sharp breath when she kissed his nipple.

When she finished unbuttoning his shirt, Caid pulled it out of his jeans and took it off, tossing it over his shoulder.

But as her fingers went to his belt buckle, he stopped her. "Let me do the rest." He wrapped his arms around her and held her close, then slowly rolled her chemise up over her head.

He swung her up in his arms again, and gently, as if she were the most delicate cotton candy, laid her on his bed. He shed his pants in one fluid motion, then looked down at her, all dark mystery and golden sinews. And he wanted her. She had no doubt about *that*.

"You are so beautiful," he whispered, his voice gritty with desire. "So very, very beautiful."

Her heart thrummed wildly as he traced delicate, teasing patterns all over her with a single finger, leaving her skin tingling in its wake.

She stirred restlessly and he threw his leg over hers, stilling her. With anyone else, she would have panicked and struggled to free herself, but with Caid she felt safe. Instinctively she knew he would never hurt her.

And deep inside her she was aware of an emptiness that only one man could fill: this man.

His gaze went to her breast and she felt warmed by it alone. "You are so beautiful," he murmured again. He tongued the pulse point at the base of her throat.

Her nipples were tight buds, and he gently rolled one between his finger and thumb while he kissed the other. Reena gasped, surprised by the blossoming pleasure.

Then he pulled her nipple into his mouth and suckled and she felt the tugging down to her toes. Her eyes went wide with surprise and her heart sang wildly with each touch of his tongue.

Clasping his shoulders tightly, she arched up into his mouth. He rubbed his lips across her bud of a nipple with a fierce tenderness that left her aching with pleasure.

The emptiness inside her throbbed insistently.

"Caid, p-please," she gasped, arrowing her fingers through his hair, trying to draw him closer.

"That's what I want to do, sweetheart—please you." He tongued first one nipple, then the other, until she was a pool of pleasure and passion.

Then he rained tiny arousing kisses all over her, gradually moving lower and lower. She tensed as he neared the curly thatch at the juncture of her legs.

But he bent over her ankle and kissed it, then rained more kisses up her legs until by the time he reached her knees she was breathless and writhing with need, wanting more, though she didn't know what it might be.

"Caid," she gasped, "come to me." A tension inside her was growing with each kiss and touch.

"I will, sweetheart, I will." He kneed her legs apart and wedged his own between hers.

Reena went still. She felt so terribly weak and vulnerable with his leg between hers—so open. She could feel the rough hair on his leg rubbing against the insides of her knees and thighs.

"It's all right, Reena." His voice was low, soothing. He kissed her deeply. "We'll go slow, I promise you."

"I-I trust you, Caid."

He returned to her breasts, teasing and taunting and suckling. She writhed beneath him, gripping his hair and silently begging him to do it again. He did.

Deep inside her the wild aliveness was growing. And the emptiness in her was howling for filling.

He trailed another line of tingling kisses down her body. "Spread your legs more for me, love. That's it." He slid down until he lay between her legs.

"What are you doing?" Reena raised her head to

watch him. She threaded her fingers through his hair.

"You'll see." With fierce gentleness, he touched her there . . . in her most private place.

"Caid!" She jerked, shocked.

He did it again. And again. Then he kissed her . . . there. And he pleasured her with his hand and mouth.

Reena gasped and trembled when he entered her with his fingers, stroking, pressing. With each stroke the wildness inside her grew. She grabbed his shoulders and hung on. Her muscles tightened until she knew they couldn't get tighter. But they did. Then he stroked her once more and she bucked wildly in a sunburst of passion and pleasure.

She went limp in his arms and her hands slid out of his hair. "Oh, Caid, I didn't know," she gasped, when she could finally speak.

He smiled down at her. "There's more." Still holding her in his arms, he moved forward, pushing at the entrance to her womb. "This is the best part, Reena." He kissed her breasts as he inched forward.

She relaxed, bit by bit, aware that the emptiness inside her was still there, still yearning to be filled.

"It'll hurt for just a moment, love, then . . . you'll see."

She raised her head and kissed the hollow of his shoulder. "I trust you. Go ahead." How could there be more?

He pulled back, hesitating when he was almost out, then he surged into her on a wave of strength and power. And this time he went all the way, swallowing her cry of pain.

Reena felt strange. Full. He was filling her where no one had ever filled her. Caid was still, giving her time to adjust to him, then he began to stroke, slowly, in and out. In. Out.

He filled her aching emptiness, filled it with power. Instinctively, clumsily at first, she met him thrust for thrust. And with every thrust, every stroke, the wildness within her grew.

Faster. Faster.

She couldn't breathe, but she had to go on. Tighter and tighter. She dragged her fingers down his back, feeling each rib as he stroked harder and faster. The wildness was growing . . . growing . . . growing.

"C-caid!" She arched up in his arms in a great, convulsive, paralyzing moment of delicious tension. Then she exploded into a thousand shimmering stars.

"Ree—na!" Caid gave an exultant yell and tightened his arms around her and exploded in his own climax.

As they drifted back to earth, Reena's fingers splayed over Caid's back. "Oh . . . Caid," she murmured, still stunned. She felt as if she'd seen all the stars in the heavens.

He moved as if to slide off her.

"No, stay." She was too boneless to move. How could he?

"But my weight." His head was beside hers and his breath wafted by her ear.

"It feels good. I like it." She could feel his chest rising and falling against her breast as he drew deep breaths. His weight was a reminder of what they'd shared when they became one. And she wanted it to go on.

He was changing within her, and she felt a stab of sadness, because with the change, their one was becoming two again.

Silently, they savored the last of being one.

"Is it always like that?" Reena asked. No one had told her about the throbbing ecstasy, about the joy of becoming one with another human being. Not her mother before she died, not Belle—no one.

Caid smoothed his fingers over her forehead and gave her a soft kiss on the cheek, then rolled off her. He lay back and drew her into the circle of his arm, cradling her against him.

"No. It's rarely that good, that wonderful." Wonderful didn't even come close to describing it. Making love to Reena had been even more than he'd dreamed. "Did I hurt you?" He had to know.

"No—I barely noticed."

She had said she trusted him, in that moment when a woman was most vulnerable to a man. To know she had given him her trust then stunned him. Emotions that he couldn't even name had filled him with a soaring warmth that was separate from his desire for her, yet enhanced it.

And even now, when he was drifting in a sea of satisfaction, he wanted to protect and adore her.

Reena rested her head on his shoulder and listened to the wonderful sound of his beating heart, so steady and strong.

She drew aimless trails across his chest, still dreamy in the afterglow of their lovemaking. She'd never felt so complete, so whole, as now, after she'd joined with him.

Reena studied Caid's profile in the dim light. He was so full of contradictions. He had the vigilance of a gunslinger, and the dedication of a lawman.

Yet with her he had both the power and the gentleness of a lover.

She turned slightly, resting her leg against his, and yawned sleepily. He cuddled her against him in his arms, making her feel safe and cherished.

It was enough—for now.

Chapter 13

❧

Caid led the ranch hands along the trail toward the creekside where they would camp the first night, but his mind was on Reena. He hadn't slept much in the two days since he'd made love to her.

He'd told Reena that he'd be working early and late, getting everything organized for the roundup, and then reconnoitering to discover where the cattle were and where they would camp each night. He didn't mention that he also was riding far and wide looking for the Simpsons' hideout. But he'd made sure that he didn't return until very late at night, after she was asleep.

Not that he had any regrets: making love to Reena had been more spectacular then he had ever thought possible.

But she'd stunned him when she told him she trusted him. He couldn't get that out of his mind, because he still didn't know if he could trust her.

Making love with her was too special for him to tarnish it with his doubts and questions about her. It was a matter of honor. Until he could give her his trust, he wouldn't ask her to give him hers.

He shook his head over the tangled web that his life had become. In Lost Gold, he had seen so much that indicated she was working with the Simpsons. But she hadn't done anything suspicious at May's ranch, and he desperately wanted to trust her—and to find out that she wasn't working for the Simpsons. That would be the icing on his cake.

"We'll camp here," he said to the ranch hands riding with him. Then he turned Diablo and galloped back to Reena.

Circling around behind the chuckwagon, he came up beside her and reined Diablo in to match her team's pace.

"I think this is far enough for the first day. We'll set up camp here tonight. Tomorrow we'll work those breaks," he pointed at the narrow finger canyons veining a nearby red mesa, "and see how many head we can flush out."

"Whoa up, boys," she called to the horses, and drew back on the reins.

Caid stepped off Diablo while Reena set the brake. He'd vowed not to touch her while they were working the cattle. He had enough trouble staying away from her, without feeling her satin-soft skin beneath his fingers.

But by the time she rose from the seat to jump down, he was standing beside the wheel.

"Come on, I'll help you." He was just being polite, he told himself—that was all. He wasn't playing with fire. He grasped her waist and lifted her out of the wagon. Reena braced her hands on his shoulders and for a second he thought about letting her slide down him. Then he set her down on the ground.

As she trailed her hands down the front of his shirt, Caid noticed she had no gloves on. He grabbed her hands and turned them over to look at the palms.

They were chafed and blistered.

"Damn it, don't you have any sense, woman? Where are your gloves? You can't drive the wagon with hands like this. What were you—?" He knew he was overreacting, but he wanted to protect her, to see that she was safe and cherished.

"Oh, shut up!" Reena whirled and stomped away, so angry she wanted to cry. She'd discovered that she'd forgotten her gloves early in the day, but hadn't said anything. After all, it wasn't anyone's fault but her own that she'd forgotten them.

Now Caid had to come along and make a big fuss. Damn him! Did he think she'd done it on purpose?

Remembering she had to unhitch the team, she turned back.

Caid stood there, his arms crossed over his chest. "And where do you think you're going?"

"To do my job!"

"Oh no, you're not! Go sit on those boulders and stay out of the way."

She tried to push past him. "Get out of my way. I need to get dinner started."

"Go . . . sit . . . down."

"But—"

"Look," he snarled, "if your hands get infected, you'll be unable to cook, and I don't need that."

"Stop shouting at me!" Everyone was watching them.

She heard the click of his teeth when he snapped his mouth shut.

"Reena," he said very quietly. "Please go sit down."

"All right. But don't blame me if you don't get any dinner tonight." She walked over and sat on one of the large river-rounded boulders and crossed her arms over her chest. How could he get her so angry so quickly?

Curly, the youngest hand, unhitched the team and led them off. After the horses were unsaddled and watered, he hobbled each animal's front legs and turned them loose to graze on the bunch grass that covered the plain.

She tried to clasp her hands together in her lap, but they stung too badly. Surreptitiously, not wanting anyone to think she was a crybaby, she eyed her palms. She'd been too busy driving the horses to notice how the rough reins were rubbing her hands raw. Now that she had nothing to do, she could feel the pain.

Caid banged the chuckwagon tailgate open, then dropped the two legs that helped support it and turned it into a table. He pulled out the wooden first-aid box and walked toward her, his features as grim as if he were going to a funeral.

Without a word he sat on an adjacent rock, unlatched the box, and opened it. "Give me your hand." His voice was flat and distant.

"That's some bedside manner you've got there." As soon as the words left her lips, she knew her word choice had been dangerous.

His head snapped up. "Funny, no one's ever complained about my bedside manner before." His tone was cool, but his eyes were hot with another message.

"I'd have to judge for myself." The danger made sparring with him more exhilarating.

He picked up one of her hands and turned it over, resting it on his knee. "I could show you," he murmured, as if reading her mind.

"I'll forego that . . . pleasure," she said dryly.

Caid took out a clean cotton cloth and poured medicinal alcohol on it. "This may hurt a bit," he said, as he hunched over her hand. "But I want to be sure it's clean before I bandage it."

Though he daubed gently, Reena went ramrod straight and clenched her fist. But she didn't cry out.

Caid didn't look at her, but she saw his Adam's apple move as he swallowed. "Sorry," he muttered in a low voice.

"I didn't mean to make a fuss." But she had tears in her eyes. "I'm all right now." She unclenched her fist and spread her fingers out. "See?"

Reena vowed she wouldn't clench her fist at his

next touch. But she did. He waited for her to un-
clench, then went on. Each time she stiffened, she
saw him swallow.

Finally they were done and he spread an oint-
ment over her palms that felt cool and relieved a
lot of the sting. "Your left hand is in worse shape
than the right, so I'm going to bandage it, at least
for a few days."

By the time he finished, her left hand was im-
mobile and looked like a white club. She was grateful he'd left her one hand to do things with.
"Thanks."

"Here." He dropped a pair of leather gloves in
her lap. "Didn't you know I was carrying extra
gloves?"

"No," she said through tight lips. She should
have realized he would have some.

He eyed her for a moment, then turned and
stalked away.

That night, as she clumsily tried to unroll her
bedroll one-handedly, Caid walked over and took
it out of her hand. He shook it out and laid it on
the ground.

"Thanks," Reena said, sitting down and flipping
back the blanket to get under it.

"You're welcome." He shook his out and spread
it beside hers.

Reena lay on her back, folded her arms beneath
her head, stared up at a thousand times a thousand
stars, and listened to the steady breathing of the
man beside her.

He lay on his side, looking at her, not the stars.

"Curly will be driving the wagon tomorrow."

"He doesn't need to. I'm perfectly capable of driving."

"That's all right. He was happy to. You can take over his job."

Alarm bells rang. "What's his job?" she asked warily.

"He's riding drag."

"Just what I want—to trail behind a bunch of cattle and eat dust. I'd rather drive the chuckwagon."

"Not tomorrow." He closed his eyes and went to sleep.

Reena had a feeling he was like a wild animal, though: part of him was still alert and on guard while the rest of him slept. She turned on her side facing him, and pulled her blanket up over her shoulder. She was sliding into sleep when she realized his eyes were wide open, watching her. Her last thought was that she was safe because of his vigilance.

Morning dawned with a light breeze and a cloudless sky.

By noon the sun had plastered her shirt to her back, but she was no longer eating dust. One of the other hands had relieved her, so she was ranging up into the finger canyons and ravines, looking for cattle.

The summer rains had brought a belly-high growth of grass, which had been seared brown by the September sun. The cattle clustered in the shade beneath juniper trees or in brush thickets, where they were hard to see. She searched for movement, like a flicked tail or ear.

Reena drove the two steers she'd found down canyon until they ran into the main herd, then she turned back to check the next canyon.

So far she hadn't spotted any recognizable landmarks, but each day brought new country, and she knew that eventually something would look familiar. And then she was determined to find her brothers' hideout and warn them.

She came upon a sheltered, south-facing swale where the last wildflowers of the season still carpeted the ground in great swaths of white and yellow and purple.

Dismounting, she took off her gloves and began picking a bouquet, using her pocket knife to cut the stems. She'd place the flowers on the chuckwagon tailgate at dinner—not that the men would notice. But she would, and that was enough for her.

She was kneeling in the middle of a patch of lavender and purple flowers when she felt the hoofbeats of an approaching horse. Shading her eyes with her hand, she looked for the animal.

He was a blood bay, and he was galloping directly toward her. He was too far away for her to recognize the rider whose face was hidden by his black Stetson. But he was a tall man and he sat his horse ramrod straight, like a military man. And with that she knew who it was.

She turned back to picking flowers until his horse stopped close to her. "Hello, Caid," she said, without looking up. "What brings you out here?"

His horse's bit jingled and his saddle creaked as he stepped off. Sand and gravel crunched beneath his boots as he walked up behind her and stopped.

"You." The single word throbbed between them.

She stilled, watching his shadow. He was holding his reins in his right hand, running his thumb up and down the leather.

"Why?" she asked softly, as she added another flower to the mound in her lap. She caught a whiff of male sweat mixed with the scent of hot horse.

Caid told himself to get back on his horse and ride away. But he couldn't. He'd watched her cooking for the men and looking for cattle, and discovered that she threw herself wholeheartedly into whatever she did—and that was also the way she made love. Wholeheartedly.

He ached with wanting her. He longed to cherish her.

But that would have to wait until he could tell her he trusted her.

"You're doing a good job, Reena. The men like your cooking." Hell, what was he doing talking about her cooking?

She arched a wary glance at him. "Is that why you came out here? To tell me my cooking is good?"

Dropping the reins, he sat beside her. He took a lavender flower from her lap and drew it over the curled shell of her ear in a touch as light as a dandelion puff.

"No, I came out here because . . . just because."

Bandaging her hand yesterday had been hell.

He hadn't allowed himself to touch her other than what was necessary. Then she'd slept beside him last night, with her sleep-softened sighs, reminding him—as if he needed to be reminded—what it was like to sleep with her in his arms.

"You should always be surrounded by fields of flowers," he said, drawing the lavender petals down her cheek. "You belong among the blossoms."

Slowly she turned her head and looked at him. "Your eyes are so big, such windows to your soul," he said. He saw her awareness of him there.

Grasping her shoulders in his hands, he bent his head to taste her lips.

She wrapped her arms around him and pulled him down on her, there in the midst of the wildflowers. "Isn't this more comfortable?" she whispered against his ear.

"Honey, kissing you will never be 'comfortable,'" he growled. He trailed a line of kisses from her jaw to her mouth, then began to sip kisses from her lips. She looped her arms around him and hung on tight as they rolled over and over in the wildflowers, kissing.

Finally he raised his head. The sweet scent of crushed flowers surrounded them. He leaned over her, cushioning her with his big hands beneath her shoulders. "Comfortable?"

"Mm-hmm." She smiled and brushed a lock of dark hair off his forehead.

He rested his head on her breasts, inhaling her scent mixed with the flowers. She stroked his hair, and he closed his eyes and relished holding her. And told himself to stop then, while he still could.

"I hate to break this moment up," he muttered, "but I think we better get back to our duties." Caid sighed as he stood up, holding out his hand to help Reena up. They picked up her wildflowers; then, when she'd mounted he handed them up to her.

"The camp is that way." He pointed. As he watched her ride away, Caid told himself to take a bath in an icy stream and stay away from her.

Because Reena deserved better than a man who didn't know if he could trust her.

Then he rode off toward a nearby ridge, where he could get a better view of the land they were combing. After a hard climb, he dismounted among the scrubby trees on the crest, took a pair of binoculars out of his saddlebags, and began to quarter the country, looking for anything—a man on horseback, a faint trail, a thin column of smoke where there shouldn't be one—that would give him a clue to the Simpsons' hideout.

He would find the Simpsons' hideout and he would find the Simpsons. And, by God, he would stop them.

It was late that night before Caid rode into camp. Reena poured a cup of coffee and carried it to him as he unsaddled. "What happened? Where did you go?"

"Just trailed some cattle, that's all." He rubbed the back of his neck wearily.

"Here." She handed him the coffee as lightning

lit up the night sky far to the north of them. "Do you think that storm is coming this way, Caid?"

"I hope not." He drank in long gulps, as if it were water, as they walked back to the chuckwagon. Lowering the empty mug, he placed it on the wagon ledge behind her.

"How about a kiss for a tired cowboy?"

"Sure. Which one do you think is the most tired? I'd say Curly, from the looks of him."

Caid groaned and dragged his hand through his dust-stiffened hair. He wasn't up to sparring with her this evening.

Not when he hadn't found a sign of the Simpsons or their hideout. He'd spend tomorrow looking for them, and the day after, and the day after, until he'd finally found them.

"You're tired." She added, "Go sit by the fire and I'll bring you a plate of stew."

He walked over to the fire and glanced at the hands sitting around, still talking. Five of them. The sixth was riding herd guard duty, he knew. But that might not be enough, tonight.

"There's a storm brewing to the north of us, boys." He accepted the plate from Reena and began to eat.

"It's far away, though," Curly said.

"It may not stay far away. It's spitting out lots of lightning, which means lots of thunder." He looked at each man in turn. "We have a herd made up of individual animals we've just shoved together. Do you think one man on guard duty is enough?

What's going to happen if that storm sweeps down here?''

"I see what you mean, boss." Curly rose and walked toward the horse line where the night horses were picketed.

The others also rose, but he halted them. "Split guard duty into three watches, with two of you on each. That way everyone should get enough sleep and not doze off on his horse. And stay alert."

He finished his last bite of stew. Rising, he carried the plate over to the chuckwagon and slipped it into the bucket of soapy water.

"What are you doing?" he asked, when Reena dumped a large mass of dough out of the Dutch oven onto parchment paper she'd spread on the tailgate.

"Getting this bread ready to rise for the last time," she replied, punching down the dough.

"Don't waste time on that tonight. Get yourself some sleep while you can."

She looked at him, her brow furrowed. "You're expecting trouble? Why?"

Caid inhaled a long breath, and caught a whiff of her lilac-and-spice scent. Amazing, he thought, considering the stench of sweaty men, horses, and cattle that permeated the camp.

"No. I'm not worried," he said, lying through his teeth, because he didn't want to worry her. She had enough to do with cooking and feeding everyone. "But I don't know what direction that storm is going. Sleep underneath the chuckwagon in case it starts to rain."

He took his blankets and bedded down beside the dying fire. His last thought was that at least he'd trained himself to be alert, even when he dozed.

A bright flash of lightning brought him awake. Caid's eyes flew open as another flash knifed through the darkness. He surged to his feet, even as he counted the seconds until he heard the thunder. Not enough of them, he thought, as a low rumble shook the ground. The storm was a lot closer.

Low clouds hid the moon and stars so he couldn't estimate how late it was. But the lightning was flashing almost continuously. Waves of thunder rolled over the land.

Caid ran from man to man, shaking them awake. "Ride! Get to the herd!"

He could hear the cattle lowing restlessly. One after another, the animals got to their feet. Nervous from the thunder shaking the earth, they stamped their hooves and lowed plaintively. The thunder was getting closer. The gap between lightning flash and boom was evaporating fast.

He ran to the fire and threw chunks of wood on it so everyone would have a beacon in the darkness. As he spun away, a lightning bolt hit a tree not far away, turning it into a one-hundred-foot torch.

"*Caid!*" he heard Reena call.

Damn, he didn't want her running around camp now! "Stay where you are!" he roared.

In between rolling thunder and almost continuous flashes of lightning, he felt the ground begin to shake. Instantly he knew what it meant. A stampede!

"*Reena*," he yelled, racing toward the horse line. "Run! Get behind rocks or up a tree. *Run!*"

He freed the snorting, rearing, terrified animals still there and swung up on one. Clasping its ribs with his knees, he whirled it and raced toward the chuckwagon. He had to be sure Reena was safe. "Reena!" He raced the animal around the chuckwagon, peering underneath to be sure she wasn't there. She wasn't. "Reena, where are you?"

"Here!" She swung down from a scrawny young juniper. He could see that it wasn't big enough to survive the onslaught of the herd if they came that way.

Leaning low over the horse's neck, he sent the animal leaping toward Reena. Caid clamped his legs around the horse's ribs and leaned off to the side as he approached her. He swept her up with an arm around her waist, clamping her against his side. She threw her arms around his neck and held on as he straightened. He could hear the thunder of the herd, so near they drowned out the sound of the thunderstorm.

He glanced back and saw horns gleaming in a momentary flash of lightning. They were headed this way! Could his horse outrun the herd, carrying two people? To the side he glimpsed the bulk of a low ridge rising above the plain. With luck the terrified animals would split and flow around it.

He'd have to risk the ridge. It was their only chance. He kicked the horse and sent him lunging

up the sandy slope. The horse scrabbled for a toe-
hold on the gravelly sand, and every time Caid
looked back at the herd those gleaming horns were
closer. He could smell their fetid fear now.

Reena clutched his shoulders. She'd managed to
wedge one foot on top of his boot, taking some of
the weight off his arm. He locked his grip on her
even tighter.

"Don't move," he shouted, hoping she heard him
above the tumult. "I'm afraid the horse will lose
his footing if you do."

He felt her lips against his cheek; still he barely
heard her. "I won't."

Behind them he heard a crash and knew the herd
had overrun the camp and knocked the chuckwagon over. Now Reena and he were the only things
in the herd's path.

Slowly, so slowly he thought they'd never make
it, they climbed the slippery slope. Suddenly the
horse stumbled over the top. Caid didn't wait for
him to take another trembling step. He dropped
Reena to the ground and jumped off after her.

"Here," he yelled, grabbing her wrist and running along the spine of the ridge toward a cluster
of wind-stunted junipers he'd seen in a flash of
lightning. They tumbled into the sand behind the
junipers and flattened out, side by side.

Caid was breathing hard and knew Reena was,
too, but he couldn't hear either of them. The
pounding hooves of the cattle shook the ground
and drowned out everything else as they flowed
around the ridge.

Then the sky opened and rain drenched them in seconds. Lightning forked out of the clouds and showed him Reena lying on her back beside him. Curls of her hair clung to her cheeks, and her shirt was plastered to her breasts. She looked at him. He saw the flash of her white teeth and realized she was laughing. Laughing!

The thunder of hooves began to lessen.

"They're past us," Caid yelled.

She rolled to her side and pressed her lips against his ear. "You don't have to yell anymore," she said in a normal voice.

"We made it!" He wrapped his arms around her and rolled her onto her back, and kissed her and laughed and kissed her again. "We made it, Reena."

"Thanks to you." She kissed him back.

"Come on, I've got to check on the men."

They stood on the ridge, looking down at where the camp had been. It was utterly black. The fire Caid had built was gone, trampled by the herd and drowned by the rain.

He listened for voices, but heard nothing—only the hard spattering of the rain pelting them.

"It stings like hail," Reena said.

"It *is* hail." He held out his hand and felt the pellets hitting his hand and bouncing off.

He made a megaphone of his hands and yelled into the darkness. "Curly! Vinegar! Anyone!" Only silence answered him. "We'll stay up here until daylight. It's all we can do until we can see what's happened."

Eventually dawn began to pink the mountains to the east. Slowly, way too slowly for Caid, the sky lightened until he could see what was left of their camp. The only thing he could recognize was the chuckwagon, lying on its side like a dead buffalo. Everything else—everyone's blankets, his black Stetson, any dishes or cups left on the ground—had been churned beneath the mud and hooves. He didn't see any horse carcasses, so he knew they'd all gotten safely away.

"I don't see that juniper I was in," Reena said in a strained voice.

"I don't either," he admitted quietly. He glanced at her. "Are you all right?"

She nodded wordlessly.

Suddenly he straightened and peered at a rider and horse as they picked their way across the plain toward the camp. Again making a megaphone of his hands, he yelled. "Curly!"

He waved in big, wide movements of his arm. Curly waved back and spurred his horse. He took the long gradual incline up the back of the ridge, and Caid knew it was because he rode a tired horse.

"Anyone hurt?" he asked, as Curly dismounted.

"No, boss—thanks to you. Your alarm got everyone mounted in time. Morning, Miss Reena." Curly nodded at her, then turned back to Caid. "We flanked the herd, and when they tired, we started turning them until they were milling in a big circle. But I'm afraid a lot of the cattle scattered back into the canyons."

"It doesn't matter. What matters is that everyone is all right. Go back to the remuda and bring some horses for Reena and me. And the team, so we can get the chuckwagon righted."

"Yes, sir." Curly gave him a half-salute, half-wave, as if he didn't know which to do. Then he remounted and trotted off.

Caid turned to Reena, worried about the strain of the past night on her. "How are you doing?"

"I'm okay." But her eyes were red from lack of sleep, and she looked as if she'd taken a mud bath.

"Why don't you curl up under those bushes where we took refuge last night, and see if you can nap. I'll call you when Curly comes back. I should have sent you with him."

"His horse was already exhausted. He couldn't have carried double." She did as he'd suggested.

Caid watched her from afar, not trusting himself when it came to Reena.

Chapter 14

⁓⧢⁓

When Curly returned, he helped rope the team of draft horses to the high side of the chuckwagon. They dug their dinner-plate–sized hooves into the muddy earth and slowly pulled the wagon back up on all four wheels. The crashes and rattles inside it told Reena she would have to spend the rest of the day straightening it out.

Then Caid left to check the cattle, leaving Curly with her.

Luckily, the tin canisters that held such staples as rice, flour, and beans had survived intact, though they had a few dents. Even the wooden box with the bricks of Arbuckle's coffee was unharmed.

Reena sent Curly downstream looking for the coffeepot and Dutch oven; with those she'd be back in business. He returned with the Dutch oven almost immediately and she set beans to soak in it.

206

While Curly was out looking for the coffeepot, Reena began to hear shots. Not a lot—just one or two, then an interval, then one or two more. She could tell the shots were coming from a revolver and a rifle. Terrified that Caid was involved in a running gun battle with her brothers, she climbed the ridge that had saved them and peered in all directions, watching for gunsmoke or a dust trail. But she could see nothing.

Finally, Caid rode back in. His eyes were red-rimmed and his face dust-caked and grim. She was sure he'd been working hard since he'd left eight hours earlier. And that was after a sleepless night. "We've set up a new campsite. I came back for you and the chuckwagon," he said.

"Did you see anyone?" she probed.

"No." He turned toward the chuckwagon, where Curly was hitching up the horses.

"Don't lie to me," she yelled, strung tight with the strain of worrying about him. "I heard the gun-shots. It sounded like you were having a running battle."

He glanced at her over his shoulder. "That wasn't a gun battle. In the stampede last night, some animals wound up with broken legs. We had to find them and put them out of their misery."

"Oh." Once again he'd surprised her.

He reached the chuckwagon and slid the Dutch oven full of beans into its niche and slammed the tailgate up.

"Wait, Caid." She hurried to catch up with him.

"Careful of those beans; that's our supper for to-night."

"You won't need to cook tonight." He handed her up onto the seat, then tied his horse to the back and joined her. "We've got beef roasting."

"How's the herd?" she asked, as he drove the team straight across the plain instead of following the track.

"Exhausted." A wheel went over a rock, flinging him against her. "The ones we rounded up aren't going anywhere for a few days, but we lost almost half. We'll have to go back into the draws and canyons we've already combed and do it again."

"They're not the only ones who are exhausted," she murmured, looking at him. Another wheel went over a rock, this time flinging her against him.

"You're right; the men are in bad shape, too. They haven't eaten or slept since yesterday."

"I was thinking of *you*," she said bluntly. "You're on your last legs. You've got to get some rest to-night, or you won't be worth anything to anyone."

He didn't say anything for a couple of miles as they were flung this way and that by the jolting ride.

Reena spotted a thin column of smoke rising ahead of them. "Is that the camp?"

He just nodded. She knew it was because he was too tired to talk.

"Who's that?" She pointed at a distant rider headed toward camp with a pack mule in tow.

"Probably Vinegar. I sent him back to the ranch this morning to get bedrolls and a change of clothes

for everyone. The way this weather's been changing, one day warm, one day cold, I didn't want the
men having to sleep on the bare ground with no
blankets."

He was amazing, Reena thought. If he'd been
running the takeover of Arizona, the Confederacy
wouldn't have been a lost cause. He was also the
reason she'd begun to think that Papa and the
twins didn't have much hope of succeeding. Not
when men like Caid were working to stop them.

Caid halted the team at the edge of camp, where
the mouthwatering scent of roasting beef greeted
them. Reena walked over to the fire to greet the
men and saw Seth talking to one of Caid's men.
What was he doing in their camp?

Caid walked up beside Reena, planted his feet
wide apart, and gave Seth a hard-eyed stare. "What
are you doing here, Biggs?"

Seth stood easily, giving Reena an oily smile.
"How's my desert thistle?"

"Prickly."

"What are you doing here, Biggs?" Caid prodded. He folded his arms across his chest and his
eyes became even harder, like silverstone.

"We had a little trouble with our herd, so I came
over to see how you'd fared. I hear you had a hell
of a stampede. Too bad you didn't have an experienced range boss to handle the herd," he added,
openly challenging Caid. "Maybe I should stay and
run this herd and let Pa run the other one."

"And maybe you should get the hell out of our
camp," Caid drawled in a soft voice.

Reena glanced at him, then at Seth. Most men would recognize the menace in that voice, but she didn't know if Seth was smart enough.

"Let him eat with us, Caid," Reena interceded. Caid looked down at her small hand on his elbow. "*Then* he can get the hell out of camp."

"If that's what you want," he waited a beat, "Thistle."

She shot him a glare that should have left a smoking hole in the middle of his forehead. For some reason, it only made him smile.

"You *do* know that dinner won't be ready for another hour or so, don't you?" He indicated the huge pit the men had dug earlier in the muddy ground. They'd burned a bed of firewood down to coals, lowered the side of beef into it, then piled slabs of muddy sod on top to keep in the heat.

Reena's eyes grew large. "That's where the beef is? You weren't kidding when you said you were roasting a beef, were you?"

"No. We had to slaughter it anyway. This way we'll have enough food to last a few days."

"Hey, boss, I got the stuff you wanted," Vinegar shouted as he led a floppy-eared mule up to the chuckwagon. He dismounted stiffly.

"Good." Caid walked toward him. He was glad the men would be sleeping on clean blankets tonight. And he would set an example for them by taking soap and a towel and his fresh clothes to the secluded spot he'd found downstream. He wasn't about to order them to bathe, but the smart ones would know they'd feel better and sleep better after washing off the mud and dust. And if they slept better, they would work better tomorrow.

"Good work, Vinegar," he said, slapping the old man on the back. "We needed these blankets and clothes." He'd managed to spare the old man the most strenuous work with the herd, and at the same time, Vinegar's task had been crucial. "Did you bring the soap and towels?" he asked, dropping the chuckwagon tailgate down to hold the mule's packs.

"Yeah, but what did you want that fool stuff for?" Vinegar unwound the rope that he'd woven back and forth over the panniers so they wouldn't slip. Caid released the near-side pack from the mule and heaved it up on the tailgate, then went to the off-side and threw that pack up, too.

"You'll see." He unbuckled the leather flaps and opened the packs up.

"All right, men," he called, pulling out the contents and strewing them across the tailgate, "come get your blankets and clothes." May had tied each man's set of clothing together and labeled it. Caid picked out two bundles and stepped back to let the men get theirs.

Reena stood off to the side, looking bedraggled and forlorn as an orphan. He handed her a bundle. "Here. May packed these for you."

A smile of delight lit her dust-caked features. "Look, she sent my jacket, and leather gloves, too." Clasping everything to her bosom, she looked up at him. "How did she know?"

"I told her. She sent this for you, too." He

handed her a bar of May's flower-scented Cash-
mere Bouquet soap and a thick towel.

"She understands what heaven it is to be clean.
I'll have to give her a big kiss of thanks when I get
back."

"May doesn't need a kiss," he growled, wishing
they weren't standing in the middle of a bunch of
cowhands. "I do." He noticed the men had collected their clothes and blankets, but hadn't walked
away yet. This was his chance.

He picked up the bar of soap and one of the towels he'd left conspicuously sitting out on the tailgate. No one had seemed to notice them. "I'm
going to take a bath at that place downstream
where the water's deeper," he announced. "That'll
really make these clothes feel good." Whistling, he
sauntered off without looking back.

He heard footsteps scampering to catch up and
slowed to let Reena stride along at his side. "Will
you let me go first?"

"Of course."

"And you'll keep an eye on Seth? And the others?"

"Of course." He felt like smiling. She obviously
put him in a different category than the others—
and he liked that.

He showed her the secluded place where the gurgling stream was completely screened by bushes.
"But remember," he said, "this water is runoff from
the mountains, and it's going to be damned cold."

"I don't care. I'll be clean—cold, but clean."

"I'll be right here. If anything happens, just call.

I can get to you immediately." He rested his hand on her shoulder. "Got that?"

She threw him a salute and a saucy smile. "Yes, sir." Then she turned and ducked between the bushes.

He listened until he heard her gasp and knew she'd stepped into the water. Then he turned away and crossed his arms over his chest. He could hear her splashing about, her *"Damn!"* when she dropped the soap, and her strangled gasp when she ducked underneath the surface to find it.

Even though he couldn't see her, in his mind's eye he could picture her very well indeed. He imagined her drawing the soapy washcloth over her breasts and buttocks and between her legs. He saw himself following the same path, his soapy bronze hands slowly gliding over her milky white skin. Very slowly. Very thoroughly. Then he'd follow that path with his lips, and—

No. He wouldn't do any of those things. He couldn't.

He uncrossed his arms and recrossed them the other way. Not until he'd found the Simpsons and put an end to their schemes.

The stampede had delayed him already; he couldn't let anyone delay him more. Especially a slip of a girl with sparkling eyes. He would just put her out of his mind.

It grew quiet behind him and he knew she'd stepped onto the bank and was drying off. The towel would slide slowly over her curves and—hell and damnation! What was the matter with him?

Couldn't he keep his mind off her for more than thirty seconds?

Oh, hell! Who was he kidding? She was always in his mind. When he rode, he imagined her riding double with him. When he lay in his blankets, he imagined her in his blankets with him.

Reena brushed through the bushes and he turned. She'd draped the white towel over her wet hair and her cheeks were pink and rosy. Even in a red flannel shirt and blue denims, she made him hard as a rock.

She gave him a smile, soft as the mist. "Your turn."

God, he wanted to sweep her up and run someplace where it would be only the two of them.

"I'll keep guard," she said solemnly, but her eyes twinkled.

"You don't need to. No one wants to watch me bathe."

"No, but Seth is dumb enough to try something."

Her resolute expression told him it was useless to try to change her mind. "Has anyone ever told you that you have a very stubborn chin?"

"Lots of people. I tell them it's not only my chin that's stubborn."

"All right." He pushed aside the low-hanging branches and slipped through the bushes.

"Remember," she teased, "just yell if you need me."

"Don't tempt me," he shot back without thinking.

He stripped and ran into the stream. The cold

paralyzed his breathing for a second, then he gave a shocked gasp. She was tougher than he'd thought, if she'd bathed in that water. He soaped up quickly.

Reena kept her jaw clamped tight until she heard him go through the bushes. Then she relaxed and let her teeth chatter. Damn, that water had been cold! But it had been worth every second of chattering teeth. She walked out into the sunlight beyond the trees and soaked it up.

Don't tempt me. An instinct buried deep inside her whispered that Caid had meant it. She smiled to herself. She could picture him running the soap over the long, lean muscles of his body, over his shoulders and arms and legs and—

No! She couldn't think about wanting him!

Not when he was a government agent. Not when he wanted to destroy her family. She began to pace, rubbing her hands over her arms.

She had to put Caid behind her. He was too dangerous. Way too dangerous.

Discarding the towel, she raked her fingers through her long hair, fluffing it so it would dry faster.

"Here, let me do that for you." Caid's voice came from behind her and she whirled in surprise. He reached into his back pocket and pulled out a wooden comb. "Turn around and I'll comb your hair."

She gazed at him. "Has anyone ever told you you have a stubborn chin?" she said, parroting his earlier words.

"Yes. Turn around."

She complied, wanting to feel his hands in her hair, knowing she shouldn't. He started at the ends of her hair, where it tickled her shoulder blades, combing the tangles out. His fingers whispered through her hair softly. Closing her eyes, she gave herself up to the delicious feelings. He parted the hair cloaking her neck, and his breath tickled the fine hairs along her nape; then his lips followed his breath in a kiss as soft as a rose petal. A shiver of pleasure washed through her.

"Caid, stop," she whispered, while her heart begged him not to.

The thud of a horse's hooves twisted them apart. Behind her, Reena heard Caid swear under his breath. As the rider neared, she understood why.

"What do you want, Biggs?" Caid's voice was colder than the stream.

"The boys wanted you to know the beef was done. I volunteered to tell you." He smirked at Reena and picked something out of his teeth with his finger.

"I'm sure you did. Ride on back and tell them to start carving and eating."

As Seth turned his horse, he added, "Easy to see why the herd stampeded, with a boss who's too busy getting some on the side to work the cattle." He kicked his horse viciously, sending him into a dead run.

Caid took a stride after him, but Reena caught his arm. "No, Caid. He's itching for a fight. You'd just be playing into his hands."

Caid took several long deep breaths before he nodded. "Come on. You must be starved and I know I am. I want us all to have a good meal, because tomorrow is going to be long and hard."

As they walked back, Reena noticed that the wind had a bite that went beyond fall. It promised winter—and soon.

"Caid," she said thoughtfully, "with the beef and the beans I started earlier, there's enough food for several days. Why don't I ride out tomorrow? I can be an extra pair of eyes looking for the cattle."

"You don't have to." He'd moved closer to her and his arm brushed hers. "That isn't what you signed on to do."

"Neither is driving a chuckwagon, but I'm doing that. And I can tell you it's a lot more interesting than waitressing."

"Chasing cattle that don't want to be found out of canyons and mountains is a lot harder."

"That's why you need me," she said quietly. "And you know it."

Caid studied her, taking his time about his decision. Finally, when she was sure he was going to say no, he nodded. "All right. I don't like having you chasing after cows and calves, but I don't like this weather we've been having, either. I think Jeter is right: we're going to have an early winter, and we need to get the cattle gathered in."

He did need her riding the draws and canyons looking for cattle, Caid thought. But beyond that, *he* needed her himself.

She kept him on his toes with her sharp tongue

and mind. It was exhilarating. When he was with her, he felt more alive. He saw more, smelled more, touched more, tasted more, experienced more.

"Caid?" Her voice had gone soft and throaty, as if she'd picked up the signals he was sending.

The siren's call, he thought wryly. He pushed it away, albeit very reluctantly. "We'll ride out at dawn, Reena. Have breakfast ready for the men before then."

Chapter 15

❦❦❦

"**T**ake your jacket, Reena, just in case." Caid led his white stallion, Diablo, and a long-legged blue roan. He'd already tied his sheepskin jacket on the back of his saddle.

She pulled her coat out of the chuckwagon, then filled an empty drawstring sack with leftover biscuits from breakfast and two of the oranges Vinegar had brought. She looped it over her saddle horn and tied her jacket behind the saddle, as Caid had done.

"You'll spoil me," she said, as Caid stood on the left side of her horse and clasped his hands together.

"That's what I'd like to do." His voice rumbled through her, warm with promises.

She glanced at him and he gave her a smoky look that took her breath away. Then she stepped into

219

his hands and he lifted her up as if she weighed
no more than thistledown. She swung her leg over
the horse's back and settled into the saddle.

They rode together along the right flank of the
herd, then split up, searching the foothills and canyons of the mountain range. Reena turned into the
first small draw, and crisscrossed it, looking for
fresh tracks. When she didn't find any, she turned
back. By that time Caid had ridden Diablo up into
the next canyon.

It went on like that for most of the day, leap-
frogging each other. In mid-afternoon Reena
passed where Caid's tracks veered off and turned
into the next canyon that snaked out of the mountains. It was V shaped, with steeply sloping sides.
She'd ridden only a short way when she found
fresh tracks in the sandy banks of the creek that
gurgled along the canyon floor. It looked like three
cows had gone deeper into the canyon with their
calves, and she followed the narrow trail.

As she rode, she felt as if the steep slopes that
rose on each side were closing in on her as the canyon narrowed and climbed higher into the mountains. She went a half-mile farther, and could see
the sheer red sandstone wall rising at the end of
the canyon. It was a box canyon.

But where were the cattle? The canyon was too
narrow for her to have missed them. She dismounted and ranged back and forth across the canyon floor until she found more tracks. They were
headed straight for the wall.

She swung back up into the saddle, scrutinizing

every bush and mesquite thicket she passed. As she neared the end she kept expecting the cows to flush and leap out in front of her, but nothing happened.

Finally, when she was almost to the base of the wall, she discovered that the canyon didn't end. It made an abrupt dogleg turn, which was hidden behind tall trees and bushes, and continued on. She looked back, marveling that she had to be at the bend itself before she saw it.

The cattle tracks continued around the turn. She pushed on, glancing up at the sky occasionally. The wind blowing down the canyon was getting colder by the minute, but buried deep in the canyon, all she could see was a thin strip of blue sky between the steeply sloping red walls. She couldn't see if there was a storm churning on the horizon—and that worried her.

She stopped to put on her heavy woolen red plaid jacket. Should she turn back?

She thought she heard the lowing of a cow and pushed on, determined to find the cattle and chase them back down the canyon to the herd. They were probably just around the next bend. That's as far as she'd go; then she'd turn back.

But around the next bend, she found another. And then another. Sure that the cattle were just ahead of her, she kept telling herself she'd just go around one more bend.

The canyon began to widen again and the grass on the floor was thick and green. The cattle were sure to be grazing knee-deep in it. Pine trees crowded the meadow from both sides. And pines meant that she was a lot higher in the mountains than when she'd started out.

Something about this canyon was beginning to look familiar. Chillingly familiar. Reena reined in and studied the red sandstone slopes and the pines, but she wasn't looking for cattle anymore.

There was only one reason why it *would* look familiar: if she'd been there with her brothers. Which meant their hideout was in this canyon.

Suddenly she was very glad she was the one who'd come up this canyon, not Caid. What if Jeff and Robby were there? Caid would have them red-handed.

Something moved behind a bush, and she circled it and flushed a cow and calf. The others must be just ahead, over the next pine-covered rise. She kneed her horse forward over it.

Through the pines she glimpsed a shack made of logs. She recognized the front porch and window beside the door, and the corrugated tin roof covered with drifts of brown pine needles.

No smoke came out of the rock chimney so she knew no one was there. She sighed in relief. She would just leave a note for Jeff and Robby and get out of there.

At the cabin she dismounted and walked up to the door. Her hand was on the latch when she heard the hoofbeats of a fast moving horse. She whirled, and her eyes widened with shock at the rider who rode into the clearing.

Caid slouched on Diablo, resting his arm on the saddle horn and eyeing her suspiciously.

The best defense.... "I think I've found the out-laws' cabin, Caid! I was going to look inside and see if I could find anything." She just prayed there wouldn't be.

He dismounted, still silent, and followed her in. The cabin was barren except for some chairs and a three-legged table that tilted because its fourth cor-ner rested on a rock sitting on a keg of nails. In the far corner a platform held a thin mattress and some blankets covered by a bearskin.

Caid glanced around the room with his too-knowing eyes. "I'll look around outside, Reena. See if you find anything in here."

She did search, but found nothing that linked it to her brothers. Nor did she find anything to write with or on. Flour, cornmeal, beans, and rice were stored in tins so the pack rats wouldn't get them, and fresh wood was stacked next to the fireplace. And it wouldn't be safe to write a message with flour on the table; Caid would probably come back in.

Meanwhile, Caid walked around the back of the cabin, looking at the multitude of boot and horse tracks. Someone was definitely using this cabin, and he was sure it was the Simpsons.

Had Reena known it was here? He had thought she was trailing some cows, but maybe she'd been headed for the hideout all along.

She was on the porch when he circled around. To keep him from going back into the cabin? But then, why was she digging at something in the wooden porch rail with her pocket knife?

"Find anything?" he asked casually.

"Maybe. Does this look like gold flakes to you?" She held her blade level, so he could see the yellow flakes on it.

"Could be." He took the knife and turned it carefully, examining the flakes. "You found this here?" He rested his hand on the porch rail.

"Yes. They could have rested a bag with gold dust in it there."

"Did you find anything else inside?" He closed up her knife and handed it to her.

"Nope." She didn't look at him, though.

"Think I'll check once more." He watched her as he reached for the latch, but she didn't tense, just glanced at him over her shoulder.

"Good idea. I could have missed something."

He knew, even before he walked in, that he'd find nothing.

When he came out, she was staring up at the sky. "Look at those clouds, Caid. Don't they look like snow?" She shivered in her jacket. "It sure feels like it."

He'd noticed the clouds earlier to the north, and now they filled the sky, a churning, heavy gray menace that he didn't like at all.

"I think you're right. Let's get out of here—I don't want to be stuck in this canyon in a snowstorm."

"I found one cow and calf—we'll need to round them up," Reena said.

Maybe she *was* innocent. "We can't take the time. We'll have to leave them."

By the time they'd topped the rise, snowflakes were filtering down through the pines. Caid put Diablo into a lope, and she followed. The snow was coming down with surprising speed.

Before they reached the sloping scarlet walls of the canyon, it swirled around them in a blowing white cloud that obliterated everything. Reena couldn't hear, let alone see, the gurgling stream they'd been following. The wind was gusting and the snow was coming at them from all sides.

Then Caid disappeared into the snow ahead of her. One second he was there; the next he was gone.

"Caid!" she screamed. "Caid, where are you?" Even as her voice was swallowed by the snow, he reappeared.

"Turn around," he yelled, as Diablo trotted up to her. "We're not going to get out of here tonight. I hope we can find that cabin before the main force of this storm strikes."

"This isn't the main force?" Snow clung to her eyelashes, half-blinding her.

"Not even close," he called over his shoulder. "Stay close to me."

"I'm trying." She lost him again. "Caid, where are you?" she yelled, frightened by the intensity of the storm. The wind was picking up, keening through the snaking canyon like a thousand banshees. Tiny bullets of ice pelted her from all sides.

Like a ghost, he materialized out of the swirling snow. Snow already crusted the shoulders of his jacket and frosted his hair and eyebrows. "Give me one of your reins," he shouted.

"Lead on." She tossed him a rein. Turning up the collar on her jacket, she hunched down into it. Even with her leather gloves, her fingers were cold and she jammed her hands into her pockets.

"It's not far now," Caid shouted.

She barely heard him. "It's all right, boy," she murmured to the skittish roan, trying to reassure him. She could barely see his dark ears turning and pricking back at her voice.

They were back in the pines, but the snow was coming down so heavily, she barely saw low-hanging branches in time to duck. Sometimes she didn't see them at all and banged her forehead against them. She wrapped her hands around the saddle horn and hunched over the roan's neck, try-ing to get as low as possible so a branch didn't knock her off the horse.

"Reena." Caid shook her. She looked at him and realized they'd stopped and he'd dismounted.

"Are we there?" She glanced around, trying to make out the cabin through the blowing snow. But there weren't any dark structures—just white.

"Yes." He swung her down, and still holding her hand, led her up onto the porch. "I'm going to take the horses around back; there's a lean-to back there for them."

"How? You can't even see your hand before your face."

"I'll manage. You go in and get a fire started."

He started to walk away, but she clutched his jacket.

"There are biscuits on my saddle."

He snagged the bag and dropped it in her waiting hands.

The rope looped on her saddle gave her an idea. "Caid, tie one end of my rope around the porch post so you can find your way back."

He glanced at her. "What's the matter?"

She clutched his arm with both hands. "I'm...." She looked down. "I'm frightened," she mumbled, not wanting to admit it. "I've never seen a storm like this."

"Like this? But I've seen huge snowstorms sweep over the Kansas prairies."

Oh, Lord, that was where she'd said the family farm was. "But then I was at home, surrounded by my family. Not alone."

"You're not alone." His voice was warm as a Hudson's Bay blanket.

"You know what I meant. Now, take the lariat and go quickly with the horses so you can finish and get back."

"All right." He tied the rope around the post, then fed it out hand-over-hand as he led the horses away. "Get inside and get that fire started," he yelled.

The cabin was just as cold as outdoors, but Reena knew that would soon change. The wood box was full, so she laid a fire, broke up some kindling, then took matches from the metal container on the mantel. She blew on the puny flames gently until the wood caught.

Then she threw handfuls of beans and rice into a cast-iron pot, went outside, and filled it with snow. She pushed the pot into the embers and piled more embers on top.

The door flew open and banged against the wall as Caid blew in on an icy gust of snow and wind, covered with enough snow to be mistaken for a snowman. "Look what I found." He held up a lantern. "It was in the lean-to, and it has plenty of oil in it."

"Good. It'll bring a lot more light than the fire. You'd better get the snow off those clothes before it melts and soaks everything."

He looked down and nodded. "You're right." He walked outside to brush most of the snow off, and returned. "This is no longer a snowstorm. It's a full-fledged blizzard." He pulled his jacket off and shook it out near the fireplace, then hung it over the back of one of the rickety wooden chairs. Reena was glad to see his blue flannel shirt was still dry, and his denim pants looked damp in only a few places.

She picked up another cast-iron pot and went to the door. "I'll get some snow to melt down and make us some coffee."

"Be careful. Hold onto the rope if you take even one step off the porch. No, on second thought, I'll do it. That wind is too strong for you." He was up and striding toward her before she could move.

"I'm not helpless. I can do it." She held onto the pot stubbornly.

"But I can do it faster." He tugged the handle away from her, then tapped her nose, teasingly. "I have bigger hands to scoop with."

He was back in a moment, sliding the pot into the ashes to melt the snow.

As she picked up the coffee tin, he rested his hands on her shoulders. "How are you holding up?"

She leaned back against him and exhaled deeply. Closing her eyes, she listened to the steady beat of his heart and absorbed him into her senses. He slid his arms around her and laced his fingers together over her waist and just held her.

A feeling that she was safe, with nothing to fear, enveloped her. "Thanks, Caid, I feel so much better," she murmured, as she reluctantly moved out of the circle of his arms. The thought of staying there indefinitely was too tempting.

"I liked it, too. Holding you, I mean."

Quietly, feeling strangely peaceful, she opened the coffee tin. The beans smelled stale, but stale coffee was better than no coffee. She threw a couple of handfuls in the grinder and turned the handle.

When the melted snow boiled, she poured it into the coffeepot with the ground coffee. "Sorry, but that's the best I can do," she explained. "And some rice and beans for dinner."

"That's fine."

The icy snow clattered loudly against the tin roof. Caid looked up at the rafters as a particularly

strong wind gust shook the cabin. "We're damn
lucky to have shelter tonight."

"What about the herd and the men? Do you
think they're all right?"

"They were out in the open, so they could see
the storm coming and had enough time to find
shelter for themselves and the herd. And that's half
the battle in a blizzard like this. Besides, we're up
higher in the mountains and in a canyon, where the
wind can really howl. It's hard to tell how bad this
storm is on the plateau." His chair screeched across
the rough planks as he sat down.

Reena sat on the other chair, suddenly tired.
Propping her elbow on the table, she rested her
chin on her palm and eyed him wearily. "You said
we'd be doing some hard riding today, but I didn't
expect *this.*"

"Neither did I. But I think it's clear why the sheriff always lost the bank robbers. That right-angle
bend in the canyon is well hidden."

"If I hadn't been following cattle tracks, I would
have turned back before I got to the turn. I thought
it was a box canyon."

"So did I, until I saw you disappear."

"Why were you following me?" Her heartbeat
accelerated.

"I saw the tracks, too, and thought I'd give you
a hand, since it was getting late in the day." He
glanced at the window as snow pelted it like a Gat-
ling gun. "It's a good thing I did. I'd hate to think
of you stuck up here alone."

"I would have been all right." She drew aimless

figures on the table with her finger. Finally she made a quiet admission. "But I'm glad I'm not. Somehow, being trapped together is a lot better than being alone."

"I was thinking the same thing. I'll pour us some coffee."

She loosened the drawstring on the biscuit bag and took out the baking powder biscuits. "Hope this will hold you until the beans and rice are done."

Caid plopped two cups of coffee down on the table, turned his chair around, and straddled it. He drank some of his coffee and found it was cooling fast.

Had she known the hideout was up here? Or had it been a lucky chance? She'd followed the cattle a lot farther than he'd have expected—or were they merely a cover for her to get to the hideout? Still, she hadn't done anything suspicious when they'd started snooping around the cabin.

He finished his coffee and a biscuit, then stood up. "It's getting dark. I'll check the horses and bring in another load of wood."

"Are they all right?" she asked, when he'd returned.

"Yes, but I'm glad they've got shelter. It's blowing a gale out there. I don't know if we'll get out of here tomorrow. Do you think our dinner is ready?"

"We can try." She placed helpings of the rice and beans on two tin plates, and they gratefully ate the hot food.

After Caid finished, he leaned back in his chair. "We've had a hard day today, and we don't know how hard tomorrow will be. We ought to go to bed. Since it's so cold and we don't know how well this tin sheet roof will hold up in this wind, I suggest we sleep in our clothes."

He crossed to the bed in the back corner. The rope supports squeaked when he sat down on the thin mattress. Caid tugged his right boot off and dropped it with a thud. He repeated the process with his left boot and looked at Reena, still sitting at the table. "Coming to bed? The only way we're going to be able to stay warm is to sleep together."

Reena swallowed twice. "Sleep together?" Her voice rose precipitously at the end.

"I don't know of any other way to stay warm; do you?" He lifted the bearskin and lay down beneath it. "Besides, it's not as if we haven't slept together already."

Why was she so nervous? This was Caid, not some weasel who'd try to take advantage of her. Besides, he was the one who'd suggested they sleep in their clothes.

She sat on the edge to pull her boots off and dropped them beside Caid's much bigger ones. He lifted the bearskin and she slipped under it.

She lay back stiffly on the thin mattress, her arms straight against her sides, her eyes wide open.

"Reena," Caid said quietly, "we're fully dressed and we're sharing a bed, not a coffin."

After a moment, she giggled. The more she thought about it, the more she giggled.

"You're shaking the bed," he grumbled.

"Sorry." But she knew he wasn't angry—and that she could sleep now. As his heat stole around her, warming her, she inhaled a deep breath and closed her eyes.

Caid lay awake long after her breathing had steadied. Reena stirred desire in him every time she looked at him. She made him edgy and alert and damn glad to be alive. He'd developed a sixth sense about her and knew where she was every waking minute. She flitted through his thoughts like a hummingbird, always just out of reach.

He smiled, remembering her giggles. He rolled to his side and rested his head on his crooked arm as he studied her. What was it about Reena that intrigued him so? He was used to kissing and traveling on. But her first innocent kiss still branded his lips.

Her profile changed slightly and he realized she'd turned her head and was watching him.

"I thought you were asleep," he said.

"I was, but something woke me." She was silent for so long he thought she'd gone back to sleep. "Thank you, Caid," she said softly.

"For what? I didn't do anything." He stretched out his arm and she pillowed her head on it.

"You made me relax."

"Go to sleep," he murmured, filling his hand with her hair.

"Caid," she said a few minutes later, "I'm cold. Would you mind if I moved closer?"

"Not at all; I'm cold too." He swept her up against his side. "Is that better?"

She nodded against his shoulder, and he knew he would sleep well that night.

It was still dark when he awoke. The fire had burned down to a few embers that weren't putting out any heat, but he didn't care.

Reena was wrapped around him, her head on his shoulder, and she was sound asleep. He pulled the bearskin up and tucked it over her, then wrapped his free arm around her.

He lay there, savoring the feel of her, enjoying just holding her—and knew he wanted to do it for more than just one night.

Chapter 16

Rowena awoke slowly, basking in the warmth of the stove in her bedroom. She felt so relaxed and cozy that she stretched lazily—and felt a hard pad of muscle beneath her hand.

Her eyes flew open. Her head rested on Caid's broad shoulder. She couldn't move without waking him—and she didn't want to do that, not when she was wrapped around him so snugly. Her hair had come loose and his large hand was tangled in it. One of her legs was between his. Sometime in the night, she'd flung her arm across his broad chest and clasped his shoulder.

Lordy, how was she going to untangle herself? She didn't dare groan for fear of waking him. She moved her chin a fraction of an inch, trying to look up and see if he was awake. His hand tightened in her hair.

"Sorry," she murmured, trying to pull away.

"For what?" He didn't loosen his arm around her.

"For turning into a leech."

He chuckled. "You feel more like a warm kitten." He drew a single finger down her cheek and across her lips.

She rose up on her elbow and peered at him. Her hair cascaded down over his shoulder and face and he wound his fingers through it.

She wanted to lean down and kiss him, to feel his lips against hers. She looked away, afraid he'd see the desire shining in her eyes.

Her gaze focused on the interior of the cabin. The cabin that was her brothers' hideout. Her brothers, who Caid wanted to put in prison.

A wave of melancholy washed over her. How could this have happened? How had she gotten so deeply, wonderfully, involved with the man chasing her brothers?

She rolled away from Caid, but the sadness followed her.

"Let's get up," she said briskly. "Maybe we can get going." Sitting on the edge of the bed, she picked up a boot and pulled it on, then the other.

"There's no hurry," Caid said behind her. "The wind is still blowing."

She listened, and heard the wind soughing through the pines. A pine bough scraped across the tin roof. "What are we going to do?"

"Wait until it stops snowing."

As Reena walked away from the bed, she could

feel Caid's gaze on her. She flung the door open and stepped out on the porch. It was shockingly cold, and she shoved her hands into her pants pockets to keep them warm. The snow was piled in sculptured drifts, some up to five feet high, and it was still coming down.

She returned to the cabin and saw that Caid was putting wood on the fire. Closing the door, she leaned back against it.

She was snowbound with the man who threatened from her nightmares—and beckoned from her dreams.

And she didn't know what she was going to do.

It snowed all that day, and all day the tension built in Reena. When they went to bed that night, she held herself stiffly away from Caid, but again woke up to find herself wrapped around him.

The morning light streaming through the window was brighter, and Reena bounded out of bed. "It looks like it's stopped snowing," she said excitedly, going to the door. She didn't think she could take another day—and night—like this.

"It has," Caid said, watching her from the bed. God, he ached for her. There'd been no hiding his arousal that morning.

"Do you think we can get out of here today?"

"I'll sure as hell try," he replied, his voice gritty.

Outside was a strange fairyland where nothing seemed familiar. The ponderosa pines' straight brown trunks marched away from the clearing like soldiers on parade. Overhead, gray clouds scudded across a gray sky.

Snow weighed down the pine boughs, bending them. One snapped with a sharp crack like a gunshot, and she jumped.

"It's just a branch breaking under the snow," Caid said from the doorway behind her.

"I know. It just startled me." Her heart was still pounding.

Because, in that instant when she'd feared it was a gun, she'd realized their danger here. If Jeff and Robby returned and found Caid, they would recognize him from the gold robbery and kill him.

For the first time, she feared for Caid's safety. Not Jeff or Robby's, but Caid's.

He passed her and stepped off the porch.

"Where are you going?" she asked, panicked. She didn't want him out of her sight. If she was with him, Jeff and Robby would hold their fire.

"To check on the horses." His steps crunched on the crusted snow.

"I'll come with you."

He gave her a puzzled look over his shoulder. "I'm sure I can find my way. Why don't you get our stuff together and we'll see if we can get out."

A few minutes later, Caid returned with the saddled horses. "It looks like the sun is trying to break through," he called through the open door. "Are you ready?"

Reena scanned the cabin. Now that they were leaving, she felt a foolish sense of sadness and loss. "Yes, let's go."

Reena led first. The wind had scoured the snow away from the trail in places so that the horses were only ankle deep in it, but in other places it was sculpted into deep drifts up to their bellies. With each step, their hooves broke through the crust.

Caid stopped frequently to give the horses a breather, and to check that they were still on the snow-obliterated trail. Huge gobs of melting snow fell on them from the pine boughs. Then the newly lightened boughs sprang back, throwing off the last bits of snow. Occasionally they heard the sharp, booming crack of a branch breaking.

"We're getting close to the pass. I'll take over here, so your horse can rest." Caid swung around her and let Diablo take the lead.

Reena stopped to let her tired roan breathe for a moment. His head hung low. "Come on, boy," she murmured, urging him forward. "It's not far now."

The canyon looked magical. Snow turned the bushes into fairy-dusters of white. The stream was just a narrow gurgle of black water between two snowy banks. Huge boulders wore snowy crowns, and the trees, even the few pines clinging to life high on the slopes, were blanketed in white.

Reena glanced up in dismay when she felt a few drops of icy rain. It soon turned into a miserable sleet, coming straight down. Reena pulled her jacket collar up over her ears, hunched down in her saddle, and followed Caid blindly, running into him when he stopped.

"What's the matter?" she asked, her teeth chattering.

"I'm worried about this sleet. This is slick rock country. If the sleet gets down under the snow those rocks will get slippery, and I don't know if the snow will hold."

"Then let's get out of here fast."

The red walls closed in on them. Caid and Reena watched them warily, keeping an eye on the thick layer of snow clinging to the steep slopes. They proceeded deeper into the pass. The walls rose higher. The sleet increased.

And what was happening under the snow? Was it becoming unstable?

There was a sharp, booming crack as a pine bough broke. It echoed and reechoed, like cannon fire booming back and forth between the canyon walls. Reena felt and heard a deep rumble, and saw a spindly pine sliding down the steep snowy slope. Then she realized that the snow was sliding too.

"Turn back! Run!" Caid yelled, as he whirled Diablo around and sent him leaping back along the trail toward her.

"Come on, boy!" Reena turned her horse and lashed him with the ends of her reins. The animal ran as fast as he could along the trail they'd already broken in the deep snow. Out of the corner of her eye, she could see a cloud of snow roaring down the slope toward them.

The roar filled the canyon, and she leaned low over her horse's neck, lashing it with the ends of her reins in fear.

"Faster," Caid yelled. "It's com—"

Snow foamed up around them in a cloud that hid everything. A stone hit her shoulder. A boulder landed on the path in front of them and her horse leaped over it. Clamping her knees to the roan's straining ribs, she leaned lower and clung to its mane. Ahead the snow cloud seemed to lighten. Was that gray sky ahead?

Suddenly she was out of the cloud, and the red slopes were spreading wide and the sleet was still coming down and the roar that had filled the canyon was gone. The world was silent.

Except for a high, wailing scream.

She pulled her horse into a snorting, rearing stop.

Looking back, she couldn't see through the sleet and still-settling cloud of snow. All she could hear was that scream, rising and falling and rising again. It sent shivers up and down her spine and made her want to cover her ears.

He is alive! her heart said, *if he is screaming.*

He is closer to death than life, her head said, *if he is screaming like that.*

"Caid!" She turned the roan and raced back. They floundered through the chest-high snow, stumbled over a boulder. The roan went to his knees and she leaped off and plunged forward. "Caid! Caid, where are you?"

She crawled over a hillock of snow, and saw the screamer—

Caid's horse.

They had almost made it out—but Diablo was buried in snow up to his chest.

Caid was gone.

Reena flailed through the snow and ice to Diablo. "It's all right, boy, it's all right," she murmured over and over again, trying to calm him.

The horse, wall-eyed with terror, kept trying to lunge forward and get out of the snow. She tried to grab his bridle, but he jerked his head free. His screams echoed off the canyon slopes.

"Caid," she yelled, "Yell, wave a hand, move a foot, something." Anything, dear God—anything! She turned around slowly, looking for movement among the hillocks of snow and boulders. Nothing.

If he answered, she didn't hear him—she couldn't hear anything besides the horse.

She ripped her jacket off and tossed it over Diablo's head so that it hung down over his eyes. He quieted and stopped lunging, and she tucked the jacket beneath his bridle straps so it wouldn't slide off.

"Caid! Caid!" She turned in a slow circle again, looking and praying.

Nothing moved.

She had to find him before he suffocated!

Then something moved at the edge of her vision—the snow humped up a bit, as if kicked from beneath, and she thought she saw a black shadow underneath. Caid was wearing black boots!

"Caid!" She lunged toward the patch of snow, staring at it intently as she ran and climbed and fell and floundered through the snowy sea, afraid that if she looked away, she'd never find it again.

"Caid, can you hear me?" She flung herself down and began digging frantically, handful after handful. Such little handfuls—so much snow!

His voice was muffled and faint. "Can you hear me?"

"Hang on. Hang on!" Reena flung snow up on the rim of the growing hole. She finally reached his boot, and felt along it until her fingers found flesh and warmth, even through her gloves. Caid flexed his leg, telling her he'd felt her touch. He was slanted downward, his head lower than his feet.

"Hang on," she yelled, "I'm digging as fast as I can."

"I'm caught in an air pocket between two boulders. I can't move my arms."

She tunneled around his legs, going deeper and deeper.

"Get my hand free and I'll help."

She scooped more snow away from his right side. Her hands brushed his arm and she redoubled her efforts, flinging snow up, away from the hole she'd made. Finally she could clasp his ice-cold hand in both hers. He wiggled his fingers against hers.

She dug down another few inches and suddenly she was in the air pocket, and Caid was working with her to free himself.

"I think I can pull you out the rest of the way." She backed out of the hole.

"You're not strong enough."

"Let me try." She lay flat on the snow and leaned down to grasp his boots, but she couldn't get enough leverage to pull him out.

"Let go. I think I can do it." He jackknifed his body and wiggled and squirmed in the confines of the hole, and finally got turned around with his head up.

"Fresh air never tasted so good." He hooked his arms on the edge and took deep breaths. Then, bracing his arms on the rim, he tried to haul himself out. He froze there, his arms trembling with the effort, and Reena realized he was far more exhausted than he was letting on.

"Here, let me help." She grabbed his arm, but she didn't have the strength to pull him out. And neither did he, with just one arm. He slid back.

"It's not working. Let go of my arm," he gasped. He rested his forehead against the edge for long, motionless moments.

Reena could see he was gathering what was left of his strength. Slowly, with trembling arms, he hefted himself up and teetered on the edge of the deathtrap.

"Hang on." Reena flopped down on her belly beside the hole and reached down to grab a handful of his pants. "Now!"

She yanked as hard as she could as he used the last of his strength to pull himself up, and finally he sprawled face down on the snow. He was out, free of his frozen hell! Reena ran her hands along his arms and legs, reassuring herself that he didn't have any broken bones. Though he didn't, his clothes were snow soaked and the sleet wasn't helping.

Free, but not yet safe. She had to get him to shelter and warm him; otherwise he would freeze in his wet clothes.

"Get up, Caid." She tried to lift him, but he was

dead weight. "Get up! We've got to get back to the cabin."

Slowly—so slowly she wanted to scream—he pushed himself to his feet. He stood there, swaying slightly. His head hung as if it were too much effort for him to raise it, and his silver-blue eyes were dark with exhaustion.

Then slowly his head came up and he squared his shoulders. He took a slow step. And another.

"Here, lean on me." She draped his arm over her shoulders and wrapped hers around his waist.

"I'm all right," he gritted, putting one foot in front of the other. "Just get my horse and bring him as close as you can."

"Diablo?" she asked, confused.

"Just do it."

She ran back to Diablo. Her jacket still covered his eyes, and now that he was quiet, she could see that in his wild lunges he'd almost freed himself. Only one or two more lunges and he'd be out of the snow. She gathered his reins, pulled the blindfold off him, then led him forward. He followed her, lunging and falling back and lunging again, and then he was free. He stood there, snorting and blowing loudly.

She pulled her jacket on as she ran back for Caid. He'd slogged along in the path she'd made, and she slipped her arm around his waist again. "Come on, Caid, it's not far now."

"Thanks," he muttered, squeezing her shoulder as he took another shaky step.

She got him beside Diablo, so all he had to do

was step up into the stirrup and swing up into the saddle. But did he have enough strength left to do it?

"Here, Caid. Just step up into the stirrup," she said briskly, trying to give him strength through her voice.

He took the reins from her and rested his hands on the horse's neck just in front of the saddle. He murmured to Diablo and touched his shoulder. Diablo went down on his front knees, as if bowing, and Caid stepped forward and swung his leg over the much-lowered saddle.

When the horse got to his feet, Caid clung to the saddle horn and jerked back and forth like a rag doll, but he stayed on.

"Thank God, " Reena murmured to herself, blinking rapidly as she dashed a tear off her cheek. He was almost safe. Almost.

She grabbed Diablo's reins and swung up on her own roan. "Hang on, Caid. Hang on."

Caid hunched over, fighting the wind-driven sleet that bit through his wet clothes like a razor. He was shivering violently, but at least he was alive—thanks to Reena.

She rode ahead of him, glancing back every few feet to check on him.

"I-I'm a-l-l r-i-g-h-t," he called through chattering teeth. The snow would have been his tomb, if it hadn't been for her. Most women he'd known would have been too hysterical to even think about looking for him. But she'd kept her head and found him. He'd wondered if he could trust her, and he'd wound up trusting her with his life.

They finally entered the pines, but they provided only slight shelter from the sleet. Still, it meant they were closer to the cabin.

Diablo stumbled so badly that Caid almost went over his head. Only his weak grip with his legs kept him in the saddle.

"Good boy," he muttered, gathering the reins he'd let lie loose on the stallion's neck. The horse was as exhausted as he was. "We're almost there." Diablo tossed his head as though he understood, and quickened his pace.

Thank God he'd taught that kneeling trick to Diablo as a young colt. When he was at West Point, Caid had known there might come a day when he was wounded and too weak to swing up into the saddle—and being afoot in either of those conditions would have made him a dead man. The trick had been crucial to his survival today.

A pine bough slapped his forehead with a wet load of snow, and he looked up. He could see the cabin just ahead.

Diablo followed Reena's horse into the clearing. When Caid dismounted, he barely landed on his feet, grabbing the saddle to keep from collapsing in the snow.

"Damn!" He hadn't expected to be *that* weak!

"Come on, Caid." Reena was at his side, supporting him. "Let's get you inside."

He took a step, thinking to show her he didn't need her help, but his legs didn't seem part of him, moving stiffly and jerkily. Caid found himself leaning on Reena when he lifted his boot up to the surprisingly high first step. Why hadn't he noticed how high it was before? And the second step was even higher. His denim pants crackled with ice.

As they shuffled across the porch, he realized he was leaning on Reena heavily. "Sorry," he muttered, trying to take his weight off her.

"Don't worry." She tightened her grip around his waist. "Let's just get you to bed." She kicked the cabin door open.

"Now, that's an invitation I can't pass up." Wanting to reassure her that he was fine, he squeezed her shoulder and grinned down at her, rakishly, he hoped.

"That's the most pathetic grin I've ever seen," she said, as if reading his mind.

When they got to the bed, Caid sat down heavily and fumbled for the buttons on his sheepskin jacket, but Reena swatted his hands away and began unbuttoning his jacket.

He wanted to protest and push her away, but it was too much effort. So he let her fuss over him, stripping off his jacket, then his shirt.

What the hell was that noise? he wondered. Slowly he realized it was his teeth—and that he was shivering uncontrollably.

Reena pushed him down on the bed and wrestled his boots off. The next thing he knew, she was kneeling over him, unbuckling his belt.

"Whoa up, girl—you'll enjoy it more if I'm awake," he mumbled, as his eyes closed.

It was better this way, Reena thought, as she opened his belt. She slid two fingers inside his waistband as she unbuttoned the top button on his fly. His skin was cold beneath her fingers.

She finished unbuttoning his fly and loosened his pants, then pulled them off him. Even his cotton underdrawers were soaked, and she stripped them off, too. Then she flung a blanket and the bearskin rug over him to keep him warm while she started a fire.

When she was sure the kindling was burning well, sending flames up into the firewood, Reena finally kneeled back and rubbed the small of her back wearily. She glanced at the bed, but Caid hadn't moved since she'd tucked the bearskin around him.

She had to take care of the horses next. She led them into the lean-to shelter in back and unsaddled them, then gave them all the hay she could find.

Filling her arms with firewood from the wood-pile, she carried it inside and stacked it near the fireplace. A soft rustle she couldn't identify came from the bed, and she saw the bearskin moving.

She hurried over and found Caid shivering violently. She felt his forehead. He seemed hot—yet he was racked by chills.

There was nothing else in the cabin to pile onto him; there was only one way left to warm him. Sitting on the bed, Reena took her boots and wet clothes off, then slipped under the bearskin. Caid was turned on his side, facing away from her. She curled against his back and wrapped her arms around him. "Please, Caid, promise me you'll be all right," she murmured. "You've got to be all right."

Gradually his shaking faded away and she felt him relaxing, stretching out his legs as he warmed up. She loosened her tight hold. Under her hands she could feel the steady beat of his heart. She rested her cheek against his shoulderblade and closed her eyes.

Caid would be all right.

He had to be.

Because she loved him.

Chapter 17

~~~~◦◯◦~~~~

Caid opened his eyes, but didn't move. First he wondered where he was. Then he realized that Reena was pressed against his back, spoon-fashion. And both he and she were naked.

She'd wrapped her arms around him and her small hands were splayed across his chest and he could feel the steady beat of her heart against his back.

Memories of his snowy tomb shuddered through him. He turned over slowly and carefully, not wanting to wake her until he could cradle her in his arms. His heroine.

He lay there for a long time, just holding her. He'd learned a great deal about trusting her that day.

The first time he'd made love to her, it had been an extraordinary joining. Now he wanted to cele-

brate trusting and life, and make love to her again
. . . and again.

Reena dreamed she was in Caid's arms and he
was kissing her. She dreamed that she drew her
fingers down over his beard-roughened jaw, and
she could actually feel the roughness. Then she
opened her eyes and discovered she wasn't dreaming at all.

He cradled her in his arms and bent over her,
kissing her gently as dawn kissing the day.

"Caid!" She ran her hand down the side of his
face—his beloved face. His cheek was rough
against her palm and she relished every bit of that
roughness. "Are you all right?"

"Yes—thanks to you. You did a good job of
warming me up." Without taking his eyes from
hers, he turned his head and kissed her palm. "A
very good job."

"I was so frightened." She spoke around a sudden lump in her throat and had to blink rapidly.

"Everything's fine, my darling." His voice was
gritty with emotion, and he rained kisses as light
as rose petals over her eyes and nose and cheeks
and lips. She could barely feel them, yet her heartstrings leaped with each one.

Then his mouth covered hers in a tantalizing, inviting kiss and her blood began to race.

She threaded her fingers through his silky dark
hair and pulled his head down, meeting his mouth
with demands of her own. Their tongues circled
and dueled in sensual combat, and all the time her
heart was thrumming faster and faster.

Need flamed between them like fire finding dry wood.

Caid rolled onto his back so that she lay above him, her hair cloaking them in gold. "I want to make love to you, Reena, but I need to know that you want me to."

She gazed at him for a moment. She wanted to make love to him, too, and though she wasn't ready to tell him of her love, she could show him. She sat up, her knees outside his hips, running her hands down his chest. As she settled into position her bottom nestled against his engorged shaft, and he groaned. She rocked teasingly, and he gasped, "Lean over me."

He palmed one breast while tonguing the nipple of the other, building anticipation in her. Then he pulled her nipple into the heated moisture of his mouth and began to suckle.

Reena trembled as waves of pure pleasure spread down to her core. Then his lips were at her other breast, sending more waves of bliss through her.

"Oh-h," she moaned, arching her back to give him better access.

He went from one breast to the other with his sweet torture. Then, when she didn't think it could get any better, he reached between them and touched the nub of her ecstasy. She moaned again and he drank her cry from her lips. He stroked her again and she shuddered with heat as her bones began to melt.

Holding his beloved face between her palms, Reena rained kisses down on him.

"I want to pleasure you tonight." She began to trail kisses down his broad chest, following the trail of dark curls lower and lower. In between kisses, she used her hair like a paintbrush, drawing it over him in lush, curving strokes that made him shudder with delicious tension.

Then she added her taunting, teasing tongue. He grew more and more taut as he waited for her touch, not knowing whether it would be a kiss or a lick or a sensual brush of her hair. She moved down the arrow of dark curls, lower . . . lower. . . .

He held his breath in anticipation of her moist warm tongue touching him.

Then suddenly she was gone. He felt for her, trying to find her, and then she started kissing and licking and brushing her way up from his foot . . . ankle . . . calf . . . knee . . . thigh. Each touch was deliciously exciting, and he quivered in reaction.

He held his breath, trembling with waiting, and knew the next place she touched with her moist, warm tongue would be—

Then she was gone again, working her way up his other leg, so slowly, until she finally reached his manhood.

He tensed as she ran her tongue around the rim, then she slowly took him into her mouth.

"Reena," he groaned. She alternated, using her tongue and her mouth, and Caid gripped the mattress tightly. Suddenly his fingers arrowed through her curls.

"St-stop," he gasped. "You're too good at this."

She rolled over on her back, pulling him on top

of her. "This is what I want tonight," she murmured, exploring the muscles and hollows of his shoulders with her fingers. "Didn't you like my pleasuring?"

"Darling, I liked it too much. If you'd gone on touching me like that, I would have exploded. This way is better."

"Prove it. Show me."

He did just that, kissing and licking and teasing and touching until she couldn't breathe and her blood was pounding.

"C-Caid," she gasped, moving beneath him. "Now!"

"Wait." And he pleasured her more with his mouth and hands until finally, when her breasts felt heavy with need, and the wildness in her cried for filling, he came to her.

He waited for her to accommodate his size, then slowly he began to thrust.

"Faster," she pleaded, wrapping her legs around his hips. "Faster." She moved with him, meeting him thrust for thrust, arcing tighter and tighter, like a bow growing tauter and tauter. Suddenly stars shimmered in her head.

"Yes! *Re-e-n-a.*" Caid held her tightly as he began to explode.

Reena felt his contractions deep within her and soared into a galaxy of stars of her own.

They were gasping and laughing and holding each other tightly as they fell back to earth.

"Reena," he gasped, drawing deep breaths into his air-starved lungs. "You are so incredible."

He wrapped his arms around her and they fell asleep together.

When Caid awakened, he could see the gray light of dawn filtering through the frost-rimed window.

He was involved way over his head, he realized. Because there was no way he could dismiss their lovemaking as ordinary.

Incredible? Yes. Ordinary? No.

The light slowly turned golden with the promise of a new day. And still he held Reena and savored holding her.

He would explore the canyon that day, see if there was another way out, or if they were trapped until the sun melted the snow blocking the pass.

Would he mind being trapped? *Hell, no,* one part of him said. He would be with Reena, able to talk and listen to her uninterrupted by the rest of the world.

Yet that other part of the world still awaited: he had to stop the Simpsons' plot before there was any bloodshed. The President was depending on him.

There was no way out—not when so many lives depended on him. Much as he wanted to stay lost with Reena, he had to go back.

Caid rode back to the cabin slowly. Reena was standing on the porch, waiting for him. Did she want to hear his news as little as he wanted to give it?

"I think we can get out today." He swung off

Diablo and stepped up on the porch. "Are you ready to go?"

Reena looked up at him and tried to speak, but suddenly tears filled her eyes and her lower lip quivered. She turned away. Caid took a step after her and caught her to him. She leaned her head back against his shoulder, and he inhaled her lilac-and-spice scent.

Would he ever get enough of holding her? He wrapped her close, feeling the beating of her heart, absorbing it into his bones.

Finally she exhaled a long breath and patted his hand. "I'm all right now."

He let go of her reluctantly. Their idyll only had lasted two days. Two days when he and Reena had been lost to the world; two days that were over far too quickly.

"Reena, we've got to go. If the pass is open, someone could be coming through from the other side." And he would be lost if they spent another night together.

"I'll see that everything is out of the cabin."

"I'll get your horse."

They were almost all the way through the pines and out in the open when Caid heard a noise ahead of them. Halting Diablo, he tilted his head and listened.

"What is it?" Reena said, behind him on her roan.

He held up his hand, signaling her for silence. There it was again. A metallic click. Again, only louder, almost a ringing. An iron horseshoe clang-ing against rocks.

He glanced at Reena. She nodded, her eyes wide. She'd heard it, too.

"Come on. We'll get off the trail and let them go by." He led Diablo down the slope away from the trail. She followed, letting her horse pick his way over the slippery pine needles.

He couldn't take a chance and confront the Simp-sons when he had Reena at his side. What would happen to her if something happened to him? If, God forbid, they got their hands on her? She was brave and resourceful, but she didn't stand a chance against men who didn't live by the laws of decency, who had never heard of a code of honor.

He got them behind a thicket of bright green bushes that had grown in a sunny spot among the ponderosa pines.

He could hear the creak of leather as a horse started through the trees to the cabin. More leather creaked as a second horse followed. Caid covered Diablo's nostrils, afraid he'd whinny if he scented strange horses. He glanced at Reena and saw that she had done the same with her roan.

Caid glimpsed the men on horseback. Each led a pack mule loaded with supplies. Just two men. He had the advantage of surprise and he could get the drop on them, but then what? What if there were more men following? What if there was a shootout?

He couldn't risk it. Not with Reena at his side.

"C-Caid, I'm frightened," Reena whispered, watching the men. "Pl-please, I—" Her heart was pounding so loud she wondered if Caid could hear it.

She had to make sure he didn't try anything. If the twins realized he was there, it would be two against one and they were expert marksmen. He wouldn't stand a chance.

She had to get him away from there.

She crowded against Caid, trembling with fear. "Pl-please, Caid," she murmured through lips stiff with fear, "don't do anything to alert them to us."

He shook his head. "I won't." He followed their passage through the woods with an intent gaze. "Not when I have you to worry about."

"M-me?" Her heart soared with relief.

"I'll protect you. No matter what."

The riders rounded a curve and disappeared from view.

Caid set off through the pines on a course parallel to the path they had come down, slowly angling over to it. He knelt beside the trail, studying the hoofprints, looking for anything unusual, like a nick in an iron shoe, that would help him identify these horses again.

"Come on," he finally said, swinging up on Diablo. "Let's get out of here." She wasn't safe yet.

"I'm right behind you."

Reena would have galloped headlong through the pass into the front part of the canyon, but Caid insisted on going first and reconnoitering carefully around each curve. It took them most of the day to get out of the canyon, and he was on edge every second, worrying about seeing someone else.

*   *   *

A day later, near sunset, they rode through the gate of May's ranch. Long before they got to the white picket fence surrounding the yard, May rushed down the front steps of the ranch house, waving at them.

Glad to see the older woman, Reena spurred her horse into a canter. When they reached the fence she drew rein and leaped off.

"Child, I have been so worried." May pushed aside the squeaky gate and clasped Reena to her shelflike bosom. "I was sure you two were dead and that we'd never find your bodies. Now you ride up as calm and pretty as you please. Where were you?"

"We were trapped in a canyon by a snowstorm," Caid explained, as he joined them.

May's brow furrowed as she looked from one to the other. "How?"

"Snowslide." Caid said. "It plugged the mouth like a cork in a bottle. We had to wait for it to melt."

May took a deep breath. "I'm so relieved to know you're both all right. I didn't know how I'd tell your mother and father, Caid. And I didn't even know where your family was, Reena. Heavens, listen to me, going on and on. Come inside and we'll get you a sandwich and coffee right quick. You two must be starved and exhausted."

"And filthy," added Reena.

"You go in, child, and I'll bring the tub to your

room and get some water heated pretty damn quick."

"Thanks, May. I'd love that." Reena turned to Caid. "I'll see you later?"

"Of course—just as soon as I've taken care of the horses." Dismounting, he grasped each horse's reins and started to lead them toward the stable.

May snapped her fingers. "Caid, I almost forgot. Tanner sent a messenger while you were missing. He wants you to come back to town; he said something about a change of plans."

"I'll leave tomorrow morning, then. Diablo is too tired to make the trip tonight."

"So are you," Reena said.

"I suppose you'll want a bath, too," May offered.

"No, I'll use the pond."

"Or you can use my tub." Reena gave him a look that made him consider her offer very seriously.

"If you'll make that coffee, May, I'll be back as soon as the horses are bedded down." He paused, head tilted, listening. "I don't hear any cattle lowing. Where are they? Where is everyone?"

"We put both herds together for the sorting and they're all over at Jeter's right now. The hands have been looking for you. They're due back in the next day or so."

"So you don't have anyone to carry the water for Reena's bath, do you?"

May waved her hand dismissively. "Pshaw, Caid, carrying a few pots of hot water isn't anything. I've done it hundreds of times."

"You don't need to this time," Reena chimed in.

"Caid and I will." She slipped her arm around the older woman's waist. "Come on, May, let's go inside and get that coffee going."

Only a few browning blooms lingered on the rosebushes edging the porch, as if fighting the coming of winter. The last roses of summer, Reena thought, even as the breeze blew a drooping bloom apart and the petals fell to the ground. Soon they'd all be gone.

Tears prickled her eyes. All gone, like the two days when Caid and she had been cut off from the world.

Reena slipped into bed and waited. Would Caid come to her tonight—their last night before they returned to Lost Gold? She lay beneath the covers, tense with longing.

The latch on her door turned softly and she knew. He walked across the room and stood beside her bed, looking down at her. Moonlight silvered and shadowed him, but there was no doubt he wanted her.

"Reena?"

"I hoped you'd come." She lifted the covers for him.

"I hoped you wanted me to come." He slid beneath them and gathered her to him and kissed her tenderly.

"Not bad. Keep it up." She stretched lazily, running her foot along his leg.

"I'll be glad to, my darling."

He urged her onto her stomach, then slowly, tantalizingly slowly, kissed her shoulder and licked her and blew oh-so-gently across her moistened flesh. Reena shivered at the tingle of pleasure that went through her. She felt a slow heat deep within her.

He continued the gentle kissing and licking and blowing across her back, following her curves, taking his time and not leaving a spot on her back untouched. Every touch sent a shiver of pleasure through her.

"Oh, Caid, what . . . are . . . you . . . doing?" she said, in a voice that was both a moan and a gasp.

Even a kiss on the back of her knee could be startlingly erotic, she found, when Caid was doing it. He kissed and touched and licked, until she was quivering with pleasure and need. Her heart hammered against her ribs like a kettledrum and the heat deep inside her had grown until it pulsed and demanded more.

"Caid," she cried, turning over and holding her arms out to him, "come to me." She spread her legs in invitation.

He slid between her legs and kissed her long and hard. "You are so very beautiful," he murmured. Every muscle, every nerve in his body was tight with the need for her. His blood pulsed like hot lava. He could feel the tight buds of her nipples pressed against his chest.

He probed her carefully, finding her slick and ready for him. He entered slowly, drawing out the anticipation, the tightening exhilaration, then drew back, back, and surged into her again. He drank her moan of welcome from her lips. Slowly, gritting his teeth with control, he began to move again. Faster. Deeper. Harder.

Reena wrapped her legs around his hips and moved with him. He couldn't breathe. His heart drummed raggedly against his ribs. Faster. Deeper. Harder.

He felt her begin to convulse around his shaft, and he gave a final, shouting thrust of explosion that carried him over the edge of a cliff and he was flying.

"Re . . . e . . . na," he cried, as he soared with her.

Slowly, slowly, he came back to earth. Beneath him Reena was panting and laughing and crying.

"Are you all right?" he demanded, running his hands over her to reassure himself that she was.

"Yes." She arched against him. "It just keeps getting better and better."

"Mmm, that it does." He wrapped her close and drifted in a cloud of satisfaction and joy and pleasure.

He felt Reena take a long, deep breath as he rolled to his side, taking her with him. He caressed her curves and hollows, needing to go on touching her, feeling her at his side. She felt so right in his arms. She felt so right when they made love.

But what would happen when they returned to Lost Gold? he wondered.

Reena lay in Caid's arms, savoring his warmth and the wonder of their joining. She held him tightly, afraid to let go, wondering if it would be the last time she held him. She felt him exhale deeply as though sighing. Did he, too, worry that this might be the last time they shared the profound joy of making love?

Reena turned in his arms and held him close, and wished morning wouldn't come. Tomorrow they would ride back to Lost Gold, and Caid would return to pursuing her brothers and once again they would be on opposite sides of everything.

She fought the tears that threatened to seep out. Time enough tomorrow for tears.

Tonight was theirs.

Chapter 18

~~~~~~~⌒⌒~~~~~~~

Reena and Caid rode back to Lost Gold side by side, but they didn't speak except in monosyllables, didn't touch except when absolutely necessary. Caid didn't even clasp his hands together to help Reena mount. She looked at him and understood. The less they touched, the better. Each touch hurt too much, when they didn't know if it would be their last.

Did they have any chance for a future?

She didn't dare hope—not when their differences were so deep, not when Caid was determined to put her brothers in jail and stop the Second Confederacy.

Did she even believe in the Cause and the Second Confederacy anymore? She didn't know.

"What have you found, Tanner?" Caid asked, as he walked into his friend's hotel suite. He dropped

266

his saddlebags on the chair beside the door. "Did the Simpsons strike again? Did you find their spy?"

"I thought you said Reena Sims was their spy." Tanner looked up from the desk where he'd been writing.

"I wondered if you found any evidence pointing to someone else." He'd been hoping, desperately.

Tanner studied him for a moment. "I'm sorry, Caid, but nothing has turned up pointing to anyone else. I sent the message because your father telegraphed you last week. He's coming to Lost Gold." He shuffled through the papers on the desk and pulled out a flimsy, yellow paper. "Here."

"My father?" Caid took the telegram and read it twice. "What's he up to now?"

"It seems the President has asked Senator Dundee to come to Arizona in his place and make a speech reassuring the people here that they're important to the United States."

"So they're taking the rumors about the Simpsons and the Second Confederacy seriously." He raked his fingers through his dust-stiffened hair.

"Very seriously. We've gotten word that the Simpsons will make an assassination attempt if the President comes to Arizona. So your father will be substituting for him."

"When will he arrive?"

Tanner laid his pencil down and leaned back in his chair. "That depends on you. He asked that you meet him in Adobe Wells, Colorado, with the private railcar next week."

Caid shook his head. "I've got traitors to catch. I

don't have time to hold his hand on his first visit to the wild west."

"You should think about going with the railcar, Caid." Tanner turned partway, resting his arm on the back of the chair. "I have a feeling there's more to this than he could put in a telegram. After all, has he ever asked you to meet him before?"

Caid shook his head. "I don't think it means anything except that he wants one more person in his entourage."

Tanner thumbed through the sheets of paper on the desk. "Do you realize how cynical you are when it comes to your father? It's so unlike you. You are open-minded and fair and observant about people. That's what makes you such a good secret agent. But I wonder if you even know your father."

"Too well." Caid moved to the window that looked out on the side street.

"Or not at all."

Caid flattened his hand against the window frame and peered out. Could Tanner be right? Was he assessing his father differently than he did anyone else? "Am I really that bad?" he asked, without turning.

Tanner studied him for almost a minute before he replied. "Yes."

Caid inhaled slowly and deeply. "I'll think about what you said. I'm willing to give you the benefit of the doubt."

"You give everyone the benefit of the doubt, Caid. Except your father."

Caid glanced at him, then turned back to gaze

out the window. "I'm *that* bad, eh? All right, if I'm
going to take the private railcar east, I want to use
the trip to set a trap for the Simpsons. That way
I—"

Movement on the side street caught his eye. A
girl in a blue chambray dress scurried toward Main
Street. Although she didn't look up, he recognized
her blond hair and the jewel-toned paisley shawl
she had draped over her shoulders.

She turned east on Main. The train station was
the only building in that direction.

"I'll finalize the plans with you later," Caid said,
heading for the door. "Reena has just slipped away
from the hotel and I want to see where she's going."

In his heart, he was afraid he knew where she
was going—and why. But he had to find out.

Reena hurried toward the train depot. As soon
as they'd returned, she had gone to the hollow tree,
hoping to find a note from Jeff or Robby. She'd
found not only a note, but a packet of money she
was to pass on to Jim Spekes, the train conductor
who supported the Second Confederacy.

A tingling along the back of her neck, as if someone was watching her, made her look over her
shoulder, but she didn't see anyone. Putting it
down to her imagination, she ignored the feeling
when it happened again.

She no longer felt proud to be working for the
Cause. Maybe Caid was right: maybe time had
passed the Second Confederacy by. Maybe they

were all tilting at windmills and fighting for something that would never come true.

Caid watched Reena from the shadows in the telegrapher's office. He saw her run out onto the platform as if looking for someone among the passengers and accidently run into the conductor—just as she had a few weeks earlier. But this time he knew it was no accident. He watched intently and thought he saw a wad of greenbacks change hands.

He had to give her credit. She was damn smooth about it—and hers was the kind of smoothness that came with lots of practice.

He turned away from the window. "Who's the conductor on the train from the West?"

The telegrapher checked the schedule. "Jim Spekes."

"Is that Spekes?" he asked, pointing at the conductor who'd come into the depot. "I want to be sure I have the right man."

"Yes, sir, Mr. Dundee, that's him."

"All right. I want to send a telegram; give me your pad." He wrote on it, and then handed it to the telegrapher, who paled visibly as he read it.

"I'll send this immediately, sir."

"See that you do. And if Spekes is warned, I'll know who did it. Understand?"

"Yes, sir. You can count on me, Mr. Dundee." He sat down at his key and began transmitting.

Caid gazed through the window. Reena was still

waiting on the platform, watching the passengers. Why?

He slipped outside into the shadows and waited, out of sight but not out of hearing.

"Do you know where I could buy a horse in town, ma'am?" a young voice asked.

"Try the stable behind the hotel," Reena replied.

Something tugged at Caid's memory. The last time he'd seen Reena at the station a young cowboy had also asked her something. He plucked at his memory, digging deep to remember.

The cowboy had asked the same question—he was sure of it. And Reena had given the same answer. So it was a code. And the two young men he'd seen were the right age to join the Second Confederate Army.

Oh, God, her involvement was much deeper than he'd wanted to believe. In the back of his mind, he had still hoped it had been an innocent collision. But now he was convinced. She wasn't just spying for the Simpsons; she was in the thick of it. She was a—

He veered away from the word, unable to even think it. He would cross that bridge when he had to.

Feeling as he'd been kicked and trampled by a herd of wild horses, Caid trudged back toward the hotel.

"Belle, I'm back." Reena slipped into the kitchen and hugged the curvy redhead.

"How was it?" Belle stepped back and looked

her up and down. Did you miss me and Miss Abigail and everyone?"

Reena laughed. "You, yes. Miss Abigail, no." She clasped Belle's hands in hers. "My chain. . . ."

"Is fixed. It's in your top drawer." Belle glanced at the clock on the wall. "I'll be done soon, then we'll make a pot of tea and you can tell me all that happened. And I don't want you to leave out a single thing."

"I won't." Heavens, she'd never considered what she'd tell Belle about the days she and Caid were trapped in the canyon. She couldn't possibly tell her about—

"Reena, you're blushing. Why?"

She waved a hand. "I'm just windburned from the trip. Look, I want to go get cleaned up. Then I'll meet you back here."

"I think we're going to need a big pot of tea." Tilting her head, Belle assessed her. "Yep, a very big pot of tea. Something happened to you."

"Well, I spent a lot of time riding horses, and you know the old saying—'There's nothing better for the inside of a woman than the outside of a horse.'"

"No. I don't know that." Belle crossed her arms over her bosom and eyed Reena skeptically. "In fact, I've never heard such a dumb saying in my life."

"It's true; I'll show you—"

"Ah, there you are, Reena. I heard that you were back." Miss Abigail's chirpy voice came from behind her.

"And ready to return to work, Miss Abby," Reena said, turning to the other woman. Work would keep her busy and she wouldn't have time to think about Caid.

"I think we'll give you a day off to get rested up." The tiny gray-haired woman crossed her arms over her flat chest. "Then I'd like you to work the eastbound train for the next week or so. You've seen the sandwich and drink packs our Lowry Girls carry on the train, haven't you, dear?"

"Yes, but what about the dining room?" She needed to be in Lost Gold on Sunday to go to the stable! She needed to talk to Jeff or Robby Lee in person, to make them understand what kind of man they were up against.

"You'll be coming back to that. But since you're already out of the rotation, I think it's easiest to put you on the train, since I'd eventually have to rotate you there anyway. Remember, you're off two days for every day you're on the train."

"That's right. I'd forgotten." And she would be back in Lost Gold on Sunday! "It sounds like it'll be fun. Thanks, Miss Abby."

"Now, why don't you go see about some dinner for yourself, dear."

Reena watched Belle and Miss Abigail hurry off to their respective duties. Taking a piece of roasted chicken and some mashed potatoes, she carried the plate upstairs to her room. There was something she needed to do before eating. Putting the plate on the dresser, she opened her top drawer and drew out the chain with the tiny child's ring.

She ran her fingers over it. The dark-haired boy had been only a child himself when he'd given her the ring. He'd appear for a few days at holidays and then disappear again. She'd hero-worshiped him, because he was handsome and didn't tease her unmercifully, like Jeff and Robby did. And he let her sit on the saddle in front of him and ride his horse.

For many years, she'd thought that if she rubbed the ring he would come. He never had.

But she'd kept the ring and worn it around her neck anyway. It was part of a past that was gone forever, but as long as she wore it, she could believe. If she took it off and put it in a drawer, she would be admitting that there were no knights in shining armor, no princes, no heroes. And that wasn't a world she wanted to live in.

She slipped the worn gold chain over her head and felt the tiny ring settle between her breasts. As she pushed her drawer shut, she noticed one of the greenbacks from her hidden store was in plain sight, and she pushed it under a pile of stockings.

It reminded her that she had felt dirty passing that money to Jim Spekes, as if she were a criminal. She couldn't go on working for the Cause. She didn't believe in it anymore.

There was no going back to the days Papa remembered before the War Between the States. The world had moved on, but Papa was locked in dreams of the past. And the twins shared those dreams. How could she get them to see that their visions for the Second Confederacy was hopeless?

Caid would fight them and the Second Confederacy as long as he was alive. And he would stop them. She had no doubts about that.

Was there any hope for Caid and her? Or was her love as doomed as dreams of a Second Confederacy?

"Oh, Caid," she whispered. "How could I have fallen in love with you?"

As Caid lay in his bed in the hotel, he pillowed his head on his folded arms and gazed up at the ceiling. In spite of all his resolve, throughout dinner with Tanner he'd kept looking for Reena.

When had she had become such a vital part of his life?

Not that he was in love with her, he reassured himself. He had seen friends fall "in love," had seen their dazed, starry-eyed looks. He didn't have that look.

What he had was a burning desire for a woman who set off sparks in him. And the more he tasted her and touched her and teased her, the more he wanted her. But that was all it was—desire. Passion. Lust. Safe emotions.

Thank God he wasn't in love with her.

Reena slipped out to the back street before dawn on Sunday. In the darkness, she waited under a sycamore tree, huddling close to the trunk so she wouldn't be seen.

The sky was beginning to lighten when the slow clip-clop of a horse's hooves alerted her to the approach of a rider. She remained in the shadows, trying to see if it was Jeff. Finally she saw the jaunty ostrich feather waving in his hat, and she stepped out directly in front of his horse.

The horse snorted and reared back, while Jeff reined in sharply. "God damn it, sis, you gave me a start. What are you doing out here?"

"I didn't want to wait for you in the stable. You never know who's lurking around there." She rested her hand on the horse's neck. "Get down, Jeff. I need to talk to you."

"Sure." He stepped down. "Got information about any gold shipments?"

She led him into the shadow of the sycamore, where it would be harder to spot them—if anyone was looking. "There's three strongboxes going out on the eastbound train. But, Jeff, I—"

He slapped his hat against his leg. "Damn good work, sis. That'll be enough gold to finish buying the rifles and ammunition for the Army. We'll be able to invade Arizona."

"No! You can't! Jeff, listen to me." She rested both hands on his arm. "It's not going to work. The government knows about your plans. They've got a secret agent out here, Caid Dundee, who will do anything it takes to stop you. Anything."

"Yeah, you left me a note about him. But he's only one man. He doesn't worry me. He can't stop us."

"Oh, yes, he can."

"Then we'll kill him."

Reena gasped and backed up a step, shocked.

She should have expected it, she told herself. She'd been focused on Caid, and on how unstoppable he was. But she knew him; her brothers didn't. "That won't get you anywhere. If you—" She couldn't say it. "If Caid is gone, there will be someone else."

"We'll kill him, too."

"Then there will be another. And another. Don't you understand? The United States government knows about the Second Confederacy, and they're not going to just let you walk into Arizona."

"The government is over two thousand miles away. Our Army is training just over the border in Mexico. We can take over Arizona before anyone can stop us. Now stop your worrying, sis. Everything will be fine. You'll see."

Reena shook her head, dismayed. "Have you heard anything I've said?"

"Sure. You warned me about the government agent. All right, I'll be on the lookout for him. Then I'll take care of him." He patted her on the top of the head. "In the meantime, don't you worry your pretty little head about the Second Confederacy. Let us menfolks take care of that."

"Jeff, you've got to listen to me." She grasped his shirt front in her hands, wanting to shake some sense into him.

"No, sis." He wrapped his hands around hers. "*You* listen to me. Stop talking all this nonsense! Hear me? Stop it!"

Reena stared up at him, shocked into silence by the hardness in his tone.

"I'll see you next week," he said, mounting his

horse. "And I don't want to hear another word of this nonsense then. Understand?" He whirled his horse and galloped off.

Reena watched him go. What was wrong with him? Why wouldn't he even listen to her?

She had to find a way to make him stop. Otherwise her brothers were going to be pitted against the man she loved. She shuddered at the picture of her brothers and Caid shooting at each other.

No one would win.

Someone would be killed.

And her heart would break.

Chapter 19

Caid leaned against the train depot wall and watched Reena walk out to the train in her black and white uniform. So she would be the Lowry girl working on the train.

Did she also know whether the Simpsons were planning to hold it up?

He knew Jim Spekes was being questioned, but still didn't have confirmation on whether she had passed him anything. There was still a chance that everything she'd done had been completely innocent.

Yeah, Dundee, and if you believe that, there's a bridge I want to sell you.

He watched her climb the steps to a passenger car, then pause on the platform and turn—as if she sensed his gaze. She glanced around and saw him. She smiled and started to wave, then dropped her hand. Her smile faded.

Deliberately, wanting her to know that he was on the train, waiting for the Simpsons, he walked out to the steam engine.

"Are you the engineer?" Caid asked, shading his eyes against the morning sun, so he could look up into the engine cab. "I'm Caid Dundee."

"Yes, sir, I am." The engineer wiped his greasy hands on an oily rag. "I was told to expect you, Mr. Dundee."

"Glad to meet you." He climbed up into the cab and held out his hand. The engineer shook it vigorously. "I want to prepare a welcome for some outlaws I think will try to rob this train."

"Yes, sir! Whatever you say, sir. I hear we have three shipments of gold on this trip." He hooked his thumbs behind the bib of his striped coveralls and rocked back and forth on the balls of his feet. "Carrying a lot of gold this trip. A lot."

Caid nodded. Tanner had done a good job spreading the rumors. "That's right. I'm going to be hiding in the baggage car, waiting for them. And here's what I want you to do. . . ." Caid outlined his plan.

"Sure, I can do that," the engineer replied. "And it's an honor to be working with you, Mr. Dundee. We need to rid the West of outlaws if the territory is ever going to be settled."

"I'm glad to know you feel that way. Now, let's get going and prepare that little surprise." Caid jumped down and started to walk away, then turned. "Oh, and if the outlaws do stop the train, keep your steam pressure up so we can get rolling as soon as possible."

"Yes sir, Mr. Dundee. I'll sure do that."

Reena leaned against the wrought iron railing of the last passenger car.

The train was carrying a huge amount of gold on this run. She'd seen Caid supervising the loading of the strongboxes. Now the baggage car door was closed and everything was quiet, but soon the passengers would be arriving and boarding the empty train.

Caid, carrying a rifle, had boarded the train between the first passenger car and the baggage car. She moseyed forward through the three passenger cars, but didn't see him.

That meant he was in the baggage car. Oh Lord, he was hiding in the baggage car. Waiting with all the gold.

It was a trap!

Reena sat down abruptly on one of the empty seats, her eyes wide with shock. The gold was bait to lure her brothers into the trap Caid had set.

Remembering where she was, she stood up, squared her shoulders, and walked back through the passenger cars again.

And with every step, her certainty that Jeff and Robby Lee were going to rob the train grew. Because *she'd* told them about the gold.

She had to stay calm and find a way to warn her brothers off, Reena decided. And she had to act as if nothing was wrong.

She tried to unlock the food locker, but had a hard time getting the key into the lock. It took her several attempts to realize that it was because her hands were shaking so badly. She wilted onto a nearby seat and clasped them tightly in her lap, willing herself to stop trembling. This wasn't the time for her to go to pieces. A noise at the rear drew her out to the rear platform. A brakeman was already on the small platform, hovering over the coupler, and another car was slowly rolling toward them.

"Are you adding more cars to the train?"

"Yeah, that private railcar that's been sitting on the siding."

"The *Senator Dundee?*"

"That's the one." He watched as the other car rolled up and bumped against the coupler. "Wanted to check that the coupling was seated properly so it couldn't come loose," he explained, as he whacked the coupler with a sledgehammer. "Don't want to lose the car someplace in the middle of nowhere."

"Is anyone traveling in the car?"

"I don't know, ma'am." He tipped his cap to her, then jumped down and walked along the outboard side of the train.

Passengers began streaming out of the station and boarding the train. Reena stayed out on the platform, watching them, but didn't recognize anyone. After the last passenger boarded, the conductor picked up his wooden platform step and boarded, joining Reena on the platform.

"Where's Jim?" Reena asked when she realized the conductor was a stranger. "Isn't this the train he usually works?"

"Jim's in jail."

Straightening, she frowned at him in disbelief. "Whatever for?"

"Don't know," he said, going inside.

The engineer blew two shrieking blasts on the whistle and the train began to roll. It was so slow, Reena had to look at the station to be sure they were moving at all. That was how she saw a passenger run out and dash to the car ahead of hers and board.

Seth? Why was the obnoxious cowboy on the train? And why had he waited until the last minute to board?

Reena stayed on the platform, holding onto the iron railing as the train picked up speed. She had to warn Jeff and Robby. If she could stop them, then there would be no face-off with Caid—and both her brothers and Caid would be safe. But how could she keep all the men she loved from shooting at each other—not only this time, but forever?

She walked up through the passenger cars, then turned back again. Seth was sitting in the first car. He'd pulled his hat down low, but it couldn't completely hide his jowls. Instead of his usual drunken sprawl, he sat straight and looked around alertly. She pretended not to see him as she passed by.

She walked back through the cars again, too restless to sit still, stopping when she reached the outside platform between the last passenger car and the private car.

Maybe if she stayed out on the platform, she could wave them off. She took a white towel from the food locker and returned to the platform. If she could just wave them off, they'd all be safe—including Caid.

Three hours later, the train slowed as they climbed into the pine-forested mountains. Reena was still out on platform, shivering in the chilly air. It was time for her to make the rounds of the passengers, she knew. Several had already walked back through the cars, looking for her. She'd do it quickly, she decided, slipping on the metal box with its wide shoulder straps.

"Sandwiches. Coffee. Tea," she called, as she walked through the passenger car. She had to take small steps to keep her balance as the train swayed from side to side.

Finally she reached the front of the first passenger car and turned to face the passengers. "Sandwiches," she called. "Coffee." Wondering why the train was slowing again, she glanced outside.

"Look! Outlaws!" A woman screamed, pointing at the man on horseback racing beside the train.

Reena recognized Jeff and her heart leaped into her throat. She wanted to yell at them, to wave them off but it was too late. They were bent on getting that damn gold for their damn cause. She slipped free of the clumsy sandwich box as the train slowed more, and came to a lurching stop.

"Don't panic, ladies and gentlemen. Just stay seated, and—"

"Outta my way," Seth snarled, shoving her aside. He opened the front door, barreled across the platform, and shoved the baggage car door open.

"Hey! You can't go in there." Reena ran after him.

The door had banged shut behind him, so she peered through the window. The baggage car was piled high with wooden crates, except for a narrow walkway where Seth stood with his back to the door, just inside. Beyond him, Caid stood with his hands raised above his head. Seth had to be pointing a gun at him.

Reena quickly slammed the door open, catching Seth in the back and knocking him forward. His gun went off as he dropped it.

Caid dived for it. So did Seth.

They rolled around in the narrow walkway, pummeling each other and struggling to reach the gun. Reena flinched at the sickening thud of fists against flesh. She watched until she saw her chance, then dashed in and grabbed the gun.

She backed away from them, then shot into the ceiling. The men froze, tangled together, and stared at her with their undivided attention.

"Put your hands up, Seth. Now!" she ordered.

"No, honey, you put *your* hands up." Jeff's voice came from right behind her. He reached around her and took the gun out of her hand.

She whirled. He laughed.

"You should have watched your back, lady," he

added, as if he didn't know her. He gestured with his gun. "Now, get over there with your pal. And here." He tossed her some strips of rawhide. "Tie his hands behind his back. And make it tight. I'll check the knots myself."

Seth sneered. "Looks like you weren't so smart after all, Dundee."

Reena edged past him with eyes only for Caid— who watched the men behind her. Jeff had said he'd kill Caid!

"Caid, you heard him," she said loudly, as she crossed in front of him, blocking Jeff from shooting him. "Put your hands behind your back so I can tie them."

She saw the change in his eyes, saw him realize what she'd done, saw him shake his head very slightly. She kept walking.

Suddenly, Caid grabbed her wrist with his left hand and—

"Get out of the way, Rowena," Jeff D yelled.

—jerked her behind him, even as he pulled his revolver with his right hand and got off a shot at Jeff.

Two shots answered him and he spun away, collapsing to his knees against a wooden crate.

"Caid!" Reena screamed. She knelt beside him, her arm across his back, shielding him from her brothers as she tried to see how badly hurt he was.

"Let me see—"

He shrugged her hands off. "Get away from me," he gritted. His eyes were blue diamonds, hard and cutting. "You—" His contempt knifed through her and took her breath away.

Gasping with her own pain, Reena scrambled to her feet and backed away.

"Is this the guy you warned me about, sis?" Jeff asked from beside her. He raised his revolver and pointed it at Caid.

"No!" she screamed, knocking his gun away as it went off. The loud blast echoed around the car.

Jeff stared at her. "What the hell?"

"Jeff, get over here and help me," Seth yelled, as he shot the lock off the loading door.

Reena looked over her shoulder as he rolled it back and Robby Lee climbed in.

"Stay here," Jeff ordered her, as he holstered his gun and turned toward the loading door.

She sagged against a crate. Caid was safe—for the moment, at least.

She edged backward to stand in silent vigil in front of Caid, hoping against hope that they would forget him. The three men manhandled the heavy strongboxes full of gold to the door and pushed them out.

The strongboxes landed beside the tracks and Robby and Seth jumped out of the car after them. Jeff looked back at her, then he jumped, too. Reena ran to the loading door and looked out.

Jeff shot the lock off a strongbox and opened it up.

The train quietly started rolling forward.

Jeff gleefully pulled a heavy bar out of the strongbox—but it was gray instead of gold. "God damn it to hell!" he yelled. "We've been had. I'm going to kill that Dundee!"

He raced alongside, gaining on the slow-moving train. Reena clung to the handhold beside the door, paralyzed with fear that he'd catch up.

Caid jerked her away from the open door and took her place. He raised his revolver and took careful aim at Jeff.

"No!" Reena yelled, knocking the revolver out of his hand. It fell, slid across the floor, and out the door.

"Damn you, Reena." Caid clung to the handhold and rested his forehead against the wall, watching as the train picked up speed and Jeff fell behind, until finally he stopped and shook his fist.

Caid released the handhold and turned slowly. He stood with his feet planted wide and his head lowered, like a bull getting ready to charge and glared at her. He shook his head as if trying to clear it.

"Rowena Simpson, I presume." His voice would have put ice on a glacier. He took a single menacing step toward her. She backed up. He took another step toward her.

He was swaying badly. He was sweating and his skin had taken on a gray-white look. On his next step, he stumbled and hooked his elbow over a wooden crate to keep from falling.

"Caid, you need a doctor." She reached out to him, but he batted her hand away.

"Keep away from me, Rowena." He raised his head and focused with what clearly was the last of his strength. "Stay away from me, or I'll—" He slumped over on the crate.

Reena took one look, then ran. She banged out the door, crossed the platform, and entered the first passenger car. "Is there a doctor on board? I need a doctor!" she shouted.

Everyone looked at her, but no one stood up; no one even answered—they just went back to talking about the train robbery.

She ran to the next car. Again, she shouted, "I need a doctor! Is there a doctor on board?"

A gray-haired man stood up. "I'm a doctor," he said, as he started toward her. "What's the matter?"

"The outlaws shot a man." She twisted her hands together, trying to stay calm. "Will you come?"

"Let me get my bag." He turned back toward his seat.

"We're in the baggage car up front." Turning, she hurried forward. She needed to be with Caid, even if he didn't want her. Otherwise she was going to shatter into a million pieces.

She knelt beside Caid and felt his forehead. It was cold, clammy. His breathing was shallow and rapid.

"Move aside, miss," the doctor said. He knelt and placed two fingers against the pulse in Caid's throat and counted for a minute. Then, taking a pair of scissors from his bag, he cut away Caid's sleeve, revealing the blood trailing down his arm from a bullet hole.

"How is he?" Reena asked, hovering over them

and wishing she could do something to help.

"I need to get this man someplace where I can clean and bandage his wound," he said, turning to her. "Are there any compartments with bunks we could move him to?"

"Yes. The last car is a private car with a bed in it."

"Get some men to help me carry him there."

Three passengers soon crowded into the baggage car and joined the doctor in lifting Caid. Reena ran ahead to open doors. With a man on each limb, they carried him through the passenger cars into the private railcar.

"In here." Reena opened the door to the bedroom and pulled back the covers.

The men deposited Caid on the bed. As they left, the doctor walked around to the other side of the bed and bent over Caid.

"What can I do?" Reena asked.

"Get me a basin of water. Hot water, if you can. And bring in some whiskey, too."

She searched the cabinets in the parlor until she found a porcelain wash basin. She filled it with water at a small sink, then carried it back to the doctor, along with a whiskey bottle. "There was no hot water."

"That's all right." Taking the basin, he began to sponge the blood away from Caid's wound. He looked up several times as Reena hovered over him. "Dear, you're in my light. Go sit down in that chair. When I'm ready for you, I'll call you."

"But—"

He stopped, sighed, and turned to her. "If you don't sit down, I'm going to have two patients on my hands. And I have the feeling you'd rather be nursing this man."

"Yes, but—"

He pointed. "Sit."

The doctor turned back to Caid and muttered to himself as he cleaned the wound. "Damn bullet's still in there." Picking up the whiskey bottle, he pulled the cork with his teeth. After pouring some over Caid's wound, he took a good long swig. He fished in his bag and brought out several sterilized instruments sealed in glassine paper.

"Can I help now?" Reena asked faintly.

Pausing, the doctor looked at her. "You're white as a sheet, child. Go outside. I'll call you when I'm through, and you can help then."

Reena escaped to the parlor, where she paced back and forth as the train thundered along, swaying on the tracks.

Finally the doctor came out, wiping his hands on a towel. "I was able to get the bullet out and he's resting. He lost a lot of blood and he's not going to feel too good for a few days. But he's a strong young man and he'll be on his feet in no time."

Reena jumped up. "Can I see him now?"

"Sure." He shrugged into his jacket. "I want to compliment you, young woman. You kept your head about you when you saw this man shot. I'm going to write a letter to Mr. Lowry and tell him what a fine young woman he had working on this train." His bag in his hand, he headed for the railcar's forward door. You might want to stay with him tonight, in case he wakes up and needs something."

"Oh, yes. I will."

A glance out the window showed the sun had gone down, so she lit the oil lamp that swung on the wall beside the bed, and turned it down low. She didn't need enough light to read, just enough to keep an eye on Caid. She pulled a chair over to the side of the bed and curled up in it.

The white bandage covering his left shoulder and upper arm contrasted sharply with his bronzed body. Even though he was unconscious, his broad shoulders radiated strength and power. And there was nothing soft about his face, only hard lines and angles and hollows.

Reena drew a shaking breath. Her brother had tried to murder him. She could understand a running battle; at least there Caid and her brothers would be evenly matched.

But Jeff had walked over to a wounded, helpless man and cold-bloodedly lifted his revolver to murder him.

She shuddered. She'd never forget the look of hatred in Jeff's eyes.

Directed at the man she loved.

Chapter 20

Caid fought the nightmare and the demons who screamed at him. *Her name is Rowena. She's a Simpson. Everything she's told you has been a lie. A lie. A lie. . . .*

"No, it can't be," he shouted, but it didn't silence them. He tried to throw something at them but his arm wouldn't move.

"Sssh. It's all right, Caid," a familiar feminine voice said. Cool hands brushed his forehead.

He awoke with a convulsive jerk. Opening his eyes, he gazed up at Reena, bending over him. His nightmare hadn't ended.

"Are you thirsty? Would you like a drink?"

"Yeah." He struggled to sit up.

"Wait. I'll help you." She put the glass down on the bedside table and reached out to him.

"Get away from me." He batted her hands away.

"I can sit up just fine." His shoulder hurt like hell, and if he'd been alone he would have groaned—but not with her standing there. Since a little movement hurt as much as a big one, he did it all at once, with grinding determination.

"You lied to me. Everything you said to me was a damn lie, wasn't it, Rowena Simpson? Talk about sleeping with the enemy!" Leaning back against the headboard, he thought about picking up the glass from the table, but it seemed like too much effort. He'd just wait until she left.

"I can explain."

"I'm sure you can. You can explain anything, can't you?" He looked around. "Where the hell am I?"

"You're in the bedroom of the *Senator Dundee* railcar."

"Ah, shit!" He turned away and stared at the blackness beyond the windows. What was wrong with him? He rarely cursed, yet here he was, cursing in every sentence.

He raked his fingers over the rough cotton threads of the sheet, remembering the nights they'd had in the cabin. Damnation, they had made love in her brothers' hideout.

He'd almost told her he needed her, then. But he had stopped himself, afraid to say the word. He'd never needed anyone.

Now he was glad he hadn't said it, hadn't made a fool of himself. What would the Simpson brothers have done if they'd ever found out their little sister had seduced him? Hell, they probably *did* know.

But it was his own damn fault, he thought, unable to put all the blame on her. He'd been around the block a few times, had fended off other attempts at seduction. This time he'd wanted her—wanted her badly.

At least he hadn't fallen in love with her. For that, he was endlessly grateful.

"You should go on the stage, *Rowena*," he sneered. "You're undoubtedly the finest actress I've ever seen. You'd be the toast of Europe and America." She didn't look up, just picked at a piece of lint on her bloodied white apron. "You'd make millions for the Second Confederacy—a lot more than those damn fools who held up the train."

She looked at him with such a stricken expression that he felt a twinge of guilt for hurting her. Then he reminded himself she was a fine actress. A splendid actress. And he hadn't been acting.

"You lied to me, too, Caid Dundee. You lied to me from the first day you got off the train and told me you were a businessman. You lied to me with your first words and you kept on lying to me every minute of every day. So don't you get up on your high-and-mighty horse, Mr. Government Agent."

She was right, but he'd never admit it. "I had to—I was fighting for what I believe in."

"So was I!"

"Don't tell me you believe that garbage that the Confederacy will rise again. It won't!"

"How do *you* know what will and won't happen?"

"Waddell Simpson is a fanatical old man who

can't see what's in front of his face. He lives in the past, not today—certainly not tomorrow."

"My father is *not* a fanatic! He's stayed true to his principles his whole life. He doesn't change like a will-o'-the-wisp, going this way one year and that way the next year."

"You've got that right: he doesn't change. But while he hasn't changed, the world has. He's still living in 1864, pretending the Confederacy wasn't defeated. Well, it was, and no amount of pretending will bring it back.

"And your brothers are as much fanatics as he is. I'm fighting for what I believe in, *Rowena*. And that means that if I have to put your whole family in prison, I will."

She stood up and gazed down at him. "I guess we both know where we stand, don't we?" She walked out.

"Damn it, don't you run away," he roared. He'd never been so angry in his life. How could she have deceived him so? "Stay here and fight! Fight, damn you!"

When Rowena returned, she threw a sandwich down in his lap and plopped a glass of milk down on the nightstand so hard it was a wonder it didn't break.

He opened the bread up. It was filled with thick slices of ham and Swiss cheese. "How do I know it isn't poisoned?"

"Eat it. If you're still alive in the morning, you'll know it wasn't." She walked out, slamming the door so hard he would have bet the engineer heard it four cars ahead.

Caid turned back to the window and its view of unending darkness. It was nothing compared to the darkness inside him. There was a heaviness in his heart as if something had died. He put the sandwich on the nightstand, not at all hungry.

He hurt. Damn it, he hurt!

The train went through several towns during the night. He would see streetlights or yellow lamplight in a window as they whizzed by, then all would be darkness again.

And through the long hours, again and again he went over how close he'd come to getting the Simpsons. He'd come so close to wounding one of them. And with one wounded, his twin would have stopped to find care for him. That would have stopped them, at least for a few days—and given him a chance to catch them.

Damn, he'd come so close. If Reena hadn't knocked the gun out of his hand. . . .

But what did he expect? They were her brothers.

Finally the sky lightened to dawn, then sunrise.

Reena came in soon afterward. She looked all rumpled, as if she'd slept in a chair. Her hair had come loose and curled over her shoulders in tousled disarray that made him want to comb his fingers through it. Damn his fingers.

She saw the sandwich still sitting on the nightstand, and her eyes rose to his. "You really think I'd poison you?"

"Of course not. I just decided I wasn't hungry."

Her eyes were red-rimmed, as if she'd been crying.

She turned around at a knock at the door. "Yes?"

"It's Doctor Rawlins."

"Oh, come in, please, Doctor." She hurried to the door, all warm smiles.

"How's my patient this morning?" he boomed, looking past her to Caid.

"Recovering." Reena followed him back to the bed.

"How are you feeling this morning, Mr. Dundee?" Dr. Rawlins sat on the edge of the bed and opened his bag.

"Fine. I'll get dressed as soon as you leave."

"The hell you will!" Reena snapped.

Rawlins looked over his shoulder at her, then back to Caid. "In this case, I'm afraid Miss Sims is quite right."

"It's only a scratch. Doesn't even hurt," he added, lying through his teeth.

"You lost quite a bit of blood yesterday. Give yourself a chance to recover." He started to pull the sheet down, then paused and looked at Reena, hovering just behind him. "Miss Sims, would you like to wait in the parlor while I examine my patient?"

"Whatever you'd like, Doctor. Can I get you some coffee?"

"Do you have hot coffee?"

"I made a pot earlier this morning."

"I'd love some. With sugar and milk, if you have it."

"Coming right up." She left without asking Caid if he wanted any.

Doctor Rawlins tossed back the sheet and began to check Caid's bandage. "Let me know if I hurt you anywhere, Mr. Dundee." He probed Caid's shoulder and arm carefully, checking to see how much movement he had.

Reena slipped in, put the doctor's coffee on the nightstand, and left again.

"Appears you two are having a lover's spat," the doctor said conversationally.

"It's more than that, I'm afraid."

"Too bad. She's quite a woman." He covered Caid with the sheet again. "You'll be fine in a few days, but stay in bed for at least three or four. Otherwise, you could have a relapse." He closed his bag and stood up. "She was very worried about you yesterday. That's why she sat up with you. Doesn't look like she got any sleep at all, does she? Well, good day to you, Mr. Dundee."

"Leave the door open, please, Doctor." Caid could hear Reena and the doctor talking, but he couldn't make out what they were saying. Then he heard the forward door close and knew the doctor had left.

"Rowena, would you come in here, please?" he called.

"Yes?" She leaned in the doorway, her arms crossed over her bosom.

"You were right. I am stuck in bed for a couple of days." Hell, he already felt dizzy from the short time he'd been up.

"So?" She looked as if ice wouldn't melt in her mouth.

"I'd like to propose a truce—at least until I'm back on my feet. My father will be meeting me today and returning to Lost Gold with me. Since I'm in no shape to go collect him from his hotel, I want you to."

"Why should I agree to this truce? What do I get out of it?" She left the doorway and sat in the chair beside his bed, then crossed her arms over her chest again.

He eyed her, wondering if she'd realized the full consequences of her actions in working for the Cause. "You won't go to prison for treason."

She paled visibly and he knew he'd been right: she hadn't ever considered the consequences.

Reena blinked several times, as if he'd slapped her. "You're bluffing."

"Try me," he growled. "I know that you're as much a renegade as your brothers, Rowena Simpson."

"You don't have anything on me."

"Oh? I know you've passed information to your brothers—who are also engaged in treason, by the way. I know you've been recruiting for the Confederate Army. And I saw you slip money to Jim Spekes." He was bluffing about that, but she didn't know it.

"I don't know any Jim Spekes."

"Yes, you do. He's the train conductor you gave money to in the Lost Gold station. Didn't you notice he wasn't on this run? That's because he's already in jail."

"A bribe isn't treason," she blustered.

"It's the purpose for which you gave him the money that makes it treason," he said, taking a stab in the dark.

"You would do that?" Numbness filled Reena's mind. She was so shocked, she couldn't think. She kept her back straight and her shoulders square, but inside, she felt utterly alone and betrayed. The man she loved was threatening her with prison.

"What do you expect?"

She swallowed around the mountain in her throat and took a deep breath. "If I get your father—then what? I drop him off at your railcar?"

"No. You'll ride back to Lost Gold with us and act as a hostess and guide, pointing out the sights as we pass them. He's never been out West before."

"Does this truce mean I have to sleep with you?" Some of the numbness was wearing off—and being replaced by an anger unlike any she'd ever felt.

"Hell, no! I've never had to blackmail any woman into my bed. I'm not about to start now."

She stood up. "In that case, I accept your truce."

"I thought you would. You're a smart lady." He watched her walk to the door. "Is there any of that coffee left that you offered the doctor?"

Reena paused in the doorway and glanced back at him. "Yes, there is. And you can get it yourself."

That afternoon Reena stepped down from the railcar and watched as the brakeman uncoupled it from the train and shunted it onto a siding. Then she walked through the dry dust of Colorado to the small, two-story hotel at Adobe Wells.

"I'm looking for Senator Dundee," she said to the desk clerk.

"That's him."

He pointed at a ruddy-faced, very well-fed man in a gray suit who was talking to another man. The senator waved a fat, acrid-smelling cigar around as he gestured expansively. His open jacket revealed a red brocade vest that strained to cover his stomach and made him look like a rooster getting ready to crow.

"Senator Dundee?" She walked up to his side.

He took his time turning and looking down his nose at her. "Yes?"

She lifted her chin, very obviously, so there would be no mistake what she was doing, and looked down her nose at him. "I'm Reena Sims. Your son asked me to get you and bring you to the railcar," she said coolly.

"Why couldn't the boy come himself? Always was like that—unreliable as hell." He flicked ashes off his cigar onto the floor. "Always flitting from town to town. Never settled down, and—"

"Caid's been hurt," she broke in angrily. "The doctor has ordered him to stay in bed."

"What happened? Did he fall out a whorehouse window?"

"No, Senator, he did not," she snapped. "He was coming to meet you when the train was held up. He foiled the holdup, but he got shot for his trouble."

Senator Dundee's eyes widened and he stared at her for several moments. Then he turned away and fished in his pockets until he came up with a handkerchief. He blew his nose, put his handkerchief away, and fumbled for the handle on his valise as if he couldn't see it clearly.

The senator picked up his valise and turned to her. "Where is he now?"

"In your railcar." She walked out the hotel doors and let them swing shut in his face.

He banged the doors open with his valise. "My son? Foiled a holdup?"

"Yes. He did." And if he had known anything about Caid, he wouldn't have been so amazed.

"Well, well." He took a deep puff on his cigar. "Will wonders never cease?"

"The car is over here on a siding, Senator," she said, striding off without looking back to see if he was coming. "It'll be added to the next westbound train, which should be along tomorrow or the next day." She stopped at the base of the steps. "I need to go back to the station and get a newspaper. I'm sure you and Caid have a thousand things to talk about."

"Hardly, young lady. He doesn't like politics."

"Maybe you should talk about what he's interested in, then." She turned away without a backward glance.

Later Reena walked back to the railcar slowly, reading the newspaper, in no hurry to hear more from Caid's father. When she finally entered it, she didn't hear any voices. She peeked into Caid's room. His father sat stiffly, his back not touching the back of the chair. Caid sat up in bed, his arms crossed over his chest. And neither was speaking.

"Come in, Reena," Caid said, spotting her. "Join us."

There was a definite note of desperation in Caid's tone. *Serves him right*, she thought "I'd rather not."

"Yes, please, do come in, Miss Sims." Caid's father turned in the chair and he looked equally as desperate, with his gray hair standing up in all directions as if he'd been raking his hand through it. "It seems Caid doesn't remember what happened when he was shot. Perhaps you do."

Her eyes met Caid's. "Caid was shot because he was pulling me out of the line of fire, Senator. Although he managed to squeeze off a shot, he was more concerned about my safety."

"Oh."

"And later, when the outlaw was going to finish me off, Reena knocked his gun away," Caid added, looking at her.

"I didn't know you remembered that." Did he also remember that she'd knocked the gun out of his hand when he'd tried to shoot her brother?

"How did you happen to be there, Miss Sims?"

"She'd seen an outlaw holding a gun on me through the door of the baggage car and barged in, giving me a chance to try to get his gun away," Caid supplied, his gaze still on her.

"I'm a waitress in the Lowry Hotel in Lost Gold, Senator, and I happened to be on the train, selling sandwiches." And trying to prevent a confrontation between the man she loved and her brothers.

"My son should thank his lucky stars that you were there." Senator Dundee turned back to his son. "And I'm sure you're tired. I'll give you a chance to rest." He popped out of his chair like a jack-in-the-box.

After he'd gone into the parlor, Reena opened up the newspaper and showed it to Caid. "Do you know about this?" she asked, holding up the paper so he could see the front page and read the headline: SENATOR DUNDEE TO ARIZONA INSTEAD OF PRESIDENT.

He groaned. "That man can't do anything quietly. He thinks every bit of publicity gets him votes."

"Do you think he gave the newspaper the story?"

"Of course. Here, let me read the rest of it." He scanned the rest of the article. "He tells what train he'll be on, where he'll be staying in Lost Gold, and when and where he's giving his speech." He shook his head. "Your brothers are going to try to take him hostage and hold him for ransom."

"No, they're not. They've never mentioned that possiblity to me. Why, they've never even thought of such a thing."

"They will when they read his itinerary. He's practically shouting, 'Come and get me, Rebs.' Especially considering they didn't get any gold from their train robbery."

"What were those gray bars in the strongboxes?"

"It was lead. It was heavy enough to fool everyone into thinking the strongboxes were full of gold." He exhaled deeply and dragged a hand through his hair, rumpling it like his father's.

"Damn it, Reena why didn't you tell me who you were?" His eyes were hooded and she couldn't tell what he was thinking.

"How could I? What was I going to say? 'By the way, Caid, I'm spying for the Cause and my brothers, and I'm a Simpson?' You made it clear what you thought of all the Simpsons."

"Not all of them. I never said anything against you, Rowena."

Leaning forward in the chair, she eyed him curiously. "No, you didn't. Why is that?"

He looked out the window, at the rugged snow covered peaks of Colorado. "Because I remembered what a sweet child you'd been."

"How could—?"

"My family spent the war on the plantation next to yours."

"What?" She fairly flew out of her chair to stand over him. "Look at me, damn you, Caid Dundee."

He did.

"Oh, my God," she whispered, falling back into her chair. Her eyes grew round. "You're the dark-haired boy."

"What?" He slanted a suspicious look at her. "What are you talking about?"

"When I was little, there was a dark-haired boy who was around only during holidays. He lived on the next plantation, and his mother always smelled of cinnamon and ginger. My mother's health was

already failing, and the dark-haired boy's mother—
your mother—would sometimes rock me to sleep."

"How can you remember that?"

"She always smelled wonderful," she said simply. "I used to love to go to sleep in her arms. She'd
tell me fairy tales about her son, who was so smart
and off at military school. And sometimes she
would cry, when she didn't know I was awake. I
think she wanted you at home."

His features went stiff and distant. "You're imag-
ining things."

"I am not. She used to sing me to sleep with
'Swing Low, Sweet Chariot.' What did she sing you
to sleep with?"

"I don't remember."

"Yes, you do. I can see it in your eyes. You gave
me a gingerbread cookie one Christmas. Do you
remember? I didn't eat it. I treasured it and put it
on my dresser, and every morning I would check
to see that it was still there. Then one morning it
was gone. Robby Lee had eaten it." She smiled,
looking back across the years. "It was a long time
before I forgave him.

"We'd see your mother often, but you appeared
only during the holidays. I didn't know your name,
so I called you the dark-haired boy."

"I'm surprised you remember me at all."

She pulled out the thin gold chain she wore
around her throat. Taking it off over her head, she
showed him the child's ring on the chain. "Do you
remember this? You gave it to me."

"And you kept it? Why?"

She shrugged. "I don't know." She wasn't about to admit that she'd hero-worshiped him.

He looked at it for the longest time. Then he reached over and touched the ring with his square-tipped finger. It was still warm from her body. Her body, which he'd adored and worshiped and loved.

He straightened, pushing away the memories. Memories that pulled him back to those days in the cabin. Memories that tugged at his heart.

Memories.

Chapter 21

❧

"**C**aid, your father and I are going to dinner at the hotel." Reena leaned in the doorway to his room. "We'll bring some dinner back for you."

"Enjoy your dinner, then." The look she gave him told him she was looking forward to dinner with his father about as much as he would have.

As soon as they were gone, he threw back the covers, sat up, and swung his legs over the edge. The doctor was being overcautious. He needed to walk around. He'd get his strength back more quickly that way.

Damn! He hated being weak and needing help from anyone. To have to ask Reena for help rankled even more.

He couldn't call her Rowena in his mind, he realized. Reena was the woman he had made love to.

Reena was the woman who fascinated him, with her quick mind and even quicker tongue. Reena was who—

Hell, man, get ahold of yourself and face facts. There is no Reena. There's only Rowena Simpson, who lied to you about everything.

Caid stood up and the room swayed as if the railcar was moving. He grabbed the bedpost until the room stopped moving, then set out for the parlor, determined to rebuild his strength.

He turned back at the door and slumped down on the bed, exhausted by those few steps. Maybe the doc was right, after all. Yawning, he pulled the covers up and closed his eyes.

"Caid, here's your dinner." Reena banged through the doorway with the tray and waited while Caid sat up.

"I was just resting my eyes," he explained, as she set the tray on his lap and whipped the metal cover off the plate, revealing roast beef with roasted potatoes and corn. "Where's my father?" he asked, as he cut his beef. With one arm bandaged, he was awkward and slow.

"He stopped at the telegraph office to send off a stack of messages for various people."

He finally cut a piece of meat free. "How did your dinner go?"

"Quite well, actually. Your father was very interesting and told funny stories about working in Washington."

"My father?"

"He's very well read, too, and can quote the ancient Greeks and Romans at the drop of a hat. Here, let me cut that meat before you massacre it." Leaning forward in her chair, she took the knife and fork from him, trying to ignore his square hands and the long fingers that would never touch her with a lover's touch again.

He exhaled slowly and his breath stirred a tendril of hair that curled over her ear, tickling her. She shook her head, trying to move the curl. It didn't work.

"Let me." Caid lifted the curl and tucked it safely behind her ear.

"Thanks," she said, looking up. She'd meant to be casual, but they were too close and she could see the bits of gray in his blue eyes and that tiny scar that snaked across his eyebrow and his lips—the lips that had kissed her with such passion.

Reena sat back. "There you go." She nodded at the cut up beef.

He didn't say anything, just looked at her for the longest time.

"I haven't thanked you for knocking that revolver out of your brother's hand in the baggage car."

"It was nothing."

"I didn't think so, Reena." He picked up the fork and began to eat.

By the time he finished, the senator had returned. Reena brought out a deck of cards and dealt them out, thinking they could talk to each other while playing.

A half hour later she threw down her cards and stood up. "Getting you two to talk to each other is as much a lost cause as the Confederacy."

"I *am* rather tired." Senator Dundee braced his hands on the chair and pushed himself up. "It's been a long day. I'll see you in the morning, Caid. Good night, Miss Sims."

Reena waited until he'd closed the door behind him, before she spoke. "I notice you haven't told him who I am. Why?"

Caid shrugged. "Why should I? You can tell him whatever you want."

She spun out of the chair and began to pace. "Are you going to hold it over my head, like a club?"

"I hadn't thought of it, but maybe I should."

"I can't believe you," she said, shaking her head.

"And I can't believe you, can I?"

"This isn't getting us anyplace. I'm going to bed. Good night."

"Wait. Are you planning to sleep in a chair tonight again?"

"I was very comfortable on the couch in the parlor."

"Not as comfortable as you would be stretched out in the bed."

She shot him a look of utter disbelief. Too much had happened. Especially since he'd threatened her with jail.

"I was just thinking of your comfort. With this snow, it's going to get colder during the night."

"You forget that the couch faces the wood stove. I'll stay a lot warmer there."

She piled two blankets on the couch, then slipped beneath them. That would keep her cozy. But by the middle of the night, the cold had penetrated them and awakened her. She lay there, shivering and telling herself to get up and put wood in the stove.

Then someone covered her with another heavy blanket and tucked it in around her shoulders. "Senator?"

"You know it isn't." Caid put more wood in the stove then padded back to his bed.

She stretched luxuriously under the covers, feeling cozy and warm.

Two mornings later they were on the way back to Lost Gold. It was a glowering gray day with occasional light snow. Just enough to make the tracks slippery and the engineer cautious.

Caid dressed. "I'm going forward to talk to the engineer, Reena," he said, as he finished buttoning his shirt.

"Don't overestimate your strength. Just because you were walking around yesterday doesn't mean you're well."

"I'll be fine. Put a fresh pot of coffee on the wood stove. I'll be back before it's gone." Opening the platform door, he walked forward to the next car.

Once he was gone, she began to pace, worried that she shouldn't be letting him be so active. "Sure, Reena, and you're going to throw him over your shoulder and hogtie him," she murmured.

"You can't do anything about it anyway, Miss

Sims." Senator Dundee looked up from the desk where he had been working on his speech. "I've never seen a stubborner, more headstrong child than Caid."

"He's not a child, Senator. It has been many, many years since he was a child—if he ever was one, which I doubt."

The senator leaned back in his chair and thoughtfully studied the pine trees passing the window. "You may be—"

Suddenly, they were both thrown forward as the train slowed violently and the ride became frighteningly rough. It was unlike anything Reena had ever felt, and she looked anxiously at the senator.

"Hang on," he yelled, as he was thrown out of his chair. "We've gone off the tracks."

She held on tight to the arms of her armchair as it bumped and bounced across the suddenly tilted parlor and came to rest against the wall beneath a window.

Outside, the screech of tearing metal mixed with the sound of splintering wood in a deafening cacophony. The railcar tilted more. Then more.

Reena froze, too afraid to scream, afraid the railcar was going to turn over. Then suddenly it fell back, hard, to almost level again.

Simultaneously a tremendous explosion rattled the windows. Then all was silent, except for the hiss of escaping steam.

She heard a low sound, like the wind soughing through the trees. Slowly she realized it was someone moaning. Then a woman screamed. She looked at the senator for one horrified, paralyzed second, then they both lunged for the outside door and rushed down the steps to the track bed where they could see the rest of the train.

The two passenger cars ahead of them were upright, although they had left the tracks and were tilted. But the lead passenger car was partially on top of the baggage car.

Caid! He'd gone up front to speak to the engineer! Reena raced along beside the tracks, slipping and falling in the gravel as she ran. Beyond the baggage car, she saw a huge tree had fallen across the tracks. But the steam engine was gone!

The tender lay on its side beside the track, but the engine was gone. *Gone!* How?

Stepping over the ice-crusted rails carefully, she passed the tender and saw the engine. It had tumbled down the slope and fallen into a stream. That had been the explosion she'd heard—the cold mountain water hitting the steam boiler.

And Caid? Her heart drumming against her ribs, she skidded down the slope and cautiously approached the tangled wreckage of the engine. The bitter taste of fear filled her mouth. She was afraid to look for him. She was afraid not to.

"Oh God, let him be safe," she prayed over and over. "Please, let him be safe. Please. Please. Please."

Caid sat up slowly and shook his head. The last thing he remembered was the engineer shouting about a tree on the tracks and yelling at him to jump.

Bracing his hand on a rock, he looked around. He lay a few feet below the railroad tracks on the snowy slope. The train—Reena!

He scrambled up to the track and sucked in his breath at the sight of the first passenger car piled on top of the baggage car. He ran toward the private railcar, grateful it was still upright.

Reena! He had to find her!

He pounded up the steps into the railcar, but it was empty. He raced along the tracks beside the other cars, calling her name and scanning the survivors who were already standing outside.

Then he skidded to a halt, staring at the tangled wreckage of the first passenger car and the baggage car.

What if she'd come forward after him? What if she was in that snarled mass of metal and wood? He spotted the engineer using a crowbar to pry open the wreckage.

"Have you found someone?" Bending over, he braced his hands on his knees and breathed deeply, trying to get his breath back.

"Yeah. All I can see is a bit of black cloth. See, there?" He pointed.

Reena's black dress!

"Let me," he said, grabbing the crowbar. "Go see if you can find more tools to work with." He grunted as he strained to enlarge the space in the wreckage.

The engineer returned with more crowbars. The

two of them worked feverishly, enlarging the hole in the wreckage until Caid could reach in. As soon as he touched the lifeless body, he knew it was hopeless. Then he realized it was a man. Wild relief washed over him, followed by the realization that she was still lost somewhere in that tangled wreckage.

"He's dead," Caid said, standing up. "Did you"—He had to swallow twice to wet his mouth, parched with fear—"See a young, blond-haired woman in a black dress?"

"No. I haven't seen anyone like that," the engineer replied. "But I'll keep an eye out for her."

Caid looked up at the passenger car above them, partially resting on the crushed baggage car. "Let's get up there and move the survivors out of the wreckage." He glanced at the glowering gray sky. "It's beginning to snow again; we'll have to work fast. Let's work from the other side. The access should be better."

"Let her be all right, please, God," he prayed, as he and the engineer scrambled over the tipped tender and around to the other side. He saw the engine then, and shook his head at the destruction. The engineer had known what he was doing when he told Caid to jump.

Caid walked close to the crushed baggage car, listening for cries or moans, but all he heard was the screech of metal on metal as the wreckage settled and shifted.

"Hey, buddy." A burly man leaned out a shattered window. "We need some help up here."

The passenger car door was blocked by a snarled tangle of seats and luggage, and Caid had to crawl past it to reach the place where the other man was working to free a gray-haired man. Caid braced his feet and helped crowbar the tangled metal up.

"Keep that wreckage levered up while I lift him out." Caid grunted as he slipped his arms around the man's chest from behind and pulled up. Slowly, slowly, the man came free.

"Thanks," the man said, looking up at him.

"We'll have you out of here in no time." Caid smashed the remaining glass out of a broken window, then slipped through it and dropped to the ground. Turning, he reached up as the burly man slid the gray-haired man out to him.

Caid hoisted him over both shoulders in a fireman's carry away from the wreckage, and he laid him down in the gravel at the edge of the rail bed.

A sharp pain shot through him. Another passenger was safe, but where was Reena?

As he turned to climb back into the wrecked car and search it, someone hit his chest going full speed.

"Caid! You're alive!" Reena threw her arms around him and hugged him tightly. "You're all right! I was so worried when I couldn't find you." Tears filled her eyes. "I thought you were dead. I thought you were blown up with the boiler!" She buried her face against his chest and her shoulders shook with deep, soundless sobs.

Caid uttered a silent prayer of thanks that she was safe. "How did you get all these scratches?"

he asked, brushing her hair off her face.

"I climbed down to the wrecked locomotive. You weren't with any of the survivors, and you'd told me you were going to talk to the engineer." She brushed tears off her wet cheeks. "I-I was so frightened. I don't know what I would have done if—"

He wiped the tears from her cheeks with his thumbs. "You're all right, and so am I. Now we need to help people who aren't."

"You're right." She stood on tiptoe and brushed his lips with hers. "Let's go. But how are we going to get word to the railroad that we need help?"

"I'm going to shinny up one of those telegraph poles and send them a message right now."

Reena watched him for a moment, then turned to help the wounded. Caid climbed back into the wrecked car to look for more survivors.

People were milling around, some dazed, some helping, as Caid and the burly man passed passengers out the windows of the wrecked car. A few complained about the delay in their travel. A young toddler leaned against his mother and wailed.

It was beginning to snow harder. Reena set one young man to gathering all the blankets he could find, then made sure that the women and children were well wrapped up against the cold.

Caid crawled out of the wrecked car with the last survivor and called everyone together. "I've sent a message, and a rescue train is on the way. It could take a while to get here, though, and it's getting colder. I see Miss Sims has already started passing out blankets. I want the women and children to go back into the private car at the end of the train. None of the windows are broken in that car, so it will stay warmer. The men can gather in the back end of the third passenger car with any leftover blankets. That's the least damaged of the passenger cars. Does anyone have any questions?"

There were none, and he turned to Reena. "You go with the women and see that everything is running smoothly. We could be here overnight and it's going to get pretty damn cold."

"Caid?" How did she tell him how proud she was of him?

"Yes?" His voice was clipped with strain.

This was not the time. "How's your arm?"

"Fine." He glanced around. "Have you seen my father?"

She gasped. "I forgot about him."

"So did I." He gave her a rueful smile. "Which he will probably never let me forget."

"Let's go look for him together."

When they found him, he was sitting on the ground playing cards with two young boys while a toddler tried to climb up his back.

"Senator? Are you all right? Any injuries?" For the first time, he realized his father was beginning to show his age. Only a few strands of black remained in his white hair, and his shoulders were beginning to look a little stooped.

"I'm fine, except that I keep losing to these young scalawags." He looked up at Reena and winked. "I do believe they're cardsharps."

The boys guffawed and punched each other in

the shoulder. "We'll take you for all you got, Tom."

"Do you believe this?" Reena murmured. "I think he's enjoying himself."

Caid nodded. "It's getting cold out here," he said to the card players, "Why don't you take this game back to the last car? It'll be a lot warmer there."

Senator Dundee looked up from dealing. "You said women and children in there. I don't think I qualify."

"Suit yourself. But that toddler climbing on your back needs to be indoors. The boys, too."

"Mr. Dundee, Mr. Dundee!" The engineer ran up to them. "I think there's a message coming through for you, sir."

After Caid hurried away, Reena turned back to the Senator. "Are you really all right?"

"Yes." He arranged the cards in his hand, then looked up at her. "And you were quite right, Miss Sims. He's a man—one that I'm very proud to know."

Reena didn't know what to say, so she just bobbed her head. "I'm going back to your railcar, Senator. Want me to take that little boy off your back?"

He nodded. "Oh, and Reena? Try to bring me some cigars if you come back this way."

Reena kept the wood stove going through the night, so the children and women filling the parlor were warm. In between feeding the stove, she wrapped up in a blanket and curled up in a chair.

Caid had been searching for her. Maybe he *did*

feel something for her. He'd hugged her tightly when she'd finally found him and flew into his arms.

Could they ever have a future together? After all, she'd carried him in her heart all these years. Surely fate wouldn't be so cruel as to let her find him, only to lose him again. They *had* to have a destiny together.

The next morning, she went looking for Caid at first light. She found him examining the tree that had fallen across the track.

"What is it?" she asked, noticing his frown.

"This tree didn't fall by itself."

"What do you mean?"

"Look at the end: it's a smooth cut, from a saw. If the tree had fallen naturally, the end would be splintered and jagged."

"Someone did that on purpose? Put the lives of all those people at risk?"

"I don't think your brothers thought the train would derail. But they should have considered that possiblity."

"My brothers," she whispered, completely shocked. She glanced at the tree again. "I don't think they did this, Caid. I know you think I'm just sticking up for them, but this isn't like them. Really."

"Maybe not. I have to admit I'm puzzled that the tree was felled here, on the shoulder of a mountain. If someone wanted to rob the train, they'd stop it on the level, where riders on horseback could get in close, then make a quick getaway. Besides, everyone knows that westbound trains don't carry gold."

"If robbery wasn't a motive, then why?"

"That's what I've been asking myself." He turned as a smoke-breathing steam engine chugged around the curve and came into view. It sounded three long shrieks on its whistle. "Here's our rescue train. Let's go back and collect everyone."

She watched him hurry away. She was so full of pride and love for him, she thought she'd burst.

But would they ever recapture the golden moments they'd shared in the cabin? She touched her lips, remembering the touch of his lips, the feel of his hands, the power of his lovemaking.

Would she ever again lie in his arms?

Chapter 22

Caid splashed Napoleon brandy into a snifter and sprawled in the chair facing the fireplace, stretching out his long legs.

He could no longer fool himself. He loved Reena. He'd known since the train wreck. When he'd searched for her in the tangled wreckage, his heart pounding uncontrollably, he'd known. The fear he'd felt had ripped away all pretenses that his feelings were just lust. When he'd feared her dead, had thought he'd never see her sparkling eyes or animated features again, that was when it had hit him squarely between the eyes.

He loved her: the Simpson spy.

They'd had two days in a hidden cabin, but he yearned for forever with her. Forever in his bed, forever at his side, forever in his heart, forever his wife.

But they stood on opposite sides of a very high wall. He was fighting for what was right, for honor and the United States. She was fighting for a dream of misguided old men and young fanatics.

Damnation! How could he hope they might have a forever, when they didn't even have a now?

Someone knocked on his door, hard enough to rattle it. The clock on the mantel showed that it was after midnight. He slipped a small derringer into his pocket before going to the door.

When he opened it, he stiffened. "Senator, I thought you'd be asleep by now. What can I do for you?"

"It *has* been a long day. That's why I want to talk to you. How about inviting me in?"

"Certainly." Caid stepped back. "Would you like to join me in a brandy?"

"Yes. Do you have a cigar to go with it?" His father followed him to the sideboard where he kept the liquor.

"I do. And that sounds like an excellent idea." Opening the wooden humidor, he passed it to his father.

"Oh ho, Cubans. You have good taste."

"Thanks." He poured a second snifter of brandy, then followed his father over to the two armchairs which faced each other.

For a few minutes it was quiet as each followed the ritual of snipping the end off the cigar, then lighting it and taking a first puff. Finally his father leaned back in his chair and contemplated Caid.

"What did you want to talk about?" Caid asked. He rested his cigar in a large ashtray.

"I wanted to tell you that I watched you at the train wreck yesterday, and I was very impressed with your actions." He gestured with the snifter, saluting Caid, before he lifted it to his lips and took a large swallow.

"I only did what needed to be done." Was he hearing a compliment? From his father?

"Leaders are the ones who see what needs to be done and do it. Followers wait for someone to tell them what to do. Not only have you grown into a man without my even realizing it, you've grown into a man any father would be proud of."

"Thanks." He'd never seen his father in such a mood.

The senator puffed on his cigar, then busied himself studying it. "I know I didn't do much to raise you. I was always too busy with Senate business. But I wanted to tell you that I'm"—his voice broke—"I'm thankful and proud that you're my son."

Not knowing what to say, Caid took a sip of brandy. "I'm proud of the work you've done in the Senate," he finally said. He knew so little about his father.

"I'd rather you were proud of me as a father— but that's something I learned too late. And for that I'm sorry. Don't you make the same mistake, son."

"Why don't we just go forward from here?" Caid leaned forward and held out his hand. "Shake?"

"Shake." His father shook his hand vigorously.

"Well, that's all I had to talk about." He started to rise.

"Maybe I have some things I want to say."

His father had the grace to sit back and smile. "I just did it again, didn't I? Assuming that because I was done, we were done."

Caid nodded at his brandy. "Want more? You're going to be here for a while."

"Actually, I think I'd like that—us talking." He leaned back in the chair. "Fire away."

"If you've come to Arizona to make a speech, you must know that Rebs are plotting to take over the state."

His father eyed him warily. "How do you know about it?"

"I uncovered it. That's why I'm here." Caid frowned. "Didn't you realize that?"

"My God! You're in the secret service? And here, all these years I thought you were pretending to write a book while you did nothing. Why didn't I know?" He dragged his hand down his face, as if removing a blindfold. "Why didn't I see what was right in front of my face?"

"How would you know? I never told you or Mother. It doesn't matter now, anyway. Let's talk about your speech. I expect the Simpsons to try something, and I want us to be prepared."

"All right. What do you think we should do? You're the expert here, not me. I haven't worked in intelligence since the war."

Caid wasn't sure he'd heard right. "Try that

again. You were in Mr. Lincoln's intelligence service?"

"I guess it's all right to talk about it now, since your Uncle Sydney's dead. We all kept quiet all these years because he was a Southerner and he had family all over the South. If they had known he'd worked for the North during the War he would never have been accepted by any of them again."

"May and her husband were involved?"

"And your mother, too," he replied proudly. "You should have seen your mother charm men she wanted information from. They never knew what hit them."

Caid was rocked by the revelation that his parents had been spies. "It looks like we have more to talk about than I knew."

"That's why we had the plantation in South Carolina. Remember it? Next to the Simpson plantation." He took the brandy and sipped it. "That's why we sent you off to military school. It was too dangerous for you there. Your mother hated sending you away, but we wanted you in a safe place in case the Confederates found out about us."

Caid leaned back in his chair and took a deep breath. "This is very interesting. I'd like to know more about your experiences."

When he saw his father to the door hours later, he was amazed at how wrong he'd been about his father.

Could he be wrong about Reena? Was there any hope for them?

*   *   *

Reena hurried along Main Street. She'd avoided Caid since their return, and she ricocheted between sorrow and anger whenever he invaded her mind—which was all the time.

In the middle of the street, near the Ranchers' Mercantile Bank, she noticed workmen building a platform. Caid stood to the side in a flannel shirt and denims, watching. He'd hooked his thumbs over his belt and seemed relaxed, but she knew him too well to be taken in.

"Is that where your father is going to give his speech?" she shouted, over the noise of hammers banging away. The woodsy scent of fresh lumber filled the air. A lock of his coffee-black hair hung down over his forehead and she wanted to push it back.

"Yes. He'll be talking right after church services next Sunday." He didn't look at her, so after a moment she walked on.

She was going by the Wild Women Saloon when a drunk reeled through the swinging doors. He staggered right into her, his arms coming down on her shoulders as he tried to regain his balance.

"Let go of me!" She tried to push him away.

"It's me," the drunk whispered as he made a production of trying to disentangle himself from her while doing nothing of the sort. "I've got to talk to you. Meet me at the stable."

"Jeff? All right. When?"

"Unhand me, young woman," he bellowed. He staggered away, bounced off a porch post, and swung around, colliding with her. "Tonight. After you finish work."

"Get away from her," Caid growled, as he grabbed the drunk by his leather vest and pulled him away from Reena. Swinging him around, Caid walked him partway down the alley beside the saloon. "Sleep it off, cowboy," he said, as he let the drunk slide down the wall to the ground.

Reena was still standing there, too shocked to move, when he returned from the alley. "What did you do to him?"

"Found him a place where he won't bother anyone. Why?"

Reena pretended she didn't hear his question as she began to walk along. He wrapped his hand around her elbow as they stepped off the boardwalk to cross a dusty side street.

She hadn't thanked him, she realized, and she didn't want him to get suspicious. "It's a good thing you came along when you did."

"Why don't you come to my room tonight? To talk—that's all."

She turned and gently disengaged her elbow. "I don't think that's a very wise idea, Caid."

She left him standing there, and went inside Hofsteader's Mercantile. And she didn't look back, although she desperately wanted to.

It was after ten by the time she finished in the dining room that evening. Since it was nippy out, she went upstairs and got her woolen paisley shawl. Wrapping it around her head and shoulders, she slipped down the back stairs to meet her brother.

The stable was dark, and quiet. She stood in the entrance, feeling along the wall for a lantern, when she saw someone wave a light at the other end. "Jeff," she called softly. "Jeff."

"Right here, sis. By the haystack." He set the lantern down on the ground and gave her a big bear hug.

"Jeff, I've got to talk to you." She grasped his shirt front in her hands and spoke earnestly. "You've got to stop. This isn't going to work. It's all wrong."

He clasped his hands over hers. "Calm down, sis. It's almost over."

"It is?" She released his shirt. "You've realized how wrong it is? Oh, I'm so glad."

"Wrong? What are you babbling about?" Grabbing her shoulders, he shook her. "We've got enough gold, and the army is ready. We're poised to invade Arizona. All it takes is a signal from me. Rowena, listen to me. We're ready to march on Arizona."

"March? Don't you understand? There will be no Second Confederacy—ever. Its time has passed. And it's time for you to give up that dream and start to live your lives—not as soldiers working for the Cause, but as men with wives and children." She reached for his hand, but he batted her away. "Pa's wrong: thousands of people aren't waiting to revolt and join the Confederacy."

"Sure they are. That's why the government is

sending more troops into Arizona. We heard they were on that train, so we dropped the tree across the tracks to stop them."

"Do you realize how many people you could have killed when that train derailed? And it *wasn't* carrying extra troops. You should have checked your facts before you put so many people at risk!"

"Rowena, there's always bloodshed in war. And this is war."

"No! Only *you* are at war. Everyone else is at peace. You're not soldiers anymore, you're outlaws!"

"What's wrong with you? I came to tell you that you can come home to the Colony soon."

"What?"

"Your work in Lost Gold is done. You can leave."

"Really? Don't you think you should have asked me if I want to leave Lost Gold? I like it here! Do you know that people in Lost Gold talk about things besides the war? They know it ended twenty years ago. They have lives, not guerrilla missions. They're not always talking about the old days and how much better things were then."

"You're just overwrought, Rowena. It's understandable with the strain you've been under, living here among the enemy. You'll settle down when you get home."

"Jeff, haven't you heard a word I said? You're not going to take over Arizona. *It isn't going to happen.*"

He slapped her. "You're a traitor!"

Her hand covering her stinging cheek, Reena staggered back, too shocked to speak.

"No, Simpson. It's you who's the traitor." Caid's low voice came from Reena's right.

Jeff reached for his pistol.

"Touch that gun, Simpson, and you're a dead man." Tanner's voice came from her left.

Jeff kicked the lantern into the haystack beside him and ran into the darkness. Caid and Tanner followed him.

Still in shock, Reena watched as flames licked at the base of the haystack. People were running by her, shouting.

The flames were growing, lighting up Caid and Tanner as they returned with Jeff handcuffed between them.

As they passed her, Jeff looked at her. "You traitor! You led them to me."

"Jeff! I didn't!" she called after him.

Tears filled her eyes. Her own brother thought she'd led Caid to him.

Caid stopped beside her as Tanner prodded Jeff on. "Are you all right?" he asked in a low tone.

As if he cared! she thought furiously. Her sorrow boiled over into anger.

She swung at him, slapping him on the cheek hard enough to make his head snap back. "You bastard! You followed me! You used me to find him!"

He clamped his hand over her mouth, wrapped his other arm around her waist, and hustled her around the corner of the stable into the shadows.

People were running down the street toward the burning haystack, but no one noticed them in the darkness.

He held her hard against his side. Beneath his hand he could feel her heart hammering against her ribs, and with every beat his heart drummed, too. Smoke eddied around them, but all he could smell was her beloved lilac scent.

"Shut up, you little fool," he growled against her ear. "Do you want everyone in town to know you've been spying for the Simpsons? That you're one of them?"

She gave him a wild-eyed look so full of fire and hate, it slammed into him like a runaway steam engine.

She held out her fists, close together. When he didn't move, she shook them furiously, still together.

"What's that for?" he asked, lifting his hand off her mouth.

"Aren't you going to arrest me, too? Don't you want to handcuff me?"

"Are you going to run away?"

"With my brother in jail? Of course not."

"Then I don't have to arrest you yet."

He saw calm steal across her face as the implications of what he'd said registered. "What do you mean?"

"I'm trying to find a way to keep from arresting you for treason, damn it!"

"Am I supposed to believe that when you just betrayed me? How stupid do you think I am?" She paced away, her arms wrapped around her waist, then whirled to face him.

"Reena, you're right: I did use you. I didn't start out intending to do that. But I have to stop your brothers and the takeover of Arizona. I could either capture them or. . . ."

He didn't have to finish. They both knew what the alternative was.

"You know, when you were lying unconscious on the train, I was sitting there wondering if you'd ever forgive me for not telling you who I was. I guess I didn't have to worry about that, did I? Your betrayal makes my lying pale in comparison. And that's what it was, Caid—betrayal."

"Reena, please, I—"

"Don't you dare ask me to see your side of things. Don't you dare. I was a damn fool, and—" She wasn't going to admit she'd fallen in love with him. She wasn't!

Turning, she ran through the darkness into the hotel gardens. There she huddled on a secluded bench and wrapped her arms around her waist, rocking back and forth as agony knifed through her. Deep, soundless sobs sucked the breath from her lungs. But even they couldn't ease her pain.

Caid had betrayed her.

The following day was a blur for Reena. She went down to the jail to reassure herself that Jeff was all right and to talk to him, but he wouldn't believe that she hadn't purposely led Caid to him.

She walked back to the hotel in a daze. Her

world was falling apart. Her brother had turned on her, because of the man she loved. And the man she loved had betrayed her. How could she even think of loving him?

As she neared the hotel, she saw the senator and Caid on the front veranda. Reena slipped down a side street rather that meet him—and felt her heart crack a tiny bit when she did.

At least he hadn't caught Robby Lee, too.

She managed to avoid Caid during the day, but that night he and the senator were seated at one of her tables. She changed with Belle rather than serve him.

She didn't see Caid the next day except for a glimpse in the lobby. And her heart cracked a bit more when she ducked down the hall to avoid him.

On the third evening he ate in the dining room at another waitress's table. She tried not to look at him as she served dinner, but she felt his gaze on her. Twice she snapped a glance at him and found he was watching her. He didn't make any attempt to turn away or pretend he wasn't.

After the dining room closed, she slipped into the library to be alone. The gas sconces were dimmed and she turned one up. A small fire burned in the fireplace, giving off the forest scent of pinyon pine and warming the room, for which she was grateful. She'd been so cold for the last few days—ever since Caid had betrayed her.

She laid another piece of wood on the fire, and stared into it, hoping its warmth would penetrate to her bones. It didn't. Inside she was still as cold.

Maybe it was the ice in her heart, leaking into her bones.

She'd known since the cabin that she loved Caid. Maybe even before that. She'd thought she had lost him when Jeff had revealed that she was Rowena Simpson, but still hoped he would listen to her, that they could work things out. Then had come the train wreck, when she had realized how all-encompassing her love for him was.

To love him and have him betray her as he had! Every time she thought about it, the crack in her heart grew. How could he?

She didn't want to think about Jeff, so quick to call her traitor to the Cause. So unwilling to listen to her—as if, because she no longer believed as he did, that she was a traitor to the family.

Why couldn't he see that she had changed since she'd been in Lost Gold?

She walked over to the bookcase to find a story that would take her away from the aching loneliness and sadness. *Ivanhoe* had been one of her and her mother's favorites, and she picked it up. Curling up in one of the high-backed chairs in front of the fire, she opened it and began to read.

She read the first page three times before she gave up. Even though she was named after the heroine of *Ivanhoe*, the story couldn't hold her interest. Not tonight. She closed the book and gazed at the fire.

She didn't even like to be called Rowena anymore; she had come to prefer Reena. It was *her* name.

Oh God, she'd lost everything. She didn't even have a home to go home to. Not when her family said she was a traitor.

Tears of hopelessness rolled down her cheeks, because her future was empty. Empty of family. Empty of love. Empty.

Someone opened the door, and she half-rose out of the chair, but it closed quickly.

Then she heard the click of a key turning in the lock and knew someone had locked the door.

Who had locked her in?

Chapter 23

~~~ೂೂ~~~

She bounced up out of the chair, prepared to pound on the door, and halted. "You!"

"Me." Caid tucked the key into his pocket with a confident air that infuriated her.

She threw her book at him. He gave her the most surprised look as he ducked.

She was as surprised as he was, and astounded at how good it felt.

He picked the book up and smoothed out the rumpled pages before closing it. "Ivanhoe, eh? I should have known."

The way he ran his fingers over the pages, gently smoothing them, reminded her of how his hands had felt on her. As if she needed reminding!

"You knew I was here." Anger, hurt, dismay warred inside her.

"Yes."

"Why are you doing this?"

"Because I had to talk to you and you won't let me." He held the book out to her. "Want to throw it again?"

"Yes!" She grasped it and raised it to throw.

He didn't cringe or put up his arms to ward it off; he just stood there, waiting. And she saw a sadness in his eyes that equaled hers.

Dropping the book, Reena whirled and stared into the fire. "I suppose I was lucky I got to throw the book at all. I won't be able to throw anything in jail, will I?"

"What are you talking about?" His voice was carefully neutral.

"You came to arrest me, didn't you?"

"No! I—Rowena." His voice was so close she knew he stood right behind her. At least he didn't touch her. She couldn't stand being touched by him now; it would finish the job of breaking her heart in two.

"My name's not Rowena. It's Reena." Rowena had been another person, a person who'd faded away as Reena had grown and learned from the people of Lost Gold.

There was a distinct silence, as though he were digesting that information.

" I want you to know that I heard what you said about the Confederacy when you were talking to your brother. I know that you don't believe in it or the Cause. I know that you've come around to my way of thinking."

She whirled, eyes blazing. "I've come around to your way of thinking? Lies and betrayal! That's your way of thinking, Caid Dundee, and I want no part of it. You used me! Was capturing my brother worth betraying me?"

He looked past her into the fire for a long time. Was justice worth losing her?

The President depended on him, trusted him to stop the Simpsons and their plot to take over Arizona. He had one Simpson in jail; soon he'd have the other.

Was it worth losing her?

"Reena, you know that robbing banks and trains for gold is wrong. Do you think I shouldn't bring them to justice, just because they're your brothers?"

"That's not what I said."

"Then what *are* you saying?" Was there any hope for them, any chance at all?

"Are you proud of using me to capture my brother?"

"Of course not." He could answer that question truthfully, at least.

"Would you do it again, if you had it to do all over?"

All he had to do was say no, say he'd been wrong. "I—" He couldn't say it, he realized with astonishment. He cleared his throat. "I—" He'd taken an oath to protect and defend the United States. He'd given his word. "When I first met you, I wanted to get to know you because I suspected you were spying for the Confederacy. But as I came to know you, to know your spirit and courage and generosity and quick tongue, I became fascinated by you. You're worth ten of them, Reena."

"If I'm worth ten of them, I'll stay and you can let my brother go."

"You know I can't do that, " he said hoarsely.

"I guess you've given me your answer, then."

"Reena." He touched her for the first time, resting his hand on her shoulder. "I don't want to lose you." He rested his forehead against the back of her head and inhaled her lilac-and-spice scent. "I've sworn my allegiance, given my word to the President. If I violate that trust, then I'm just as much a traitor as they are."

He felt her draw a shaky breath. She shook her head, stepped forward, away from his touch, and turned and held out her hand. "I'll take that key now."

He gazed down at her small white hand. If he gave her the key, she would walk out of his life. How could he give up the woman he loved? Yet as much as he wanted her, he couldn't betray his country and everything he'd worked for all his life.

He reached into his pocket for the key, knowing that it was the end of his hopes.

He'd found the woman he loved—the woman he'd love for all the days of his life.

But she would never be his.

He held out the key. He heard her tiny sob, so quickly swallowed, and realized she also knew it was the end.

He watched her walk out the door, out of his life.

"I love you," he whispered as the door shut. "I'll always love you."

"Caid, how long has it been since you slept? You look like hell," Tanner said, at breakfast.

"I don't know. Why?" Caid moved a piece of fried egg around on his plate, but didn't eat it. "I'm fine."

"Then you've suddenly gone stupid—and I don't think that's the case." Tanner stirred his coffee.

Caid chewed a piece of tasteless bacon. All right, he hadn't been sleeping well. But he couldn't let his personal feelings interfere with his job. He just hadn't expected the black, raging emptiness when he lost her.

"Tanner's right, Caid. You don't look good," Senator Dundee added.

He threw down his napkin and stood up. "Can't you two let a man eat in peace?" Grabbing his hat off the rack by the door, he stalked out into the lobby.

He would check on Sheriff Huddle, see if he had all his men in position. He glanced at the clock on the wall. His father's speech would be ending in about three hours—if everything went as planned. And that was a big if.

Reena walked in the front door as he approached it.

He stopped.

She stopped.

He nodded at her.

She lifted her chin in that endearing way she had, that made him want to sweep her up in his arms. Her eyes met his, and shards of ice knifed into him.

Grasping her skirt and swinging it so she wouldn't touch him, she swept around him.

He paused on the veranda to slam his hat on his head and stalked down Main Street, studying everything as he went. It was a frosty fall day, so people were wearing coats and jackets. He didn't like that. They could stand around the platform where his father gave his speech and hide too much under those coats and jackets.

"Come on, Reena, don't you want to hear what the senator is going to say?" Belle leaned on the counter in the butler's pantry, tapping her foot.

"No." Not if she might meet his son there. "Besides, I'm not done cleaning up my tables from breakfast yet." Reaching into a drawer, she took out a handful of fresh silverware.

"You *are* done." Belle took the silverware out of her hand and put it back. "Reena, you can't spend your life avoiding Caid."

"Yes, I can." Even thinking about him hurt so much. They'd come so close. Every beat of her heart echoed with the message. So very close. She turned away to look in the glass cabinet doors and pretended to fix her hair.

"I mean it, Reena. You are coming with me." Belle grabbed her wrist and tugged her toward the door. "Come on. Do we need to go back upstairs to get your coat?"

"No. It's in the cloakroom."

"So you were thinking of going, weren't you?" Belle said, as they shrugged into their coats.

"I like the senator. Once you get past that crust of his, he's a softy inside. Too bad his son wasn't the same."

"You wouldn't love him if he was any different." Belle led the way down the stairs to Main Street.

"What are you talking about?"

"You said it was too bad Caid wasn't a softy on the inside, like his father. But you're wrong. If Caid was different, you probably wouldn't have fallen in love with him. It's what makes Caid Caid that drew you to fall in love with him."

Reena opened and closed her mouth. "How did you get so smart, Belle?"

"A lot of broken hearts. But I don't give up. Someday I'll find the right man for me. And you will, too."

"Are you saying a broken heart heals?"

"Most of the time." She towed Reena along behind her until they stood at the base of the platform. Caid and his father were already on it, throwing cigars to the men in the audience. "Hey, Senator," Belle yelled, "we'll take some of those cigars, too."

"Here you go, ladies." Caid knelt at the edge of the platform above them and handed down two cigars. "Morning, Reena."

Reena nodded, unable to say anything around the lump in her throat. She busied herself looking around—anywhere but at Caid. But she watched his shadow, and saw him continue to kneel on the platform for several heartbeats, before he finally stood up and walked away.

"Why didn't you at least say good morning?"
Belle asked. "He was trying."

"I couldn't," she said, her voice still tight and
scratchy.

Senator Dundee began his speech. "Ladies and
fine gentlemen of the great Territory of Arizona,
I . . ."

People crowded closer to hear him. Reena found
herself caught between an older woman who was
shaped like a double whiskey barrel and a man
who stank of beer. They pressed closer and closer
until she felt as if she couldn't breathe.

"I have to get out of this crowd, Belle," she whispered. She worked her way along the platform until she could break free of the press of people.
Standing back from the edge of the crowd, she listened to the senator as he droned on and on.

Growing restless, she glanced around and noticed men with rifles on the roofs up and down
Main Street. Caid wasn't taking any chances, she
thought. Absently she watched two riders coming
down Main Street. Slowly, aware of something familiar about them, she focused on them.

Was it Robby and Seth? She couldn't be sure. Instead of joining the crowd listening to the senator,
they turned off onto a side street and she lost sight
of them.

Should she warn Caid? She went to the back of
the platform, looking for him. He wasn't there, but
a man told her he'd gone down to Sheriff Huddle's
office.

Nagged by some instinct she couldn't identify,

Reena hurried toward the sheriff's office. She was becoming more and more certain that she should warn Caid. But she didn't know about what.

She had nearly reached the office, when a blast blew out the front door and window of the building, and knocked her off her feet. Reena scrambled up just as Jeff, Seth and Robby ran out of the sheriff's office.

Robby glanced at her and yelled. "Rowena!" He held out his hand to her. "Come with us."

She shook her head, stunned.

"Put down your weapons. All of you!" Caid's voice came from the porch opposite them. He stepped out of the shadows into the sunlight, his rifle trained on them. Behind him, more men stepped out of the shadows. And they all had rifles or revolvers.

Reena saw Robby move, but didn't understand what he intended until he wrapped his arm around her waist and pulled her in front of him. "All right, everyone, just back away. Or she gets it."

"Robby! What are you doing? Don't hold me so tight!"

Reena heard the metallic click of a revolver hammer being drawn back, then he pressed the cold barrel against her head.

"*Robby*! My God, have you gone crazy? I'm your sister!" This couldn't be happening.

"Not anymore. You're a traitor to the Cause. Jeff told me how you led them to him. *You led them to Jeff!*" She could feel him trembling with rage.

"Drop your rifle, Dundee! Or she gets it," he yelled at Caid.

Caid studied Robby in the bright sunlight. Then he dropped his rifle into the thick dust on Main Street. "Everyone, drop your weapons," he yelled. "He's threatening to kill a hostage." He spread his arms wide, as if to hold back the men behind him.

Slowly the men dropped their guns.

"The men on the roof, too!" Robby yelled. "Send those rifles down to the ground. Now!"

"You heard him," Caid shouted. "Do it!" All the time, he didn't take his eyes off Robby.

"We need four fresh horses," Robby yelled. "And keep that crowd back." He gestured at the crowd coming down the street from the senator's speech. Jeff put a shot into the ground in front of the crowd, stopping them.

"I'm going to walk into the street to talk to the crowd, Simpson," Caid said. "But I'm doing it unarmed. See?" He didn't take his eyes off Robby and Reena as he unbuckled his gun belt and dropped it beside his rifle.

"Robby," Reena gasped, "I'm your sister. You can't be doing this."

"Shut up." He jabbed her with the gun barrel. "I can and I am. You will not get in the way of the Cause."

Tanner rode up to them leading four horses.

"Mount," Robby said, gesturing with his gun.

"I'll just hold you back. I can't ride hard like you."

"Shut up and mount or I'll put a bullet in Dundee," Robby growled, watching her. "Oh ho! I *thought* there was something between you two. No wonder you turned traitor. Now, mount up."

She did as she was told. Robby had always been the hard one, the dangerous one. Now she knew exactly how dangerous.

As they galloped out of town on the road to the east, she looked back. Was Caid coming after her? Would he?

Chapter 24

Caid stood in the middle of Main Street, watching them until they disappeared over a slight rise. All he could see was a dust cloud, rising in the still morning air.

He'd never felt so helpless in his life. What kind of bastard used his own sister as a shield?

God damn him to hell! He'd see Robert Lee hang for his crimes. By God, he would.

"Caid." Tanner punched him lightly in the arm, bringing him back from his thoughts. "Caid! I've got a posse forming. We'll go after them. We'll catch them this time."

"He'll kill Reena," he said quietly, with absolute certainty. He watched the dust cloud, still visible, but already melting away.

"What? What do you mean?" Tanner shook him. "Caid, snap out of it!"

"He'll kill Reena." He picked up his gun belt from where it lay in the dust and buckled it around his waist. "If the posse gets too close, he'll use Reena as a shield again. After all, if it worked once, it'll work again. But the posse will be too excited and angry by that time. Bullets will fly. She'll be killed."

"What do you want to do? I can't call off the posse. The sheriff's already deputized them and sent them to get their horses."

"Try to hold it back. The Simpsons don't know that I know where the hideout is. They're heading for it, but I'm going to try to get there ahead of them and prepare a surprise." He bent to tie the leather strips that secured the bottom of the holster around his thigh. "Tanner, it'll be up to you to control the posse. But if he kills Reena and me, don't let any of them get away." Picking up his rifle, he added, "The hideout is a couple of days' ride east of here. Follow the road toward May's and watch for my sign. That's where you'll turn off. I'll leave a trail you can follow."

Caid saddled Diablo and galloped out of the stable.

As he pounded down the road, he wondered if Reena believed that he would follow them. Did she know he would come for her?

No matter where they went, they wouldn't escape. No matter how long it took, he would find her.

*   *   *

Reena clutched the saddle horn as they pounded out of town. Robert Lee held the reins to her horse, which told her how little he trusted her. She would have to be careful around him.

But one thing was uppermost in her mind. Caid had let her brothers go, rather than endanger her. Caid had let her brothers go!

And no matter where they went, no matter how long it took, she believed he would come for her. He would find her.

Two days later, Caid drew rein at the cabin. He'd pushed Diablo and himself hard, but they'd beaten the Simpsons.

Now he had to prepare their surprise. He went through their supplies, leaving the beans, rice, and coffee, but taking every box of cartridges they had cached in the cabin.

Without bullets, they'd be in deep trouble. If his plan didn't work and he and Reena were killed, at least the Simpsons would still be unable to fire back when the posse cornered them.

He moved back into the pines to wait for them.

Within hours he heard them. Robert Lee and Jefferson were laughing, not even trying to be quiet, as they rode through the pines. He noticed Reena's hands weren't tied. Good. She'd cooperated with them, then.

After they dismounted, Seth took the horses around back and unsaddled them. A few minutes later, Reena came out of the cabin carrying a coffeepot and the cast-iron Dutch oven that they'd used to melt snow.

She walked across the grassy clearing to the stream and knelt to fill both pots with water. As she did, she gazed up into the pines, slowly scanning them, as if she knew he was there and was looking for him.

He couldn't signal her yet. Soon, though. Soon.

As if also sensing him, Robert Lee came out on the porch, carrying his rifle in the crook of his right arm. He leaned against a porch post and watched Reena.

"Hurry up, Rowena. We're hungry."

"Coming." She didn't look at the pines again, just picked up the heavy Dutch oven and coffeepot and walked back to the cabin. She paused and looked up at her brother, but he didn't offer to help her with either pot. Kicking her skirt out of the way so she didn't trip, she marched up the two steps, across the porch, and into the cabin.

Robert Lee turned to follow her. She kicked the door shut in his face.

Caid smiled and nodded approvingly. That was his Reena.

He waited as the sun set and twilight faded into night. Then he crept to the corral in back and lowered the rails, quietly shooing the horses out of the enclosure, freeing them.

Finally he eased down to the cabin and peeked in the window. It looked like Reena had made a huge pot of rice. The three men sat around the table, drinking coffee, their dirty plates still in front of them.

Reena sat in the far corner on the bed. Good girl, he thought, impressed once again by her smarts. She'd made sure she was out of the line of fire when he came for her.

He eased up to the door and drew his revolver. Taking a deep breath, he kicked the door open, and burst into the room.

They just stared at him, their mouths open. "Hello, gentlemen," he said. "I hope you'll enjoy the little surprise I've prepared for you. You don't know what I'm talking about, but you will; very soon.

"Reena, before I go on, do you want to come with me? Or do you want to remain with your brothers?" He wanted her decision out in the open.

Reena looked at Jeff and Robert Lee, then Caid. "I want to come with you, Caid," she replied firmly. She stood by the bed, still out of his line of fire. "Shall I get their guns?"

"No, I don't want you in arm-grabbing range." He took a step into the cabin. "Wait for me outside."

As Reena edged toward the door, giving the three men at the table a wide berth, Robert Lee's fingers tightened on the tin coffee cup he held and he flung the hot contents at Caid. But Caid was prepared. Stepping aside, he fired a single shot that knocked the cup out of Robert Lee's hand.

Robert Lee shook his stinging hand. "You son of a bitch!"

"Next time it won't be the cup, Robert Lee," Caid said, levelly. "And I'm hoping there will be a next time."

"Caid," Reena said from behind him.

"Outside, Reena." He waited until he heard her steps cross the porch.

"All right, I'm going to offer you three a deal. I'm taking Reena and riding out of here, and you're not going to follow us."

"Why the hell not?"

"Because I have all the cartridges you cached in this cabin."

They looked at each other, then Jeff dived for the supplies and pawed through them frantically. Finally Jeff knelt back on his heels. "They're gone. Every damn box of them."

"That's right. And only I know where they are."

"I'm going to kill you for this, Dundee," Robert Lee gritted through tight lips, half-rising from his chair. "I should have killed you when I had the chance when we were kids, Runt."

"Shut up and sit down. Here's the deal: you ride out of here and go back to Mexico, and that's the end of it. I won't pursue you into Mexico."

Robert Lee snorted contemptuously. "You couldn't anyway."

"Yes, I could. The government would never know about it—it would just be me and you, Robert Lee. And you know I'd come." He backed up a step toward the open door.

"And if either of you ever sets foot in the United States again, I will pursue you—to the ends of the

earth, if I have to. I'll see you jailed, and then I'll
see you hang for the murder of that black family
on the Atlanta road."

Jeff jumped to his feet. "You know about that?"

"Yes."

Jeff turned to his brother. "I told you not to shoot
them. I told you I'd seen Runt Dundee—"

"Shut up." Robert Lee leaned back in his chair.
"He's bluffing. It happened twenty years ago. It's
way past the statute of limitations. He can't do anything about it."

"There is no statute of limitations on murder,
Robert Lee. And I would be happy to testify that
that's what it was: cold-blooded murder. Remember that the next time you think about coming up
here. I'll be waiting—and hoping."

He backed another step out of cabin and saw
Reena. She'd been pressed up against the cabin
wall, listening.

"One last thing—there's a posse not far behind
me. If you pursue Reena and me, you'll run into
them. As for your cartridges, there's a paper under
the hay in the lean-to telling you where they are.
But you're going to wait here five minutes before
you move, because you won't know if I'm standing
just outside the door—waiting for you."

He pulled the door shut. "Come on," he told
Reena. They ran from the cabin. "This way." He
dodged behind a pine and leaned against it, watching the door with his revolver still in his hand.

"Diablo is behind the ridge. Get him and bring
him back here. I'll watch the cabin." He listened to

her moving through the trees, then the sounds faded into the night.

The cabin door opened a crack and he fired a shot at it. It slammed shut.

He looked around, straining to hear something besides silence. Where the hell was she? It shouldn't have taken her so long to get Diablo.

"Caid." She rode up to him.

"What took you so long?" He swung up behind the saddle, wrapping one arm around her waist and cradling her thighs with his.

"I went to turn their horses loose."

He chuckled. "I already had."

"So I discovered." She ducked to miss a low branch, barely visible in the light of the half-moon, and felt him duck also.

"They'll come after us as soon as they find the cartridges, you know."

"Nope."

She looked up at him over her shoulder. "I hear a smile in your voice. Why not?"

"Because the paper I left them will send them to another clue. And when they find that one, it'll send them to another clue, then another and another."

"Like a treasure hunt?" She reached up over her shoulder and gently drew her hand down his cheek.

"Exactly. It'll take them all day to find their cartridges."

He bent his head and inhaled her special scent. He had found his own treasure.

"Caid, I heard what you said about that black family." Her voice was hesitant. "I understand why you were so intent on capturing them."

"I'm sorry you heard. That's why I told you to go out on the porch."

She twisted her fingers in the horse's mane. "I never knew."

"I know that, Reena. It wasn't the sort of thing they'd ever admit to."

"But my own brothers." He felt a shudder go through her.

"Forget it. It's over." He dropped a tiny kiss on the top of her head. "Forever."

She leaned back against him and his blood began to rush. He felt the tension in him rising and tightened his arm around her.

Soon. Soon.

They arrived in Lost Gold two days later and went directly to the hotel. Reena had a long hot bath in Caid's suite while Caid did some errands.

She'd put on his blue silk dressing gown and was curled up in a chair in front of his fire, rehearsing what she'd say, when she heard his key in the door and he walked in. He carried a large package wrapped in brown paper and tied with string.

"What's that?"

"A little something for you." He dropped it in her lap.

She fumbled with the string. "Damn, I don't have my pocket knife."

"You are the only woman I know who carries a

pocket knife." His voice was full of warm sunshine as he broke the string for her.

"Well, they're useful." She tore back the paper and stared at the gown made from the emerald green velvet she'd admired at the dressmaker's. "Oh, Caid, it's so beautiful," she murmured, stroking the rich velvet.

"Go try it on."

Reena retreated to his bedroom and slipped on the most luxurious dressing gown she'd ever seen. She turned this way and that in front of the mirror, admiring the changing hues of green in the golden lamplight. It was cut low in front, exposing her scant curves and making them look sexy, she thought.

She pulled the sash tight around the waist and returned to the parlor. Caid's gaze slowly moved up the gown to her face, and his eyes told her that he liked what he saw.

"Thank you, Caid," she murmured, brushing her hand down over the rich nap. "I've never had anything so nice."

"Glad you like it." He walked toward her and she gave him a very womanly smile.

He cleared his throat. He hadn't expected to be so nervous. Of course, he'd never asked a woman to marry him before . . .

Her long blond hair foamed over the velvet like waves on a deep green sea. He rubbed a curl between his finger and thumb. Her pulse throbbed against the silken skin at the base of her throat. He touched it with a single finger and felt the movement as she swallowed.

He trailed his finger lower, hooking it under the fine gold chain that disappeared into the shadow between the swell of her breasts. Pulling the chain up, he looked at that child's ring from so long ago.

"Reena, I think it's time I gave you a ring that fits your finger."

She stared at him, too surprised to speak. Then she threw her arms around his neck and kissed him. "Caid, I thought you'd never ask."

He smiled and caught her to him. "Well, now that I've asked, what's your answer?"

She kissed his right eye. "Yes." She kissed his right cheek. "Yes." She moved to his left eye. "Yes." And his left cheek. "Yes."

That was all he could stand. He swept her up in his arms and carried her across the room to his bed. "Are you sure?"

"Very."

"Good." He laid her down on the bed. She was completely covered by her emerald velvet wrapper, yet she looked as wanton and desirable as any woman in his dreams. She was his.

Her golden hair tumbled across the pillow in glorious disarray. Slowly, tense with anticipation, he undid her sash and pulled it away, freeing the two halves of her gown.

He slowly pushed back one half of her emerald green velvet wrap, then the other, unwrapping his treasure.

"My God, you are so beautiful." Stretching out

beside her, he rested his head on one hand and simply gazed at her, drinking her into his senses.

She held out her arms to him. "Hold me. Just hold me."

He did, gently stroking her, relearning the curves and hollows of her—as if he'd forgotten any of them. He shifted onto his back, and she curled over him, resting her head on his shoulder and draping her long, smooth leg over his rough-textured one. Idly she ran her foot up and down his leg.

She teased him, letting her fingers curl through the soft curls on his chest, slowly, slowly exploring lower and lower. "I want to pleasure you tonight, Caid."

He spread his arms wide and gave her a devilish smile. "Do with me what you will. I'm yours."

She brought her mouth down on his in a kiss that started out as fiercely tender and slid into fiercely demanding in seconds.

She moaned softly when his tongue invaded her mouth, and curled her fingers through his hair and held on as their kiss turned to fire. Her heart began to gallop.

Finally, she pulled away from the mind-drugging glory of his mouth and rained gentle kisses all over his harsh features, then slowly worked her way lower, kissing the hollow of his shoulder, the thick muscles that padded his broad chest.

Each kiss sent a spark of fiery pleasure through Caid. Finally she strung fiery kisses up the length of his rod, sending fierce jolts of pleasure with each one.

Reena found it as exciting to pleasure Caid as it was to have Caid pleasure her. Every time he groaned, her bones softened a bit more.

He drew his thumb across the tight berry of her nipple, sending a shock of pleasure through her as she leaned over him.

"Caid," she gasped, even as she arched against his hand. He kissed her nipple, then softly laved it with his tongue. When he blew gently across the moistened tip, he sent an exhilarating shock wave of heat tumbling through her.

"Oh . . . h . . h," she moaned, as another quiver of pleasure and heat went through her. "Now," she urged.

"You're in charge," he reminded her.

She smiled down at him as she positioned herself, then slowly took him within her. It was a different feeling, strange and strangely exciting.

Slowly she began to move up and down. His eyes were glittering slits as he watched her, moving over him, then he began to move with her. His hands cupped her breasts, adding a new dimension of pleasure to her.

Then he slid his hands to her hips and turned over, taking her with him and suddenly he was on top and he was thrusting and she was meeting his thrusts with her own.

He demanded much. He gave much.

Their joining was sweet and savage and wild and tumultuous as a storm blazing across the Grand Canyon.

"R-e-e-n-a," he shouted, as they came together in an explosion of stars.

And they soared together.

Caid wrapped her close and held her as they slowly drifted back to earth.

"I have just one question for you, Reena." Caid combed his fingers through her wild tangles of golden hair.

"What?" She asked drowsily, turning her head and kissing his wrist.

"How soon are you going to make an honest man of me?"

Chapter 25

⁓⁓⁓

The next morning, Reena walked into the dining room on Caid's arm. Miss Abigail herself showed them to a table beside the window, where they could look out at the trees dressed in shimmering shades of red and gold.

"Honey, you look beautiful this morning," Caid said as he sat beside her. His eyes twinkled as he added an echo of their first meeting, "Or don't you want me to 'honey' you?"

"You can 'honey' me anytime." She gave him a cat-drank-the-cream smile.

He eyed her intently, then leaned close. "Don't smile at me like that unless you want to go back to bed, honey." His voice stroked her like rough velvet.

Reena knew she was blushing; she could feel the telltale heat in her cheeks. She gave him a shy sidelong glance.

"You're making it worse," he murmured. "I won't be able to get up from this table for a while."

She snickered. "Poor darling."

"Good morning," Belle said, as she poured their coffee. The fresh-brewed fragrance tantalized them. "What would you like for breakfast?"

Reena laughed when Caid's eyes met hers. She knew what *he* wanted for breakfast.

"It's a very good morning, Belle." Caid smiled up at her. "Are you coming to our wedding?"

Belle almost dropped the coffeepot. "I-I don't know. When is it?"

"In five days."

"Five days!" Reena yelped. "I can't get a wedding dress so quickly."

"Does the kind of dress you're married in matter?" Caid asked, picking up his cup.

"Yes—though not as much as the kind of man I'm marrying," Reena retorted.

Caid eyed her over the rim of his cup as he drank.

"After breakfast," he said, "I'll walk down to the church and talk to the minister. Why don't you and Belle go down to the dressmaker's and see about buying the most wonderful wedding dress you can find?"

"Sounds like a good plan to me."

Belle cleared her throat loudly.

Concerned, Reena glanced at her. "Do you have a cold?"

"No! I was just trying to remind you two that I was still here. Now, order some breakfast, before

Miss Abby wanders over to see if anything is wrong."

After Belle walked away with their orders, Reena leaned over and tapped the back of Caid's hand. "You know, Tanner and your father are having breakfast at another table. They keep glancing at us and smiling. Should we invite them to join us?"

"Hell, no. I told them to get their own table and stay away from us."

"Oh." Reena sipped her coffee. "Did you mean what you said? About my ordering a wedding dress?"

"Of course. And a trousseau, Reena. With lots of silk chemises and nightshifts. You should always have silk next to your skin. Ah, here comes Belle with our breakfast."

After that, they didn't have much time to talk, because a constant stream of Lowry girls came by to congratulate them and give them their best wishes.

As they sat with their final cup of coffee, Caid lit a cigar and leaned back in his chair. "Where would you like to go on our honeymoon?"

"We'll have a honeymoon?"

"I thought we'd couple the railcar up to a train going in the right direction and go wherever you'd like. You said you wanted to go to new places and meet new people, so we will."

"Oh, Caid, you remembered! I'll have to think about where I want to visit first." Reena laid her linen napkin beside her plate. "I'd like to ask May to stand up at our wedding."

"I think that would be wonderful. By the way, my father cabled my mother while I was out chasing you, and she's on the way to Lost Gold."

"Then almost all the people you and I love will be here for our wedding." She looked up at him and tears filled her eyes.

He covered her hand with his. "Reena, you know I would give you the moon if I could. But I can't give you your family back."

She sniffled, fished a handkerchief out of her purse and dabbed at her eyes. "I know, Caid. We all make our choices. I made mine, they've made theirs."

He squeezed her hand.

"I've been thinking about buying a ranch around here. You like this country, don't you?"

"I love it here." She'd found her love here.

Belle came back to the table, minus her white apron. "Come on, Reena, let's go to Madame Fifi's and see about a trousseau and a wedding dress for you."

"I'll walk you down there," Caid said, standing and pulling Reena's chair out for her. He trailed his fingers across her nape in a gentle caress.

Reena and Belle looked at Madame Fifi's pattern books all morning and Reena fell in love with a dress that made her think of Cinderella going to the ball. That was how she felt, sometimes. Madame Fifi promised her that she would have her special wedding dress in time.

Later that day, when Reena and Caid went to

dinner, they spied May and Jeter at another table.

"What a pleasant surprise, seeing you in town," Reena said. "I was going to send a messenger out to you, May. Caid and I are getting married."

May looked up from her roast chicken. "It's about time! I was beginning to wonder what was wrong with you two."

Reena glanced at Caid. "We had a lot of things to work out. I'd like you to be my matron of honor."

"An old warhorse like me?"

"Yes, because you are a dear, dear lady and a friend to both of us."

"Why don't you run away, like Jeter and me are planning to?"

"You're getting married?" Reena gave May a quick hug. "That's wonderful. When?"

"When we run away, right, Jeter?"

Jeter looked up from the thick slab of roast beef he was inhaling. "Damn fool woman wore me down. Wanted me to put a ladder up against her second floor bedroom window and carry her away, romantic-like. But I said a step stool by the first floor window would have to do."

"I'm sure you two will have a wonderful marriage." Reena's eyes met Caid's. "It's obvious how you feel about each other."

"Yup. I even got Jeter's wedding present already."

"You do?" Reena exclaimed. "What is it?"

"A box to stand on so he can kiss me," May declared, with a twinkle in her eye.

"Waste of a good box, if you ask me," Jeter grumbled, going back to his roast beef.

"Stop complaining," May said, forking up mashed potatoes. "Now, when's your wedding?"

"In five days." Caid took over. "And we'd like you both there, and you to stand up with us, May."

"My pleasure, Caid. You know, I'm going to be moving over to Jeter's place. Would you be interested in running my ranch?"

Caid nodded. "Might be, May. Why don't you and I talk about it later, over a cigar?"

"You're on."

As Caid and she walked away, Reena couldn't keep from smiling. "I hope they're half as happy as we are."

On the morning of her wedding day, Madame Fifi delivered a satin wedding gown with train and veil to the hotel and Belle brought it up to Caid's suite, where Reena was staying.

"I can't believe it," Reena kept saying, as she turned this way and that, looking at the stunning white satin gown. "How did she do it in time?"

"We all worked on it," Belle said shyly.

"What?"

"All the Lowry girls worked on the seams—there was someone sewing on it around the clock. Even Mrs. Hofsteader sat up all one night sewing. And Miss Abigail. Most of the women in town worked on it, Reena."

Reena blinked rapidly. "You all did this for me?"

"Now, don't go getting teary-eyed. You haven't

even seen your groom yet. Wait for him if you want to get watery-eyed. Actually," Belle added thoughtfully, "I've seen some brides who *should* have cried at their weddings. Or run away."

"Oh, Belle, you're terrible." Reena hugged her.

"Come on, I want to get you to the church."

In the vestibule Belle adjusted Reena's veil and train, and gave her a bouquet of white roses, white orchids, and fragrant white orange blossoms. "Where did you find these?" Reena exclaimed, astonished by the fragrant blooms.

"I had them brought in from California for you," Tom Dundee said, as he entered. A tall, patrician woman with white hair in a strikingly simple blue dress accompanied him. "And this is Caid's mother, Eileen."

"How do you do, Mrs. Dundee?"

"Hello, Reena. I think my son has chosen very well. And I hear that I used to rock you to sleep when you were an infant. I know you're in a hurry now, but we'll talk more later."

Senator Dundee was dressed in a formal gray morning coat and had a white rose boutonniere. "Ah, Reena," he said, bowing slightly as he lifted her hand to his lips. "You look lovely today, my dear. I've never seen a more beautiful bride. Except for my own Eileen, of course. I'd like to welcome you to the family." He cleared his throat several times. "And, since your father is not here to give you away, I wondered if I might accompany you down the aisle and do the honors?"

"Why, thank you, Senator." Reena swallowed

around a sudden lump in her throat. "I would like that very much."

The rich sound of an organ swelled into the rafters as Belle opened the vestibule doors. Golden sunlight slanted in through the high windows and lit the interior. Most of the pews were full, for it seemed that everyone in Lost Gold was there—all the Lowry girls, Miss Abigail, Mr. and Mrs. Hofsteader, and Madame Fifi. And everyone was smiling.

Reena's eyes met Caid's, and she walked down the aisle confidently, for her love was waiting for her.

In front of the minister, Caid's father placed her hand in Caid's.

He clasped her hand tightly and smiled down at her as the minister began their vows.

Tears filled her eyes as she listened to the phrases joining her and Caid forever.

"I do," she whispered, looking into Caid's eyes.

"I do," he said, gazing deep into her eyes. Then he lifted her veil and kissed her. It was only a light-duty kiss as their kisses went, but the room still whirled around her for a second.

Then they turned to make the walk up the aisle, and Caid stopped.

"Reena, there's something I'd like to say in front of everyone." He clasped her hands with his and gave her a look as warm as summertime. "This town is called Lost Gold," he said in a firm voice that carried to the farthest corner. "but I found gold in it. My own special gold—you."

They walked up the aisle to the sound of clapping and cheers.

Outside Caid handed Reena up into a shiny black carriage, driven by Tanner, who drove them to the private railcar.

When Reena stepped out of the buggy, Caid swept her up in his arms.

"I want to carry you across our first threshold," he explained, climbing the steps to the railcar door. "But you'll have to open it; my hands are full."

Laughing, she unlatched it and he lurched through, almost knocking her veil off in the process.

"Put me down," Reena said, giggling. "You're dangerous."

He did, slowly letting her slide down in a sensuous rustle of silk and satin skirts. Then he rested his hands on her hips. "I just need more practice carrying you off to bed."

She stood on tiptoe and brushed a light kiss over his lips. "And I need more practice being carried off to bed."

Something banged into the front end of the car, almost knocking them off their feet.

"What was that?" Reena started to walk forward.

Caid snagged her wrist. "We were just coupled onto the eastbound train. Look out the window—we're starting to move."

They stood together, watching the landscape outside move by at a faster and faster pace. Finally Reena sighed and pushed away from him reluctantly. "I better change."

"Yes, you'd better." Caid swept her up in his arms again and walked toward the bedroom.

"Caid, what are you doing?"

"Practicing carrying you off to bed."

And he did.

Later, as the train raced east into the night, Reena lit the oil lamps in the parlor. She wore her emerald velvet dressing gown and her tousled hair curled over her shoulders.

"Reena," Caid said quietly, "you have one more wedding present. This is a special one." He handed her a triple-folded heavy parchment sealed with golden wax. "It's from the President."

"President of what?" she asked absently, as she broke the seal.

"The United States."

Her eyes widened and she blinked. "The United States?

He nodded.

She unfolded the parchment carefully and read it before she looked up at him, then returned to it. "It's addressed to 'Reena Sims Dundee, born Rowena Simpson.' "

"I didn't want any mistakes as to whom the President was referring."

Reena ran her thumb over the embossed gold seal at the bottom. "This really *is* from the President, isn't it?"

"Yes. He's the only one that can do that."

She read it again. "This is a Presidential pardon,

Caid," she said in a strained voice, "for all treason-ous acts."

"Yes."

Reena didn't know whether she was going to cry or cheer. Caid had realized her secret fear. "Why?"

"I don't want you to live with me because I'm holding a sword over your head. I want you to be mine because we love each other. And when we're sitting by the fire in fifty years, I want us to be married for only one reason. Because we love each other."

"Oh, Caid, don't you know?" she said softly. Resting her hands on his broad shoulders, she gazed up at him with all her love shining in her eyes. "I did marry you because I love you. You're my hero."

He threaded his fingers through her tousled hair and kissed her. "And you will forever be my Ari-zona renegade."

Dear Reader,

Julia Quinn is quick becoming a rising star here at Avon Books, and next month's Avon Romantic Treasure TO CATCH AN HEIRESS shows why. A case of mistaken identity provides Caroline Trent with the escape she needs from her stuffy guardian. But Caroline escapes right into the very strong arms of sexy Blake Ravenscroft. Julia is pure fun to read, and if you haven't yet joined in the fun you should!

Lovers of Regency period romance shouldn't miss Suzanne Enoch's BY LOVE UNDONE. Four years ago, Madeline Willits was found in a compromising position. Now she's rusticating in the country, but when handsome Quinlan Bancroft arrives at the estate she's once again caught up in passion and discovered in *another* compromising position! Poor Maddie...all she ever seems to do is fall for the wrong man—but then Quinlan proposes marriage...

If you're hooked on THE MEN OF PRIDE COUNTY series by Rosalyn West, then you know you're in for a treat with next month's THE OUTSIDER. Starla Fairfax has returned to Pride County with a secret. She accepts northerner Hamilton Dodge's proposal of marriage for one reason only: he can protect her from her past. But Dodge has more in mind than a marriage of convenience...

Contemporary readers: be on the lookout next month for Hailey North, an exciting, new writer. Hailey's got a winning writing style, and in BEDROOM EYES, her debut book, she's created a magical, sensuous love story. A prim-on-the-outside attorney, Penelope Sue Fields has dreams of finally meeting Mr. Right. But lately all the attention she's getting is from Mr. Wrong—ex-cop Tony Olano. Will Penelope ever find true love?

Enjoy!

Lucia Macro

Lucia Macro
Senior Editor

AEL 0698

Avon Romances—
the best in exceptional authors and unforgettable novels!

Avon Romantic Treasures

Unforgettable, enthralling love stories,
sparkling with passion and adventure
from Romance's bestselling authors

✳✳✳✳✳✳✳✳✳✳✳✳✳✳✳✳✳✳✳✳✳✳✳✳✳✳✳✳✳✳✳✳✳✳

Discover Contemporary Romances at Their Sizzling Hot Best from Avon Books

SIMPLY IRRESISTIBLE
79007-6/$5.99 US/$7.99 Can
by Rachel Gibson

LETTING LOOSE
72775-7/$5.99 US/$7.99 Can
by Sue Civil-Brown

IF WISHES WERE HORSES *by Curtiss Ann Matlock*
79344-X/$5.99 US/$7.99 Can

IF I CAN'T HAVE YOU
79554-X/$5.99 US/$7.99 Can
by Patti Berg

BABY, I'M YOURS
79511-6/$5.99 US/$7.99 Can
by Susan Andersen

TELL ME I'M DREAMIN'
79562-0/$5.99 US/$7.99 Can
by Eboni Snoe

BEDROOM EYES
79895-6/$5.99 US/$7.99 Can
by Hailey North